THE HIDDEN GIRLS

Rebecca Whitney

PAN BOOKS

First published 2020 by Mantle

This paperback edition first published 2021 by Pan Books
an imprint of Pan Macmillan
The Smithson, 6 Briset Street, London EC1M 5NR
EU representative: Macmillan Publishers Ireland Limited,
Mallard Lodge, Lansdowne Village, Dublin 4
Associated companies throughout the world
www.panmacmillan.com

ISBN 978-1-4472-6588-7

1 3 5 7 9 8 6 4 2

A CIP catalogue record for this book is available from the British Library.

Typeset in Sabon by Jouve (UK), Milton Keynes
Printed and bound by CPI Group (UK) Ltd, Croydon, CR0 4YY

Visit **www.panmacmillan.com** to read more about all our books
and to buy them. You will also find features, author interviews and
news of any author events, and you can sign up for e-newsletters
so that you're always first to hear about our new releases.

THE
HIDDEN
GIRLS

Rebecca Whitney's debut, *The Liar's Chair*, was published in 2015. As well as novels, Rebecca writes short stories and features, and also teaches creative writing. She lives in Sussex. *The Hidden Girls* is her second novel.

Also by Rebecca Whitney

The Liar's Chair

For my mum, Jean Whitney, who holds us together.

The tapping has been going on for days now. It's coming from behind the sink in the downstairs toilet, where a walled-up recess runs under the stairs. Ruth puts her hand to the surface, feels the vibrations from the other side; a persistent banging, like someone's trying to get out.

'Tam?' she says with her mouth close to the wall. 'Is that you?'

Tap. Tap-tap.

Ruth tries to work out the code, but her thoughts are whirling so fast they won't land on anything tangible. Ruth and Tam always knew what the other was trying to say, though, communicating sometimes with just a look, a sort of telepathy passing between them. That's how it is with sisters or how it had been with the two of them, right through to their teens, Ruth only a year younger, so close in age people used to mistake them for twins. And now, after all this time, Tam's come and found Ruth. Clever Tam.

Tap-tap-tap. Tap.

1

Ruth puts her lips on the wall, lets the vibrations run into her. 'It's OK, Tam,' she says. 'I think I understand.'

Another noise is coming from the lounge, something else that needs Ruth's attention, although she can't grasp what it could be. She opens the toilet door to look. There, on the floor in a Moses basket, is a baby – oh God, Ruth's baby, Bess; she'd forgotten all about her – and the little girl is making the worst noise of all. Ruth puts her hands over her ears, squeezes her eyes shut, tries to balance her spinning head, but the crying is so loud it's inside her, filling her up to almost drowning. If Bess quietened, even a little bit, Ruth would have space to think, only the baby never ever stops. Tam would know what to do, though. Tam always knew how to sort things out.

Behind Ruth the tapping has become a thump, like Tam's beating her fist against the wall.

'All right, all right,' Ruth calls back to her. 'I'll deal with it.'

In the kitchen, Ruth opens the utensils drawer and takes out the largest knife, the one she and Giles use to slice watermelon or carve the chicken for a Sunday roast. The knife is a single piece of metal from end to end, part of an expensive set given as a wedding present from Ruth's workmates. Ruth grips it, the cool handle almost painful in her burning palm, and she takes it back through to the lounge where the baby's watery eyes follow her, little mouth wide and wailing, face a painful pink. *Is she even mine?* Ruth thinks. After the caesarean four weeks ago, Ruth was so out of it, the surgeon could have passed her anyone or anything – an alien child perhaps, or the devil.

'Shhh.' Ruth tries to make her voice gentle, but the noise comes out spitty and Bess's cry grows hysterical. Ruth wants to help this baby, she really does, but she's terrified to touch her because the little girl is so small that Ruth could crush her with one hand. 'Please, please, just be quiet.'

Ruth edges past the baby into the downstairs toilet and slams the door, sealing the crying away from her on the other side. Above the sink is a shelf of moisturizers, nappy-rash creams, liquid soap. Ruth clears them off with one swipe of her wrist and the bottles scatter on the floor. Now she has the room she needs. She launches at the wall with the knife, paint chipping and flaking under the blade as it bites into the surface.

'I'm coming.' Ruth's breath is ragged with the effort. 'I won't leave you this time, Tam.'

The wall is made of plasterboard, not brick as Ruth had thought, and the dent quickly widens and deepens as she attacks it with a feverishness, elated that getting Tam out is going to be so much easier than she'd imagined. After only seconds, the knife breaks through. Ruth stands back, expecting a rush of water as the hidden recess empties itself out, but there's not even a drop. She brushes her hand across the damage; the wall is bone-dry.

'Tam, are you there?' Ruth puts her mouth over the hole. 'I'm sorry, OK? But you should have let me tell them.'

Silence on the other side. Ruth moves her eye to the gap. Inside it's dark, but there's an elusive occupancy to the space, like something just passed by and disturbed the air. She pokes a finger through. Her skin connects with warm flesh. Ruth screams, yanks her hand away, knife spinning out of her sweaty palm and clattering to the floor. She takes a breath, crouches, grabs the sharp shiny blade and glimpses in it the reflection of a woman, crazier than anyone Ruth's seen in her life.

'Christ.' She touches her face that's salted with paint, and her reflection in the knife follows suit. 'What is happening?' This strength she possesses, and her wild rushing thoughts; she could do anything to anyone – even that baby – and it would all be out of her control.

1

A scream splits the 3 a.m. silence, two long bursts, high and wild. A woman's scream. Even as Ruth listens, propped up in bed on soggy pillows with her colicky six-month-old sucking the last from a bottle, she doubts the scream exists; it's just her sleep-starved brain tossing out fantasy again. But she'll have to call the police, if only to confirm the noise is her imagination.

She lays Bess next to Giles in the bed and takes the phone into the next room. Her little girl mustn't wake, and Ruth hasn't the energy for Giles's judgement.

'Where did you say the noise came from?' the controller asks, after Ruth tells her what she heard.

Ruth's eyes turn to the ceiling as she recalls the daytime noises that carry to her house: the intercity trains speeding past allotments at the back, a constant rumble of traffic on the North Circular, men's voices who work the car wash at the end of her street.

'From the petrol station,' she says.

'Was it from inside the building?'

'I'm not sure. It's not a petrol station any more, it's a car wash during the day now. But the noise came from thereabouts. I mean, I think I heard something. Has anyone else reported a disturbance?'

'No, madam, just you.'

Details are taken, the call ends, and Ruth returns to her bedroom to wait at the window with the curtains open. The old gym T-shirt she now uses as a nightie trembles with her fluttering pulse, the sensation in her chest similar to the butterfly of her baby's first movements, only it's travelled up to her heart, as if she's pregnant with anxiety. Ruth will cry if she gives the feeling much attention, so she pushes her face against the cold glass to concentrate on outside. In the netherworld of the night the minutes warp and flatten until eventually a blue light blinks on the tarmac – a premonition of the response car that follows. The vehicle cruises into view, and from inside the car, officers shine their torches over the hedgerow that lines the opposite side of the street. Ruth imagines the policemen or women cursing and their tired eyes blinking as they follow up another of her calls. The car passes out of sight, then the noise of the engine turns into the dead end at the top of the road where the terrace numbers reach the early hundreds, before the vehicle glides back past her house, leaving behind a silence somehow emptier than before.

She waits for a few minutes to see if the police return. They don't. She shuffles into the small space left over in the bed where Bess fidgets between her mum and dad, the little

6

girl in a feathery sleep. If Ruth moves her to her cot, she's bound to wake, so it's better to lie in discomfort than have her baby cry any more. The clock shunts on in slow minutes. Ruth palpates with exhaustion, yearning for the old habit of sleep, but her off-button's been taken away and she's being forced to watch the static. In less than three hours it will be time to get up again.

Eventually Ruth's breathing slows and a small dream settles – a circle of trees swinging in a dark wind, a figure running through the undergrowth, just out of Ruth's reach as she chases behind – only to be disturbed again by another scream. This time Ruth doesn't react. The police have confirmed the noise is simply her brain malfunctioning, another aftershock from the illness she suffered since giving birth. Now she's certain of her uncertainty, she feels a small camaraderie with this auditory hallucination, or paracusia as she's learnt it's called. Nothing else exists in this witching hour except for Ruth, her baby and the scream; all other members of the sane world are dreaming of sex or sorrow, or yesterday's faux pas. Ruth wonders what would happen if all the forests caught fire, smoke and ash blanketing the sun, and this darkness remained. Nothing would grow. Supplies would run out and she'd be forced to forage for food with her daughter strapped to her back, this being to whom she's bound with the greatest urgency, but is yet to love. Which of her neighbours would be first to take up the pickaxe? How long would they all go hungry before they started eating each other?

She squeezes her eyes shut against the spiralling thoughts and attempts to mould the pillow into a comfortable shape.

Giles turns to face her and Ruth peeks at him; a dream-smile flickers on his lips. She grinds her teeth at his brand of tired, of having a tough day at the office with too many tasks and not enough time. She remembers feeling that way herself and thought there was nothing else to measure the exhaustion by: the flop on the sofa with a glass of wine after the assault of the week, moaning about office politics and clients' expectations, while privately acknowledging she'd aced the lot. That was before this new type of wipeout, a need for sleep that buzzes inside every cell of her body but is rarely satisfied. She is wired with tired.

Giles mutters and chuckles as if he's continuing a fascinating conversation at the pub. Ruth puts out a hand to settle him in case he wakes Bess, but she's afraid that too might disturb their little girl, so she pulls back to let Giles ramble on. In Japan they say a child is a river that flows between the parents, completing their landscape, but the valley that's been carved in Ruth's marriage is canyon deep. The couple call to each other from opposite sides of the divide, each of them straining to understand their partner's new language.

It's a 6 a.m. start to the day and Bess wakes with a cry that's impossible to ignore, unless you're a sleeping father. This petty carving up of time – who gets what and how much – deflates Ruth. It's not the person she wants to be, nor is it any part of herself she recognizes from the past, though it would bother her less if she had the energy to turn it around. She takes her daughter downstairs for a feed and sits with Bess on the sofa, her mind revisiting last night's call to the police, the shame more resonant for having opened up her fears to public scrutiny again. She's been well for several weeks now, was convinced she'd finally cheated the monkeys who'd set up in her head after Bess was born, but it seems the old paranoias still have some power. Or perhaps it's simply the insomnia that's brought them back. She can't tell any more.

Ruth keeps the TV on low in the background, the rolling news repeating images of a bobbing island of plastic junk, backlit by blue sky and sunshine. At least the world's still turning outside of Ruth's four walls, though what it's turning into, she despairs. Giles ambles down an hour later and the couple share a breakfast of sorts. He makes tea and toast and holds charred jammy triangles up to Ruth's mouth in between sending work emails. Her mug sits on top of paint charts and brochures for kitchen and bathroom fittings, the renovations they started with such enthusiasm having since stalled through lack of time and money. Before Bess, she and Giles had been too busy establishing careers and having fun to possess the foresight to save up a decent deposit, always assuming they'd get on the property ladder when the market settled, but it never stopped going up. Then, with a baby on the way and Ruth about to go on maternity leave, the couple dashed from a spacious rented flat with friends round the corner and cafes nearby to an affordable area too far away for anyone they knew to pop in. Ruth spends her days staring at bare plaster walls and woodlice that lurk where the skirting board should meet the floor.

'How are you feeling today?' Giles says with a smile so

small it's almost invisible. 'You're looking a bit brighter. The new medication must be really suiting you.' He mimics the sing-songy tone that all the medics use, dumbing themselves down to what they believe is Ruth's level. 'Perhaps we could go on a bit of an outing this weekend?'

His polite caution sinks inside her; an ice cube creeping towards her stomach. She wonders if she and Giles have ever really known each other, or if they've always been children playing at grown-ups. Before Bess was born, a passion for adventure and faith in love was their cornerstone, only now that things have got serious, the best Giles can muster is a polite peck on the cheek. She wants to shake him and shout, 'Remember when we laughed at couples on Valentine's, eating at candle-lit tables in silence?' Giles's back is straight in the armchair opposite, legs together, hands clasped at his knees as if bracing himself for some new terror that might need containing.

The baby's bottle slips in Ruth's sweaty hand. She tightens her hold. 'Yes, I'm feeling really great.' Her tone is bright, magnified. She checks it down a notch. 'Getting back to my old self.'

A frown glances across Giles's face before he disguises it with his newly learnt toothy grin. Ever present in the room with them is Ruth's illness, a feral child who dragged them to unspeakable places, only recently tamed. Neither she nor Giles signed up for this rebranding of love to duty, though both are unable to escape. She stays because Bess is her new reality, and Giles can't leave because he's responsible for his wife and, in turn, the safety of their daughter.

'Are you sure you'll be OK for a bit today?' Giles says, leaning over to hug Ruth with limp arms. She smells his bed-hair and a memory rushes in of long lazy weekends, box-set marathons and takeaways, retreating to the bedroom whenever they chose, whispering to each other because their love had the volume to knock them sideways. 'I'm only popping into the office,' Giles continues. This last month he's been testing leaving Ruth for periods alone, like a toddler dropped at nursery for a few hours at a time. 'I can come home if you need, you just have to call.' She knows this, it's the same shtick he gives her every time he's about to go, his face trained to a blank, but Ruth reads his itch to get out of here and sample normality. The weeks spent managing his wife were never supposed to be part of the bargain, and the stress has taken its toll. But the fact that he gets to take a break and dip into the real world is a hot coal of resentment in Ruth's fist. She can't blame him though, she'd run for the hills if she had a choice.

'I'll be fine, don't worry,' Ruth says, her words always out of step with the truth, a habit of self-sufficiency with a longer history than the duration of this relationship, her stoicism more of a compulsion, dating back to her teenage years when she'd had to muster every ounce of strength to lift herself out of a tragedy of her own creation. More recently though – having fallen so short of expectations – pretending to cope like she used to has become her only dignity. She envisages the lonely hours that stretch ahead, the death of a day where she'll be consumed by chores that reanimate as soon as they're completed – the nappy changing, the feeding and washing, the laundry and cooking – like fungus resprouting from a cracked pipe.

'Righty-ho then.' Ruth's not heard Giles say this before and she goes to tease him about it, imagining the chuckle that would rise in his throat, the giggle they'd share. But this new medi-speak, along with his clumsy brightness, defeats her, although at least he's trying. She's grateful he cares because who else ever did?

Giles pats Ruth's arm before going into the downstairs toilet. There, fixed to the wall above the sink, is the medicine cabinet. His cough isn't loud enough to mask the squeak of the doors opening, where inside he'll be checking she's taken today's prescription. Ruth's been on the tablets for nearly five months now, and even though she's over the worst, taking them every day keeps her illness in check. Whole tranches of her memory have been erased by the psychosis, leaving only one sure image from that time: the sister she thought had been bricked up in the recess under their stairs, who Ruth imagined communicated with her by tapping on the wall. Ruth once tried to get her out. 'Do you feel trapped by motherhood?' asked the psychiatrist who diagnosed Ruth. 'Walled in by expectation? Is there a part of you that's waiting to be rescued?' Only now, on the better side of illness, is Ruth able to absorb the totality of the message she was sending herself.

So these current nips at independence are a huge step forward from Ruth's weeks in the mother-and-baby unit, followed by round-the-clock home supervision, and in light of where Ruth's illness took her tiny family, Giles's monitoring of her medication is understandable, only she can't help being humiliated by the necessity of any of it, which amounts to nothing other than her constant and irreversible failure as a mother. The muscles of her jaw are already aching this early in the day. As soon as Bess has finished feeding, Ruth will need to fetch her night guard or she'll end up grinding her teeth to stumps.

Presumably satisfied her dose is on target, Giles comes back into the lounge and stuffs his computer and coiled accessories into bicycle panniers, then straps on his cycle helmet. The edges of the hard plastic hat squeeze his face, pushing his cheeks towards his nose, and random grey hairs poke from the sides of the helmet. He's aged a year for every month of their daughter's life, partly a result of having had to work a job from home that needed him full-time at the office – though mostly it's the worry that whatever has taken his wife from him may never give her back.

'I need to go,' Giles says. 'I've got a meeting at nine.'

'Be careful out there.' It's the joke they used to share before they became parents. 'Don't die or anything.'

'I'll try not to.' He laughs. He still finds it funny. Leaning closer, he whispers in her ear, 'I love you, Ruth.'

She pauses to process the phrase, replying a moment too late, 'I love you too.' She hopes she does, she knows the feeling can't have gone far; it's buried somewhere, that's all, and when she has the headspace she'll send out a search party.

Giles kisses Bess's head. 'Goodbye, munchkin.' His eyes glisten with love. 'Be good for Mummy.' He strokes Ruth's cheek and leaves.

She watches him through the front window as he unlocks his bike in the concrete yard of their Victorian terrace. Their property search had always been couched in terms of *finding the right fit* and *falling in love*, but in the end the decision to buy this micro London house on the edge of railway sidings was steered as much by budget and urgency as it was by any DNA the house might possess. Giles pushes his bike through the gate, straddling the saddle with the excitement of a boy going out to play. With a grin, he mouths, 'Have fun,' then he disappears down the street to his job at the charity he fought hard to win.

Bess, sated and exhausted, drops her head back from the bottle, keeping the teat in her mouth for comfort. Her cheeks are wet and her eyelids jitter in a junkie-haze of food. There's huge pleasure in the peace that follows feeding, and sitting with a quiet, milk-heavy child in her arms allows a pulse of love to pass from Ruth to her daughter. The feeling's elusive though, disappearing as soon as Ruth's fears worm back inside. Bess's velvet skin, doll-sized features and the biscuity warmth of her little head are all laid out in front of Ruth like an abstract code she's yet to decipher. She kisses her daughter, lips barely brushing the baby's fontanelle. 'I'm getting better,' Ruth says. 'Things are really going to change round here.' She wishes more of their time could be as simple as when Bess is sleeping.

Outside, the flash of a white car passes on the street. Ruth's stomach seizes – was it a police car or one of those big white SUVs? Ruth's neighbour Liam bought a white Range Rover recently, but he lives at the beginning of the street, and Ruth's house is too far up for him to chance a parking space. If it's the police, it means something's wrong, perhaps something to do with last night's scream, a threat that might hurt Bess. Ruth strains her neck to see out of the window as a man passes in the opposite direction to the car, cigarette in mouth, plume of smoke the volume of his lungs. It's Barry from next door, one of the many dog walkers who amble up and down the street rather than bothering with the local park. He checks over his shoulder in the direction of the car. There's no panic to his step, no concern on his face. The emergency Ruth imagined was simply her trigger-happy adrenaline.

She reaches for the cup of lukewarm tea, trying not to unlatch her little girl from the bottle as she stretches. Bess wakes, starts to cry, face turning red in an instant, and Ruth decides it's easier to forgo the drink. There's a corner of toast next to the tea, slathered in butter and jam, just as Ruth likes it. Her mouth salivates. With the medication has come a lust for sweet, starchy foods, and her body has mushroomed over her trousers. Stretch marks on her stomach and thighs are battle scars from a war she'll never win. She still wears her elasticated maternity clothes because they're the only things that fit her new outline, and she's no money to buy new stuff since her leave has run out and Giles has become the solo breadwinner. A bobbly cardigan she hates and has thrown away on more than one occasion always ends up being taken out of the charity bag because nothing else is as easy to wear. Ruth's never been concerned about putting on weight, it's simply that she's always been slim, and now she finds the shape she's grown into is such an unknown she doesn't

15

recognize herself. Part of her identity has been lost with the change, exiting at such speed, it's as if she's gone to seed.

A knock at the door. Ruth shuffles to the entrance with one hand still holding the empty bottle in Bess's mouth so her baby doesn't wake again. Their front door opens directly into a little galley kitchen and standing outside is a uniformed woman with POLICE COMMUNITY SUPPORT OFFICER written across her jacket.

'Mrs Woodman?' the officer says, raising her eyebrows.

'Yes. Yes, that's me. What's happened?'

'Nothing to alarm you, I've just come to give you this.' The woman holds out a business card. 'It's a number to call in non-emergencies. It's my extension. You can leave a message if I don't answer or try 101.'

Ruth stares at the card, wondering if she should explain that since Bess there's no such thing as a non-emergency.

On the other side of Ruth's garden gate, two neighbours walk the pavement with their baby in a pushchair – Sandra and Liam, the friends she and Giles made when they moved in. Sandra's hair is a silky black curtain reaching halfway down her back. She turns to Ruth with a little wave, mouthing, 'You OK, honey?' Sweet Sandra, Ruth's guardian angel, the only friend who's truly looked out for Ruth even though she has her own baby to take care of. Their friendship's been tricky recently; Ruth's noticed a cooling off from Sandra's perspective – phone calls rarely answered, and when she does pick up, noticeable pauses when Ruth suggests meeting, any plans she tries to put in place cancelled last minute – perhaps understandable in light of Ruth's neediness as she's never been able to pinpoint an actual moment of offence. Ruth's reassured now by this tiny exchange, and she wonders if again she simply got it all wrong, that Sandra's still there for her and always has been. She nods quickly at her friend before ducking inside the door, hoping to hide her shabby outfit and unwashed hair, feeling guilty even though she hasn't done anything wrong, fault hardwired into her. Her worry is the couple will think she's been shoplifting – or worse, hurting her daughter. They know she's been ill. She wouldn't blame them for jumping to conclusions.

'Mrs Woodman?'

'Yes?'

'The card.' The policewoman thrusts it forward.

Sandra's already walked away. A kindness, Ruth thinks, to intuit her need for privacy. Liam has one arm round his wife's shoulders and he pushes the buggy a little awkwardly with his other hand, like a butler to his princess. He's overattentive to his family and there's something false about his need to play the part of perfect dad in front of this audience. He stops and holds his phone up to take a selfie of them all. Such a good-looking couple, with an air of confidence that it's all going to come their way, disappointment not even a word in their life vocabulary. As Liam goes to take the shot, Sandra stops him and repositions herself to get her best angle, then he holds the camera up again and gives his wife one of those awkward schmaltzy kisses, reminding himself and all his followers of the power of his love and the treasure of his possession. Not for the first time, uneasiness flits through Ruth at Liam's need to assert ownership over his family. Inside the pram is their quiet little boy, Ian, who always sleeps when he's supposed to, who eats buckets of food that fill out his cheeks, who's sunny and smiley to be around. Ruth's failure flares momentarily – *it's not fair*. She presses her lips together, hoping she's not actually mouthing the words.

'Is everything OK?' the officer asks.

Ruth snatches the card. 'Yes, fine.'

'Next time you hear something, just ring this number, please, Mrs Woodman. We'll get to it when we have time.' The officer smiles but her eyes don't match the uplift of her mouth.

'I'm really sorry. I was sure I heard a scream.'

'The call-log from your house has become prolific this last month and we need to save our manpower for real events, not suspicions. If we receive any more false alarms, I'm afraid our next course of action will be a fixed penalty notice.' The officer shifts her balance to the other foot, speaking in the same lightweight tone. 'There can only be so many paedophiles living on one street.'

Behind Ruth's lips her brain gallops: *I used to be someone. I had responsibilities, budgets, an assistant. I did lunch and shopped at Liberty*. Even in the last days before Bess was born, Ruth didn't rest, she'd have been bored within seconds of putting her feet up anyway. Her talent had always been hard work, the trickiest clients, the longest hours.

The officer pats Ruth's arm with a smile, and Ruth suspects that this time some of her words had been audible.

'I'm sorry, Mrs Woodman.' The woman's voice slows and she annunciates each syllable as if she's teaching phonetics. 'I didn't mean to upset you. It's just routine in these situations. Is there someone I can call? Do you have a friend nearby who could be with you?'

The last person Ruth wants to know about this is Giles, who'll clock her failure with his usual tired resignation. Plus he thinks she's improving, and she can't bear to disappoint him. The only other friend available is Sandra whose petite figure is already shrinking into the distance with that quick-footed, breezy pace, as if she's filled with helium and Liam needs to hold her down. If Sandra came over, Ruth could inhale a little of that buoyancy, but today it's better to be alone than have her own inadequacy laid bare. Ruth's imposed too much already, and she senses Liam's irritation at the amount of Sandra's time she absorbs; a mute rudeness emanates from him whenever they meet and Ruth's constantly trying to second guess what he's thinking. Everyone else Ruth knows is at work, their lives set to a different clock, but even if they weren't, there's not a single one of them Ruth would want to sit with this morning. If she's going to fail, she'd rather do so with no one watching. Letting people in, admitting her need, has always been a challenge, and even in the past, those who had the potential to be solid friends only seemed to end up as acquaintances. 'You are hard to know,' a colleague once told Ruth, but since her teenage years and the black hole that opened in Ruth's universe, she's needed to keep a piece of herself back. No one would ever be able to get as close to her as her sister.

'I'm fine,' Ruth replies. 'I won't call any more.' She takes a big breath and looks the policewoman directly in the eye. 'I really have to go now.'

As she reaches to push the door shut, the PCSO leans towards Bess. 'So sweet! Your daughter is beautiful.' The woman strokes Bess's head and glances at Ruth. 'Sorry, I couldn't resist.' Another smile, this one more gentle. 'It's lovely when they need you all the time, isn't it? I never wanted mine to grow up. This is the best age, don't you think?'

Ruth discovers tears are falling down her cheeks. She rubs them away but they keep coming; somehow it's always easier to open up in front of strangers whose sympathy she can bear because she'll probably never see them again.

'It's just so hard.' Ruth laughs a little through her tears, annoyed at herself as now the officer will think she's a time-waster. 'I mean, it's like I've become invisible, and I've forgotten what normal feels like. How come everyone else knows what to do and I don't?'

The woman puts her hands in her pockets, bedding in for the kind of session she hadn't expected and – by the look on her face – doesn't want. 'I know it can feel like it at times, but no one's keeping score.'

'Well, they are of me.' Ruth's hand hovers over her mouth, wanting to take back the volume.

The officer leans away a touch. 'One day you'll look back on all this and wish you'd cherished these moments. Before you know it you'll have a grumpy teenager on your hands who won't want to know you any more.' The radio attached to the PCSO's jacket crackles into life and she fiddles with the knob, bending an ear to listen, eyes rolling to the sky. 'Never a dull moment, eh!' Ruth wants to hold on to the woman, keep her there for a little longer with all her access to life outside Ruth's tiny courtyard. Instead, Ruth presses her nails into the heel of her hand; any harder and she'd draw blood. 'Be kind to yourself, Mrs Woodman,' the officer says. 'Make yourself a cup of tea. Relax for the rest of the day. And please, please, leave the policework to the police.'

The tall wooden gate squeaks shut behind the officer as she walks up the street, back to her car and her full life. Ruth closes the door, returning to the laundry-filled lounge, and she navigates unpacked boxes containing books and knick-knacks, some labelled 'kitchen' and 'bedroom' stacked three high against the wall. Several containers have been ripped open, the cooking and cleaning essentials scavenged from the top. She looks inside one box: a wedding photo in a cracked frame, a jar of antique marbles bought from a charity shop. So much junk that Ruth forgets what it all is – certainly nothing she needs or misses. She may as well put everything of her old life in a skip rather than get it out to gather dust. If the fog of medication would lift, at least there'd be the impetus to tidy even if the opportunity didn't present itself. How can one tiny being take up so much time?

A stack of old magazines is on the floor next to the sofa. Sunlight staggers across their spines, illuminating a series of small golden steps. Ruth holds up her phone and pivots the viewfinder of the camera app to get the best shot. Her fingers twitch as if they're waking up. She presses the shutter and the moment freezes on the screen, the frame elevating the mundane into a moment of beauty. When Bess was first born, Ruth had posted her shots on social media, but she's banned from Instagram and Facebook now; all that self-comparison kept dropping her down to rock bottom. Then when she'd been really ill, she lost any filter for her bitterness. 'Your diatribe is poisoning my feed,' one now ex-friend messaged. Without an online presence, though, Ruth feels like she's disappeared from most people's lives, or at least that her experiences are seen as less valid – even to herself, even if what she had posted in the past was lies – because she never gets those little endorphin hits of approval from the 'like' button. But neither she nor Giles made any rules around Ruth taking photos for herself, and she fantasizes that one day, on the other side of all this, she'll exhibit these pictures, the images by then history, and she'll be able to reflect on how far she's come, the mountain she conquered.

Bess pumps her tiny legs up and down and her face turns red. Her squawks are ones that can't be satisfied by milk. The doctor says it's wind – it's been this way since she was a couple of weeks old – and no amount of patting will bring anything up. The only method that works is holding Bess over Ruth's shoulder and pacing the room until she settles. Ruth puts her phone to one side and takes her baby into the kitchen where she boils the kettle to make a fresh cup of tea, stirring in three sugars. The drink spills and burns Ruth's one free hand. Tears spring into her eyes, but she refuses to give them any attention when the day is sure to bring bigger and badder problems. She puts the cup to one side to cool and walks the well-trodden avenue through the mess in the lounge, tripping over her dressing-gown cord and resigning herself to another day stumbling at the coalface of motherhood.

2

It's 10.30 a.m. when Ruth finally leaves home, each earlier attempt frustrated by another feed or nappy change. From her gate she takes a right to walk the remaining forty terraces that line one side of the street towards the petrol station at the end of the road, the business now decommissioned and used as a pop-up car wash. After that, she'll carry on to the high street to cruise the charity shops and pick up a coffee.

Morning sun dissolves last night's fears and the scream is consigned to the background of Ruth's thoughts. She's revived by the chilled air and picks up pace, the buggy's wheels over paving stones acting like a train on tracks, lulling Bess, and Ruth exhales into the peace of believing she can be the mum she wants to be.

There are rules to follow since recovering from her illness and leaving the house unaccompanied would be a black mark. Walking, though, is one of the few things that blocks Ruth's anxiety. Since Giles has started returning to work for periods of time, she reasons with herself that getting out is justified; she won't go far, she won't get lost, she'll take supplies. Before she was diagnosed, she used to love taking Bess for a spin round the block in the pram, even though post-caesarean she should have been taking it easy. But as her illness quickly progressed, the act of forward motion became mesmerizing, so that on several occasions Ruth found herself stranded miles from home with no money and no idea how she'd got there. Night had been coming in as she'd made bewildered calls to Giles to rescue her, with Bess hysterical as Ruth's head had been so full she'd forgotten to feed her. The third time it happened, Ruth was sitting in the car after Giles had tracked her down, and she'd turned her hands over and over, staring at her skin that had become hypersensitive from the elbows down, as if her limbs were no longer her own. A terror had gripped her; what might these hands be capable of now they were out of her control? She begged Giles to stop the car, slap her face, bind her arms, anything to bring her back into her body, but only the speedometer reacted, spinning up to 50 as Giles jumped amber light after red light, driving her straight to the nearest A&E. No one had prepped Ruth or Giles for the outside chance of post-partum psychosis, and even if the couple had been warned, things like that didn't happen to normal people who'd just sunk their limited savings into a little house and were happy to be making a family. The bread-making, finger-painting and picnicking fun Ruth had planned was all wiped out in one diagnosis. From there on, all Ruth's energy was poured into keeping afloat. That was just under five months ago.

To Ruth's left on the pavement is a tall hedgerow that hides the back gardens of houses on a parallel street. Last summer, the bush had chattered with life as birds zipped in and out of the leaves. Now its winter branches are knotted and bare. To Ruth's right she glimpses her neighbours' front yards through slatted fences, like a Victorian zoetrope, though there are no dancing gymnasts or running horses here, only bins and overgrown gardens. When she and Giles moved to the road, they loved the spiky horsetail plants that sprang up in their raised flower beds, only what they didn't realize then was that the shoots quickly turned shaggy and brown. So they set about clearing the plants from their garden, but each time Ruth pulled one up, another two grew in its place from the network of roots underpinning the whole street, the subterranean empire widening daily, and it soon became clear why most of their neighbours had given up weeding. The boggy soil would need to be poisoned half a mile in each direction to bring the infestation under control.

During those first weeks in their new house, Giles had searched library vaults for old maps of the borough, and like a boy discovering a lost kingdom, he'd papered their floor with a geological survey and yellowed deeds. 'Look, we're here!' His face was flushed as he pointed to the place their house now stands, where a hundred and fifty years ago a river had followed the course of the road; a valley at the bottom of gentle hills, part of the countryside buffer around London. Giles's finger traced another line through woodland. 'This used to be one of the main trade routes in and out of London. Apparently highwaymen used to lie in wait in the woods to ambush travellers.' His eyes flashed with excitement as he looked out of the window at the metres of sidings that were all that remained of that wood, a number of mature trees still standing. 'I wonder how many murders took place just over there. How many undiscovered bodies are still buried in the earth.' The rail line conveniently took the place of the old road and cottages were built for the workers as the water was redirected into a culvert underground, where it still rushes below their feet. Sometimes Ruth thinks she hears the hidden river, like a bath left running in a distant room. Though since there's no longer a natural valley for the weather to empty itself into, and the surrounding hills have now been forested by tarmac and bricks, there's nothing left to absorb the rain, so their street's become the storm gutter of north-west London, an energy sink where all the bad stuff gets stuck.

A flock of birds cruises through the sky, away from London, like an exhalation. Ruth presses ahead, peering into gardens, trying to guess from the plant pots, mopeds, old fridges or garden furniture what kind of people live in each house. She vaguely knows a few of her neighbours. Monica and Barry's terraced house connects directly with hers on the left. The couple have four children, the last of whom is a newborn. Monica's friendly in an arm's-length sort of way, and Ruth senses she's over the newbie mum phase, with bigger kids whose door-slams reverberate through their shared wall. She hasn't the time for Ruth's fuss and bother. *Been there, worried about that, worked it all out*, is the look Monica gives Ruth when they chat over the fence, but even so, there's a fatigued kindness in her eyes. Monica's husband, Barry, is skinny and small, as if no one bothered to feed him when he was a kid. He throws stones at a fox that slopes around the pavements and over a small strip of land just beyond the back gardens, which everyone here calls the allotments. 'Foxes are worse than rats,' Barry says, his eyes never leaving Ruth's breasts as he speaks. 'Vermin. They attack your kids, you know. The council should put down traps.' In the summer, Ruth used to watch the fox from Bess's bedroom window; he lay curled asleep on the roof of a dilapidated chicken shed in her own allotment that butts the railway fence, his sun-cooked fur shimmering. Since the weather's turned, the fox has got skinny. Ruth leaves leftovers in her back garden at night, and in the morning the bowl is licked clean.

Walking up the pavement towards Ruth is an elderly woman who lives on the other side of their house. An alleyway divides their terraces, so thankfully they don't share a wall. This woman is the mum of Liam, mother-in-law of Ruth's friend Sandra. Ruth's only ever seen her in her garden or allotment, tending her vegetable patch, taking photos of birds with a clunky Soviet-era camera, or in passing like now. The woman always keeps her head tipped forward, like she's expecting the wind – or anything else that cares to have a pop – to give her trouble. Liam says his mum's batty, and Sandra scowls at the very mention of her name. 'Bloody witch,' Sandra says. 'She'll try it on with you, Ruth, if you give her half a chance. Fill your head with nonsense about us, but you should ignore her.' Ruth focuses on the distance in case today Liam's mum should decide to say hello. Avoiding the enemy, neighbour though she may be, is the least Ruth can do to repay Sandra's friendship. They pass without catching each other's eyes, and Ruth breathes again.

The final house on the road is Sandra and Liam's, only metres from Liam's childhood home, the location of his mum and her trickiness when he'd been growing up, behaviour Sandra says continues to this day. He bought his place for peanuts ten years ago – 'Before you lot bumped up the prices.' His mum has health problems so he needs to be close apparently, although actually he only seems to visit her when he has to collect computer parts that get delivered to her address as his work takes him out and about, fixing laptops and other tech in the homes of 'the morons', as he likes to call his clients. Occasionally, when Ruth's neighbour's not been in, the postman delivers to Ruth, and she grudgingly accepts. The parcels are addressed to Mr Smith, c/o no. 40 – his mum's house – and Ruth always experiences a kind of static coming off the packages as they sit on her worktop, in anticipation of Liam's outline appearing on the other side of the frosted glass panel of her front door. When he eventually arrives, she can never stop apologizing as she hands the parcel over; for what she's sorry she doesn't know, but something about his expectant quietness makes her want to fill the space with words.

A roughly constructed brick wall surrounds Liam's property where a fence should be, with trellis on top making it impossible to see inside, the perimeter fortified by a solid gate with entry buzzer on the street. Ruth's never been invited over, any socializing between the couples always having taken place at Ruth's or in the pub, but she imagines that inside their home it's immaculate, unlike her own. Everything about Sandra is neat and safe, and Ruth yearns to spend time at her friend's place where she's sure she'd be purified by an osmosis of calm. Sandra recently admitted that it's Liam who won't allow visitors – 'You know what blokes are like, wants me all to himself' – and there was even a hint of pride that he loves her enough to need only her in his life. Once, when Ruth had been really unwell, she'd built up a rage about never having been inside, paranoid that Sandra was hiding something from her – what, though, she had no idea – and she snuck round the back of her friend's house, held her phone up over the high wall and clicked the camera shutter a few times. Even now, weeks down the line and on the better side of illness, Ruth blushes at her craziness and the shame of spying on a friend.

As she passes Sandra and Liam's today, she lowers her head, afraid if she sees either of them she'll have to explain the earlier police visit, and she's too tired to invent a more rational, less humiliating reason why the officer came to her door, scared too that having the police round might reverse Sandra's renewed friendship – no one round here likes or trusts the police. Ruth has been building up to asking Sandra outright what she'd done to upset her, and now that she won't have to, she wants to keep it that way. She pushes the buggy at speed.

A car's been abandoned on the road, its broken windscreen shedding onto the pavement. Bored kids probably, slashing seats and tugging out wires for the hell of it. Why not, there's nothing else to do here, though Ruth can't fathom why they keep crapping in their own pool when a few streets away are posher houses, each a rich well of opportunity. Most nights, groups of lads race up and down this long straight road on mopeds, the noisy engines like wasps in a jar, and sometimes they set fire to wheelie bins. By the time the fire brigade arrive, the gang have escaped down an alley to stash their bikes in the allotments at the back and run into their houses. No one on the street likes what they do but no one's going to dob them in to the authorities either; there's only one thing worse than being a victim and that's involving the police. Occasionally Ruth's seen figures on the railway sidings and once a campfire. At least the kids have some wilderness, somewhere to escape to and be real children without bothering anyone else.

Bess's pushchair crunches over the glass gravel and a couple of rough-cuts lodge themselves in the plastic wheels. This is Bess's normality; it might be all she ever knows. Ruth questions for the millionth time how she and Giles thought a good place to set up home was on the industrial edge of the city, so deep north-west it's possible they're not even in London. But before having a child, colonizing what they thought of as edgy or undiscovered parts of town had been exciting, like missionaries in the cult of gentrification. They were the early adopters, front runners of the still affordable, only this road has yet to see a glimmer of the place it's predicted to become. There've been rumours of a big new development on the acres of railway sidings that parallel the backs of the houses, though every application so far has got snagged in council planning. No Costa has yet appeared on the high street, no M&S Foodhall, but when these shops do arrive, Ruth and Giles will have made their money and can ship out if they choose. Houses these days are investments, not homes, and this particular buy is a step towards their dream of a spacious semi in a leafy suburb. No wonder all the families who've lived here for generations scowl at Ruth's potted Japanese maple and pastel-coloured watering can. They see the aspiration, they know what's coming. They don't want a makeover, they're fine as they are.

Bess has pulled off her hat and is waving it in her hand. Cold wind sweeps across her head, her dark hair wispy like the half-grown feathers of a baby bird. Ruth peers down at the soft spot of skin covering her daughter's still-forming skull. Only millimetres of cells separate the baby's essence from the outside world – such poor design – and Ruth's heart contracts with a feeling closer to terror than love. She stops to put the bonnet back on, crouching to plant a kiss on Bess's cheek, lips sinking into the baby's pillow of skin, a little mole on her cheek that makes her look even more adorable. Ruth begins to unravel the plastic rain cover to keep the air from touching her baby, but Bess predicts what's coming and kicks her legs, hurling the mohair hat – Ruth's favourite, an expensive gift from a work colleague – into a puddle of black water. The material soaks up the scum. No amount of disinfectant will ever make it clean again. Ruth stands, walks on, leaves the hat where it lies.

Ahead is the car wash that's taken over the petrol station.

A grubby banner has been tied to the rear wall: RAY'S HAND WASH AND VALET. The sign has come loose at one end and flaps in the wind. A small queue of cars edges into the main road, waiting to join the conveyor belt of soaking, scrubbing, rinsing and vacuuming. The process takes place underneath a floating roof that's propped up by a peeling plaster colonnade; a modern-day Acropolis. Ruth wonders how long the station's been out of service, how many years it's taken for the weather to pick at the paint like this. An old-fashioned mangle stands in one corner of the forecourt and the workers crank the handle to wring blackened water from their cloths before wiping down the cars.

Shouting and beeping as traffic slows to pass the queue in the road. Men on the forecourt call to each other across the mechanical hiss of the jet wash. These same sounds reach Ruth's house every day, signalling the start of a world that moves to a different rhythm than her own, her shift seemingly never-ending. One of the workmen flicks his rag in the air and the sonic boom reaches Ruth as a gunshot, jolting her back to a memory of last night's scream. The scream she's been told to ignore, the scream that didn't exist, the very hearing of which is proof of her fragility. Her brain overlays an image on the forecourt of a woman running in the dark, being chased, grabbed, thrown to the ground. Ruth's come to a standstill, her hands tight round the handles of the pushchair. But nothing happened last night. Ruth knows that, even if part of her refuses to believe it. Bess kicks her legs to move on and Ruth jerks forward.

Customers whose cars are being washed sit on plastic

chairs outside the shop, and they glance up at Ruth as she approaches. The permission to pause in the cold sun on a fume-thick road seems to be giving them enormous pleasure. A woman in a business suit with briefcase at her side is bewitched by her smartphone. A man leans on a wall eating crisps, staring at his car being vacuumed. He gives Ruth the briefest attention before returning to his interesting day. 'Don't forget to lift the seats to get the crumbs,' he calls to a man using an industrial vacuum cleaner with eyes painted on the machine that seem to follow Ruth as she passes. Cleaning man nods and car man nods back. Ruth wonders if the driver has children, and if they know he loves his car more than them. To one side of the shop, two Mercedes are parked, shined to a mirror. They're here most days and must belong to the owners. Next to these vehicles is Liam's white Range Rover, a big step up from the nondescript sedan he used to own when Ruth first met him. Sandra says they have a deal with the petrol station to park here where it's easier to find space than outside their own gate.

Ruth's thirsty, and she rummages in her bag for the bottle of water she filled before leaving the house. She's packed an item for every possible Bess-emergency but forgotten the one thing she needs for herself. A section of the old shop at the petrol station is open to the public for basics: toilet roll, plastic bread, nuclear margarine. Customers getting their cars washed and kids on the street use it mostly, as does Ruth in emergencies, and today it's easier to buy some water than go back home. Manholes patchwork the forecourt and planks have been laid over the uneven surface where the petrol pumps used to stand. Bess's head wobbles as they cross the pitted and crumbling tarmac, her little neck hidden inside a roll of chubby skin. The gravel kicks up an ancient tang of petrol and Ruth strains not to rush from this toxic fog; there's only home to go to and it's better to be here than reunited with her own four walls so soon.

On the main road, a vehicle jumps into a space in the queue. Ruth opens the door of the shop as, behind her, two men shout at each other through car windows. Inside the shop, a man in a shiny tracksuit reads a paper behind the counter and another man in a business suit stacks the shelves. They look up as Ruth enters. The man in the aisle is shoving cans next to bread, squashing the loaves into un-buyable shapes. His colleague behind the counter is well groomed, eyelashes thick and mascara-dark, verging on pretty. Behind him, a glass-panelled door opens onto a small room where several men have plates of food on their laps. They're relaxed and chatting, perhaps on their break, their clothes grubby from cleaning. Desiccated moths darken the plastic of a flickering strip light and an untidy desk at the back of the room is heaped with dog-eared tabloids and a couple of mobile phones. Hanging from the door handle is a spotty silk scarf, the femininity incongruous in the unapologetically masculine environment. Perhaps a customer dropped it by accident and it's being kept here in case she returns.

Business must be booming, Ruth thinks, to fill all these people's time, plus pay their bills and buy expensive cars. What would a wage from a place like this be? Would they need to supplement their income with another job? Perhaps some of the men have to sleep rough on the floor here, and if they do, maybe they heard the scream last night, the scream Ruth's already assured herself didn't occur, although assuring and convincing are two different things. She wants to ask if anyone heard, imagines filling the air with the question, the words perverse in this snug of Heinz and Hovis and Cadbury. Then, as if it doesn't belong to her, Ruth's mouth begins to move.

'Does anyone stay here overnight?' She blushes.

'No.' Pretty-man frowns behind the counter. 'Of course not, this is a car wash.'

Ruth's eyes flit around without landing on anyone. 'I know, I just wondered – for security, I mean.' She picks at the foam handle of the buggy. 'Because I thought I heard something last night and I was worried.' She looks up. 'I called the police.'

One of the men sitting in the back room catches her eye and stops eating. Shelf-stacking man walks behind the counter. He's taller and wider than the other man, with a puffy booze pallor. His suit bags around the elbows and knees as if he's slept in it. The two form a wall in front of Ruth.

'It was probably foxes,' shelf-stacking man says, his voice smooth and reassuring. 'They sound like screaming. There are animals here, because of the railway and the land. Lots of empty land.'

Reflected in the glass panel of the door behind them is Katty, the eldest of Monica's children. She's only about thirteen, but seems older, probably because she's always out on her own, desperate for space away from her siblings in their tiny house. Katty's at Ruth's back, and her reflection shows her holding her index finger next to her head and rotating the digit in a *she's cuckoo* way. Ruth turns and Katty instantly drops her hand, the teenager well practised in the art of piss-taking as well as avoiding getting caught. In Katty's other hand is a vaping pen. She walks to the counter, chooses a packet of Haribos from the multiverse of sweets, opens and eats them even though she hasn't yet paid.

'Hello, Katty.' Ruth tries to keep the nervousness from her voice. 'How's your mum? How's your baby brother?'

'He's in hospital, got some lurgy.' Katty looks Ruth up and down without moving from her relaxed position. 'Went to see him today.' She talks through a mulch of sweets. 'The doctors don't know what it is, but he's got spots all down his throat.'

'Oh God, that's terrible! I'm really sorry.'

'Yeah.' She turns to face the counter and continues eating.

The men watch Ruth in silence. She leaves the pushchair at the counter to get a bottle of water from the chiller and her mouth salivates at the cans of Coke. She grabs two, the tins deliciously slippery with cold. Bess grizzles. Ruth turns to see Katty with her finger in Bess's mouth. Bess is sucking hard while Katty smiles at Ruth.

'All babies like it when I do this,' Katty says. 'It kept my brother quiet for ages at the hospital.'

Ruth grabs the handles of the pushchair and swivels the buggy fast so that Katty's finger plops out. Bess cries. Ruth begins to speak but the words stopper-up in her throat. She pushes towards the door, the drinks sliding in her free hand.

'You need to pay,' pretty-man says.

'Of course. Yes, I do, I know. Sorry.' One of the cans falls to the floor as she fumbles with coins in her bag. Bess's cry ramps up. 'Oh God, never mind.' She laughs, more high-pitched than she expected, placing the second drink on a pile of newspapers by the door. 'I'll get these later.' The dropped can rolls to the middle of the floor. Nobody moves to pick it up. Ruth's face holds the rictus of a smile as she heaves open the door and rushes outside.

She steers the pushchair in the direction of the doctor's surgery, and when she's out of sight of the shop she stops to smear antiseptic cream on Bess's lips and cheeks. The baby screams, little pink mouth stretched into an angry O as Ruth slathers on the ointment. She wipes away the excess so Bess doesn't swallow any, no idea if it will do any good, but something's better than nothing, so she squeezes more from the tube to layer on Bess. Then Ruth remembers she can't just turn up at the doctor's as they'll tell Giles she's been out without permission. She heads towards home, concocting an excuse as she runs. She'll call the surgery and tell them Katty came round the house – they'll probably have a record of the girl's brother's illness and will understand it's urgent. Ruth will insist they do a home visit, which they will because she's high on their 'to watch' list. Antiretrovirals are probably what Bess needs. The buggy's wheels skitter at speed over the rough pavement.

When she reaches home, Ruth bundles the pram into the house and leaves Bess in her seat. The little girl is crying, but she's buckled in and safe at least, freeing up Ruth to phone the surgery. The receptionist answers. Ruth tries to explain what happened but can't find a way to take the hysteria from her voice. 'I just need to talk to a doctor. Please put me through. It's an emergency.'

'All the doctors are with patients at the moment. If it's urgent, you need to call 999.'

Ruth has a flash of the police officer from this morning telling her no more emergency calls. Did that include a medical emergency? How many ambulances has she called since Giles has been returning to work, the paramedics nodding with a *what seems to be the problem today?* as they amble through her front garden.

'Is this Mrs Woodman?' the receptionist says. 'Would you like me to get in touch with your husband for you?'

Giles mustn't know she's got herself into a state; he'll suspect something's amiss with her medication. He'll want to stay home and watch her, tetchy that he can't get on with his work, that she's unable to be normal, that her mothering still falls way short of anything approaching satisfactory. Ruth bangs the receiver down.

On a pad she makes two columns, one with the header 'P' for probable, and the second with an 'I' for improbable. Under 'P' she lists, 'Katty's filthy hands, germs attacking Bess's immune system, poisoning by antiseptic cream,' but there's no one to ask for verification, no one to advise her without raising the alarm over her own health and whipping up the inevitable blizzard of interference. Or perhaps the doctors will finally agree that it's time to take Bess away from this useless mother who can't seem to get through one day without falling apart. Ruth leaves the 'I' column blank as she lifts her baby from the buggy, taking her into the downstairs loo to wash her face at the sink. Bess howls at the water as Ruth rubs and rinses a soapy hand over her anyway. 'I'm really sorry, sweetie. Nearly clean now.'

The tap continues to run as Ruth recalls the looks on the men's faces in the shop when she was acting crazy. She goes to stick her hand back into the water, but the stream's now gushing hot and she snatches her fingers away, a thought burning through her worry. She only mentioned hearing a noise last night – they were the ones who called it a scream.

3

Ruth lays Bess on her play mat on the wooden floor, checking inside the baby's mouth for spots. There's no room inside her immediate panic to unpick any more of what was or wasn't said at the shop. Bess's bottom lip quivers, and Ruth kisses the little forehead, testing the baby's temperature with her own lips; she's hot, but that could be because she's been crying. Ruth leans back on her heels, attempting to slow her breath. Directly underneath where Bess lies, where her precious head touches the floor, is the dusty void of the foundations.

When Ruth and Giles first moved in, they had to complete a damp course, and the workmen pulled up some of the ancient pine floorboards to check for leaking pipes, finding only an anaemic root of a horsetail breaking through, its tendril as broad as a finger, blindly searching for an outcrop of sun. It had shocked Ruth that underneath their feet the foundations consisted of only a hollow foot or so before a layer of concrete shored up the mud. How close they live to the earth, how little of substance props up their world. Centimetres below the footings, the soil is a mess of dead things; a molecular memory of everyone and everything that's passed over this place, perhaps generating a kind of energetic interference that's been wiping Ruth's intuition, like a ship losing contact with land as it sails through the Bermuda Triangle. What if one of the highwaymen stood on the very spot where Bess now lies? What if he killed and buried someone there? Ruth scoops up her daughter and paces the room with the little girl over her shoulder.

One-handed, she powers up her computer and googles *virus, infection rate, incubation period*. Layer upon layer of childhood rashes pass her inspection as she falls down virtual wormholes of looser and wilder association. Her fingers grow tacky, the keypad seemingly as infected as the images it summons. She forces herself to close the laptop, palm warming on the lid. These past months, Ruth's learnt her triggers, she has insight into her illness, and this obsessional behaviour is a red flag. Her astoundingly creative worry fuels so many potential catastrophes, though she's yet to understand the purpose of this huge rehearsal for the unlikely. At times she almost wishes the worst would happen, then at least she could deal with a tangible problem, with the impetus to mop up her flooding adrenaline. But not Bess being ill, that would be a horror too far.

She takes Bess upstairs and manages to settle her in her cot. With the baby finally asleep, the house is quiet, and Ruth's nerves stagger back to partway normal. She goes downstairs and splashes cold water on her face in the small downstairs toilet. Inches from her nose is a roughly patched area of wall, evidence of how she'd once tried to break through to the recess under the stairs, where she'd been convinced her sister had been bricked up. That day, months ago, she'd used the big kitchen knife to hack at the plasterboard, managing to make a hole that had opened onto a bead of darkness. 'Tam, are you there?' she'd whispered into the crack, willing her sister to answer. 'I'm sorry, OK? But you should have let me tell them.'

She turns off the tap and barely dries her hands before pulling the toilet door shut behind her. Even at that brightest point of madness, a tiny part of Ruth had stood outside the main beam of her brain's invention. She remembers glancing at her reflection in the blade of the knife, her face unrecognizable in its determination, body as well as mind almost completely out of her control, and she knew then that she couldn't be trusted. If she could damage a wall, then if pushed, if she truly lost her sanity, what might she be capable of doing to Bess? She'd dropped the knife where it clattered on the floor, and ran to gather all the other sharp implements she could find – the rest of the kitchen knives, two corkscrews, a broken mirror, even an old fountain pen – and placed them in a tea towel before bundling them up and taking them outside, through her small back garden, across the path and past the old chicken shed on her allotment to where tall scratchy weeds met the railway fence. One by one, she threw the items onto the sidings, where she'd never be able to reach them again, and never be able to use them to hurt Bess.

A train rumbles past in the distance and a bird screeches,

startling Ruth back to the present. Her thoughts open again onto the scene at the shop, the moment having bided its time until she's had the space to examine her unease. Is it embarrassment? It's highly probable she misheard the man – though her darker suspicion is that he knew about the scream. In the middle distance of her front yard, shrubs and climbers planted in the spring are now spindly and bare, the world outside as dull and pedestrian as before, her wild speculation ridiculous in contrast.

Two men walk the pavement at a slow pace. They wear sportswear with stripes and ticks that mimic expensive brands. High-tech trainers, bulky and luminous, hit the pavement in sync. Ruth recognizes both of them from the car wash. They lift their heads to look through her window, past the dreamcatcher she's hung from the latch – a present posted through her letter box after Bess was born with no card to say who it was from – to where Ruth stands in her lounge. One of them is the man who stood behind the counter, his kohl-dark eyelashes accentuating his stare. He says something to the other man, who nods. Ruth's teeth and jaw ache.

Her mobile bursts into life. She yelps as the phone skitters in a vibrating circle on the table. The display flashes up *No Caller ID*. She reaches for the handset, but the ring cuts out before she gets to it. Outside, one of the men puts something in his pocket. She cranes her neck as they pass, wondering if it's possible to make out the shape of a phone in his trousers, but only his bunched knuckles show through the fabric. The two disappear from view.

Ruth makes a fist and thumps it against her forehead. *Enough of this.* Paranoia is sneaking up on her and she knows only too well from past experience that if she gives it enough room it will come inside and make a home; the man was most likely warming his hand in his pocket, and how would either of them know her number anyway? She wakes up her mobile to check the display. There's no message, the call probably telesales or international from her dad.

The light's been left on in the toilet and an arc of yellow shines under the door, making a still life of the toys scattered on the floor, their shadows elongated, the tableau almost comical. She opens her camera app and takes a couple of shots, then snaps a picture of the chaotic table: laptop surrounded by breakfast plates, garden out of focus in the background. The winter day is grey with cold, perfectly summing up her mood, but inside she brightens a little, as if by capturing the worst of her surroundings on her phone she no longer has to give her issues the same attention. She circles the room with a growing energy, taking more pictures of the clutter and mess, the photo frame elevating the banal and transforming the domestic into scenes of beauty, encouraging her to believe she matters even though she has no online presence and no one to be her witness; she lives unobserved, uncelebrated, invisible, apart from this. One day she'll reflect on these photos as a difficult time she passed through, nothing more insidious than that, though that future version of herself seems impossibly distant. And because the past is equally remote, inspiring only a kind of grief for the endless freedom Ruth had before Bess and might never experience again, it means that being present, here in this moment, is her only mooring. The sun comes out from behind a cloud and the light shifts from blue to golden.

Ruth pulls up her last dialled numbers and clicks on Sandra's name, chancing that Sandra's earlier wave when Ruth was on her doorstep was a positive sign. The phone rings only once before Sandra answers.

'Ruth!' Sandra's voice is high and girly with that breathy sexiness Ruth imagines men go nuts for. 'I was just thinking about you.'

Sandra's lost the vagueness of recent weeks, and Ruth's fears of being frozen out for some mystery infraction seem to be unfounded. She exhales in relief.

Sandra breaks the pause. 'You OK, honey?'

Ruth dissects the pretence she's about to set up, the prospect of feigning ease after her morning of stress, deciding instead that what she really needs is to confide. 'Oh, I've been in a right state.' Her voice shakes with relief. 'Things have been really getting on top.'

'Oh no, poor you. What's happened?'

'Nothing really, just nonsense. Bad dreams probably.' She stops herself there, unwilling to go full tilt just yet.

'Nightmares?'

'More than likely, didn't seem like it at the time, though. Got myself in a bit of a tight spot with the police too, but then you saw them here this morning.'

Sandra laughs. 'You been stealing make-up from Boots again?'

Ruth giggles. It feels good. 'I wish it was that simple.' She runs a hand through her unwashed hair and switches the phone to the other ear. 'I've been getting myself in knots.' She hears Sandra inhale sharply – Sandra, her one and only friend – and Ruth leaps in to reassure. 'Not like when Bess was tiny, nothing as bad as that. Just worrying about anything and everything. You know how it can get.' Although she doubts Sandra does. 'Please don't tell Giles, though, he'll freak. I've got a handle on it now.'

'Don't worry, honey.' In the background, Sandra's house is perfectly quiet and Ruth thinks about the hoops her friend must have had to jump through today to make her home immaculate and keep up her baby's routine, and whether that silence implies sanctuary or sterility. Sandra continues with a small sigh. 'I know how aggy blokes can get.'

'Who, Liam?' Sandra sometimes jokes to Ruth about certain rules she has at home, like once when Liam didn't get back when he said he would, she simply threw his food, plate and all, in the bin. She hints that he likes the boundaries, that it makes him attentive. Ruth worries about raising the inconsistency now for fear of offending her friend – it's not the first time Sandra's given out mixed messages – but she wants to check with Sandra that everything's OK at home. 'I thought you said he only gets in a strop with other people and not you?'

Sandra is silent on the other end of the phone and Ruth imagines her friend momentarily levitating out of the contradiction before she cuts back in. 'Let's not spoil the day by talking about him, eh?' Sandra speaks fast, with no space for Ruth to question even if she wanted. 'Why don't we pop to

Brent Cross? You fancy it? We can have a coffee and you can tell me what's been worrying you. Sound good?'

One day, Ruth will press for more understanding of Sandra's set-up with Liam – it seems to be as much about complaining as complying – but for now, what she really needs is to leave the house. 'Sounds great.'

'I'll drive up to yours in about ten minutes. Do you want to let Giles know or shall I?'

'You do it. It'll come better from you.'

Sandra's been vetted by Ruth's team, she's a go-to friend who's trusted with Ruth, with emergency numbers to contact if Ruth gets in a fix. She even has a set of keys in case she should need to get into Ruth's house, although she's never used them. Sometimes, Sandra gives Ruth a conspiratorial wink if Ruth wants a little longer out of the house or confesses to slightly wonky thinking. 'Don't worry, hun,' Sandra says. 'I won't tell anyone unless I think you're in danger.' Sandra being on-call means that the two of them can go out. Ruth's not driven for so long she doesn't trust herself behind the wheel, and her and Giles's vaguely vintage Saab idles outside the house. Giles has talked about giving it up altogether. 'Who really needs a car in London?' he said. 'The amount it costs to tax and insure hardly makes up for the use we get out of it.' 'But what about when I'm back to normal?' Ruth replied. 'What if I need to get away?' Giles's raised eyebrows posed the question he didn't need to speak aloud: *From what do you need to escape?*

When Sandra arrives it's with her usual bundle of goodies for Ruth. Sometimes, it's cast-offs from her house or wardrobe, other times, a small gift she thinks Ruth might like.

'I couldn't resist,' Sandra says, handing over a branded paper bag.

'Oh wow, thanks!' Ruth takes the roped handles and peers inside. It's a small Clarins moisturizer and cleansing set. The whole while Ruth had been anxious her friend didn't want to see her any more and Sandra must have been thinking of her all along. 'Just what I needed.' She absent-mindedly touches her face, worrying if this is a little nudge from Sandra for her to make more effort.

'It's a pleasure, honey. I remember what it was like to scrimp and save, and you deserve a treat.'

'It's really kind of you.' Ruth puts the bag on the dining table and picks out a couple of the bottles, her pleasure at receiving the gift marred by guilt at never being able to reciprocate, or the sense that she needs to pay Sandra back in some other way, with loyalty perhaps, or compliance. The creams are small enough to have been a freebie Sandra received when buying something bigger, but still, she could have kept them for herself and Ruth's grateful.

'That's what best friends are for,' Sandra says, already making her way out of the door to the car, missing the surprise on Ruth's face.

Ruth would never dare admit out loud how precious Sandra's friendship is in case the feelings weren't mutual, ashamed too that she needs Sandra more than vice versa; she always assumed Sandra hadn't introduced her to any of her other friends because she wasn't up to their standard, but perhaps a group of mates isn't Sandra's style after all. Nevertheless, this current elevation to best-friend status is both flattering and a little unnerving. Ruth has much to live up to.

She glances inside the bag one more time before leaving the house, anticipating trying out the new creams when she comes home later, promising to take more care of her appearance, like Sandra does.

Two wheels of the Range Rover are parked up on the pavement. The car is wide and stakes a bigger claim on the road than the other vehicles nearby. Ruth loads Bess's car seat next to Sandra's son, Ian. The little boy is plump and rosy-cheeked compared to Bess, and he nonsense-chatters from his own seat. Bess responds with squawks and her legs jiggle a dance. Ruth strokes her daughter's happy cheek, holding back the tears, not wanting to spoil things with Sandra by letting everything out too soon.

She pulls the seat belt over Bess's carrier, the seat higher off the ground than she's used to, and she has to fumble around the space to secure the belt as Sandra's gym bag is in between the babies. 'Is Liam OK with you borrowing the car?'

'What's it got to do with him?'

'Sorry.' Ruth winces. 'I didn't mean it like that. I just thought he might need it for work.'

'You set?' Sandra asks.

Ruth hesitates, giving her friend space to tell her not to worry, that she's understood Ruth's comment was just a gaffe and she's not offended, but she doesn't. Sandra does this evasive thing sometimes, and Ruth can never tell how far she's overstepped Sandra's line, or if her friend simply didn't hear. Today, Ruth decides to try and be less needy – she did say the wrong thing, after all. She climbs into the passenger seat. 'Absolutely.'

Sandra turns to Ruth and smiles, and Ruth quickly returns the grin. Whatever just happened, if anything happened, it doesn't seem important to Sandra.

Sandra's petite frame is a wisp in the car's huge interior, and she accelerates noisily and pointlessly towards the junction where she has no option but to slow down. A Dyno-Rod van is at the turning, clearing the drains that seem to be permanently blocked round here, a stink hanging over the place, and images come to Ruth of fatbergs clogging up the sewers, condoms and baby wipes set in lard.

Cars queue at the petrol station for their turn in the wash and, inside the shop, figures wait at the till. A woman swings a loaf of sliced white at her side while behind her a man stands in line reading the paper he's about to buy. Everything normal, nothing threatening. As it should be. Ruth's earlier exchange with the men who work there shifts forefront in her mind. She examines the incident from a safer standpoint, noticing the memory's lost some clarity. With the benefit of a few hours' distance, she's convinced the man didn't mention a scream at all; her own spongy brain simply soaked up what it wanted to hear to validate her crazy suspicions.

Sandra pulls out onto the main road, the G-force pushing Ruth's head back on the headrest, and her friend drives with a fluttering racetrack-excitement in this beast of a car.

Sandra's daring is infectious and Ruth fizzles with it, as free in this ounce of time as she's ever been, slipping back momentarily into the person she used to be: confident Ruth, witty Ruth, Ruth who had the emotional space to care about people outside of her own tiny family.

Sandra blows a bubble of gum, offering Ruth a cube from the packet of strawberry Hubba Bubba she always keeps in her bag. Ruth's jaw aches as she chews, the pressure kinder than the molar against molar she's used to. Sandra switches on the radio and they travel to the shopping centre with Sandra's tone-deaf singing trouncing the terrible pop. Ruth leans into the back and checks the babies. Both faces are frozen in smiles of awe.

They park in the multistorey and Ruth puts Bess into a papoose across her chest. Sandra loads Ian into a swanky pushchair.

'That new?' Ruth asks.

'Yeah, the old one got a bit dirty. You know Liam, he's a sucker for the latest model.'

'He certainly is! Looks fancy.'

Sandra crouches next to her son, wrapping a softer than soft blanket round his knees. Her reply comes a beat late – 'Suppose' – and again Ruth wishes she would stop coming out with such tactless remarks.

Neon strips in the ceiling reflect in Ian's eyes as Sandra finishes clipping her quiet, pliant little boy into his seat. The lights buzz inside Ruth's ears and she imagines the electricity popping her brain cells. She holds a hand over Bess's head as if it could make a difference.

'You ready?' Sandra says.

Ruth snaps back to the present. 'Yep.'

'Anywhere in particular you want to go?'

'Not really.' She rocks from leg to leg to keep Bess quiet, staring at her own feet, the rhythm a comfort to herself as well as she stacks up a list of things to talk to Sandra about, normal stuff that's not about her worries and failings, so as not to bore or scare her friend away.

'Do you need anything from the shops?'

'Don't think so.'

'Perhaps a bit of a wander then and a cuppa somewhere?'

'Yes, why not? Great.'

'You OK, Ruth?'

Ruth flicks up her head. 'Oh, sorry.' She tries to laugh. 'I'm a bit useless today. Can't seem to get it together.'

Sandra rubs Ruth's arm. Her nails are long and newly painted, and Ruth feels safe in the care of this organized and capable woman.

'Don't worry about it. I'm here for you.' Sandra smiles and turns, already moving towards the entrance, and Ruth is drawn along in the slipstream of her best friend.

Inside the mall, the two women wade through crowds of shoppers purchasing more than anyone surely wants or needs – a whole planet of Easter Islanders. They pass endless displays of perfume and crockery; obscenities of delights. Shop window after shop window attempt to outdo each other with a slightly different cut of trouser or frill of dress. Ruth relaxes in the outlets' generic glow, assured by the sheen of money and order; nothing bad could happen here. She covets the Skandi crockery she'd once imagined using to serve up dinner to a group of friends, and the skinny jeans on an emaciated mannequin that would have fitted her a year and a half ago, but even if she could afford these luxuries, or had some place to use them, it's not the jumper, coffee pot or lipstick Ruth wants; it's the normality they represent, a fraction of which would remain with her at home until she peeled off the cellophane.

Sandra glides across the concourse, stopping occasionally to point at a sparkly top in a window or touch a toy that's excited her little boy. Through the sea of heads, Ruth spots a man she vaguely recognizes. He walks towards her with his arm round a woman. As he comes closer, his features snap into focus – he's an old boyfriend. Ruth finished the relationship shortly before she met Giles, and the man had been heartbroken. She catches her reflection in a shop window, shocked at the disparity between what she wants to look like and the reality. Her back is hunched over the papoose, stomach sagging underneath. Thin, unwashed hair, face weathered by sadness. She turns swiftly towards the shop until the couple have passed behind. Her ex probably wouldn't have recognized her anyway, but if he had, she'd have had to chat, and all the time he'd have been unable to disguise the pity in his eyes and his smile as he hugged his attractive new girlfriend, thinking, *I got off lightly there.*

'You OK?' Sandra touches her friend's back.

Ruth starts. 'Yes, fine, just a bit tired. Need a coffee.'

'OK, let's go to Costa then, it's the closest one.'

Sandra nods at the cafe on the other side of the concourse and down an escalator. A drowning distance. Ruth ducks her head and pushes forward, focusing on the task ahead: get to the cafe, order a drink, have a regular conversation with her friend. She senses people staring and whispering, and checks herself for twitches, hugging her arms round Bess's back. Being in a crowd amplifies Ruth's differences that get worse the longer she's out of regular company. Her failure as a human and a mother at times like these is an open wound, and she wishes she'd stayed home after all. Wherever she ends up is always less comforting than she'd hoped it would be, and at each new location she discovers she's brought along her same sad self.

Inside the cafe another group of mothers sit and chat while their babies lie in pushchairs rattling toys. Underneath the table is a minefield of raisins. The women sip biscotti-adorned lattes and wear suede ankle boots, ripped jeans and logoed sweatshirts; the uniform of the still connected. Since school, Ruth's never felt hugely comfortable in a big gang, but even so, pre-Bess, she'd have held space on a table like this, with a silly joke and one special friend at her side. Now, the impossibility of being part of this sisterhood is a hunger. One of the women reaches down to pick up a biscuit her child has dropped and her eyes connect with Ruth. The woman smiles. Ruth intuits only judgement – she's failed to make the grade – and she scowls back. The stranger's face drops as she twists back to her coffee. It's very possible that this contest – the difference between who Ruth wants to be and what she's currently capable of – is hers alone, and if this is the case, she hates herself even more.

Ruth finds a table away from the group and slumps down. A TV on the wall is showing an Arctic documentary on silent: an emaciated polar bear scavenges in a bin, icebergs airbrushed by soot calve into the sea. A subtitle scrolls across the screen: 'The polar ice caps have melted faster in the last twenty years than in the last 10,000.' Ruth imagines in the very near future how the rivers might burst and her road and the sidings will flood with water, turning into a lake, her house quickly filling up, and she'll have to grab Bess and run upstairs to escape the rising tide until only the roof is left. And where to go after that? She catches conversational snippets from the tribe of women at the other table as they swap recipes for butternut squash casserole and Spotify playlists, as unconcerned that they are all going to die as Ruth is hardwired to the truth.

'Tea or coffee?' Sandra asks.

'Coffee, please. And a muffin.' Ruth's fists tighten under the table. 'Something big and sweet and fattening. I don't care.'

Sandra stares without blinking, pausing momentarily inside what she wants to say before sighing and drifting away. As she crosses to the counter she stops to chat to one of the other women, touching a toy, turning it over in her hand, probably complimenting the colour and asking where it's from. Ruth's sure Sandra doesn't know any of them, but Sandra's smiling anyway, and all eyes have turned to her. The group lean forward, some with their lips parted as if attempting to inhale a little of her glow, that knack she has of offering friendship even though Ruth's rarely seen her follow through, choosing fat mad Ruth over this group of interesting women. Perhaps Liam's possessiveness only allows his wife so much free time.

Ruth slumps back in her chair, her perpetual failure boiling in her stomach. She bets that most of those women had drug-free births, unlike her who fell at the first hurdle by having an emergency caesarean, the shock of major abdominal surgery leaving her with a fear akin to PTSD. 'Don't be so hard on yourself,' her health visitor had said during those early days at home. 'The most important thing is that Bess is safe and well. As are you. You wouldn't have a tooth out without an anaesthetic, would you?' 'A baby is hardly the same as a tooth,' Ruth had replied, still so fresh out of the workplace that competing to meet targets – new ones she'd interpreted as essential from the antenatal facilitator: to resist intervention, to stay pure and present even through pain, even in an emergency – was the only system she worked to, as if after giving birth she'd get a promotion for endurance, unaware then that being a mother didn't have a finish line.

Bess's cry irritates like a mosquito in a hot room. Ruth unclips her baby from the papoose to sit her on her lap, asking the passing waitress for a jug of hot water to warm the bottle of milk. Ian continues to sleep soundly in his pushchair as Sandra joins the queue at the counter, phone to ear, talking rapidly and gesticulating as if she's commanding an army. The waitress trudges back to Ruth with a steaming bowl and Ruth immerses the bottle into the water before pushing both out of Bess's reach. For a fleeting moment, her hand millimetres from the handle, Ruth imagines throwing the scalding water at a man sitting at the next table, and her muscles tense with capability. It would be so easy, the outcome so catastrophic. What's stopping her? And if she could think of doing that to a stranger, might she be capable of the same impulse with Bess? She flinches in horror, pressing her palm flat to the table as she surveys the room of customers preoccupied with their coffees and conversations and smartphones. Each moment of every day, all these people make choices between impulse and rationale, between wrong and right. If her sister was here, she'd understand Ruth's internal debate, this sideways thinking that's her habit. They used to talk about taking chances, had a way of egging each other on, but never into real danger, at least that's what Ruth believed at the time.

'Everything OK, Ruth?' Sandra's standing at Ruth's side with a laden tray.

Ruth snatches her hand from the table. 'Yes, I'm fine.'

'Really? You look upset.'

'Oh, right.' Ruth rubs her arm. 'It's nothing. I just banged my elbow.'

Sandra settles in her chair, eyeing Ruth. 'Poor you.' She places two muffins on the table and Ruth lays into one between gulps of her coffee. Such guilty pleasures in front of petite Sandra, but then two cakes have been bought today, so for once it seems her friend is going to indulge. Sandra sips a mint tea, the steam settling in a dew on her foundation, before she takes a Tupperware box from her bag. It's a salad she's brought from home. She pushes the other muffin to the centre of the table and smiles kindly at Ruth. 'I won't manage it, but if you want it, feel free.' Ruth lays a hand on her stomach and waves the cake away as if eating two would be ridiculous, when really all she wants to do is cram the doughy blob into her mouth whole. Sandra says, 'They made a mistake and put another on the tray. Only charged me for one, though. Might as well make the most of it.'

'Really?' Ruth looks at the harried baristas, all probably studying for degrees while doing a double shift. She places three pounds on the table. 'Will that cover it? I don't want anyone getting into trouble on my behalf.'

'Ruth!' Sandra says, removing the lid of her salad box. 'You're such a goodie two shoes.'

The waitress stops next to the table and says to Sandra, 'I'm sorry, madam, but you're only allowed to eat food bought in the cafe.'

'But my baby is lactose and gluten free. It'll go through to my milk.'

The young woman looks as though she's barely resisting rolling her eyes to the ceiling. It's probably the tenth time she's heard this today. 'Right.' She clomps away.

'I didn't know you were still feeding?' Ruth asks. 'And when did you give up wheat and dairy?'

'I haven't and I'm not.' Sandra pours vinaigrette on the leaves, the smell wincingly strong, probably all vinegar and no oil. 'But I'm not going to let that Polish bitch tell me what to do.'

Ruth holds her breath.

Sandra chews and swallows. 'Look at your face!' She winks at Ruth with a little laugh. 'I'm only joking, silly.'

The moment to say something is now, but Ruth can't think how to phrase her shock, unsure what tack to take if Sandra was only making a joke, a joke in very poor taste nonetheless. Even though she and Sandra have ridden out some tough times, it seems Ruth knows less about her friend than she thought, and any disapproval she voices will be a new angle to navigate. Ruth never used to find it tricky to be direct when something was so obviously wrong, but it's different now she so desperately relies on this one person, a friend who's been patient and generous with her too. Sandra crunches through her seeds and sprouts, making chit-chat about Ian's weaning and Liam's gym routine, as if by giving her previous comment no attention, the words have no charge, or perhaps never even existed. Ruth doubts herself yet again, but saying nothing makes her complicit. She tips her head to one side and opens her mouth, but before she can speak, Sandra snaps forward, her voice loud enough to be heard by anyone sitting close.

'So, what's been going on? You not coping at the moment?'

Ruth's jolted by the exposure, losing the thread of what needed to be said. She fumbles with crumbs on her plate, having hoped for more of a warm-up to this topic. 'Well, it's complicated.' She's never liked talking about herself, even less so now that everything is in the negative. She clears her throat. 'It was night-time, that's all, and I got confused.'

'Not sleeping?'

'Not really, but then Bess is still waking quite a lot.'

'Really? I thought your health visitor helped you get her into a routine?'

'I got a handle on things for a bit, but . . .' She sighs – this picking over the inconsequentialities that are the sum of her days ruins her almost as much as her catastrophizing. She closes her eyes a moment before continuing. 'Every time I get my head around her naps, she moves on to another stage.'

'Perhaps an extra dose of Calpol will do the trick. That's what I do with Ian. Can't hurt anyway.' Sandra opens and shuts her eyes lazily, as if she's worn out, and sips her tea. 'And what about the other stuff? What were the police doing round your house?' Ruth blushes. Sandra leans across the table and lays a hand over Ruth's, saying more softly, 'I'm sorry, honey. I didn't mean to embarrass you. I just thought you might want to talk about it. I'm here for you, Ruthie.'

Ian makes a tiny cry and Sandra puts her salad to one side to lift her baby from his pushchair. 'Oh, you're such a bubba.' She kisses him and pops him over her shoulder, rocking back and forth in her seat until he calms. 'Such a little crybaby.'

Ruth checks the room to see if anyone's listening to their conversation, but no one is remotely interested.

'So, what did they want?' Sandra licks her top lip, her lipstick intact even after eating, and Ruth's momentarily distracted by the magic of Sandra remaining so well put together. If Ruth herself learnt a few of these tricks, perhaps she'd be more attractive to Giles. Sandra carries on without noticing Ruth's stare. 'Of course, you don't have to say if you don't want to. But if you need to get it off your chest, you can trust me.'

'Well . . .' The crumbs on Ruth's plate have grown fudgey

under her fingertips. 'You see, it was almost like one of the hallucinations I used to have, but it wasn't. Don't worry, I know the difference.'

'Really? What happened?'

'I heard a scream. At least I thought I did. A woman screaming. It really freaked me out.'

'Have you spoken to the doctor?'

'No. Look, I'm not unwell again. I can't be.' Ruth dips her head and lowers her voice. 'I've been taking all my medication.'

'But they could up your dose? Maybe get you over this sticky patch.'

'God, I'm sluggish enough already. And I can't bear the thought of putting on any more weight.' Ruth doesn't tell Sandra how she worries the medication might be damaging her physically; all those toxins being filtered through her kidneys, accumulating in her liver, deposited around her body as fat. And then there's the fear of the fear. What's that doing to her health, her sanity?

'So, this scream,' Sandra says, moving in and out of Ruth's focus as she rocks Ian on her chair. 'Did the police find anything? What did they say when they came round?'

'They told me to stop calling them, that I was becoming a nuisance.'

'Oops.' Sandra winks again at Ruth.

Ruth sighs and slumps in her seat. 'It sounded so real at the time, but telling you about it now, it's obvious it was just a dream.'

'Well, I'd stop calling the feds if I were you. The less

they're in your life the better. Came after my dad when all he was trying to do was provide for his family and I'll never forgive them for that. I mean, it was only money, no one got hurt or anything.' She pats Ian's back. 'No, best keep your nightmares to yourself.'

'Don't worry, I will.'

'And listen, I get it.' Sandra eats her salad one-handed. 'Liam hates it if I get fat.' She speaks so loudly that the man on the next table throws a concerned look. 'I mean, your bloke's got to fancy you, right? You've got to put out even if you don't feel like it, otherwise he'll go elsewhere. They're men, they need it, can't help themselves.' Behind them, a barista drops a cup. It smashes. Bess startles, Ian doesn't even stir. 'But you need to make sure you keep your head together too. You really can't afford to get ill again.' Her mouth turns down. 'Sorry, honey, I'm just being practical.'

'I know.' Ruth rakes a hand through her hair, a little unnerved at the idea that Giles could be the same as Liam and she never realized before. 'Really, I'm fine, I probably just needed to offload. God, it's good to talk it through, blow the nonsense out of my brain. I just get so down sometimes, you know? It can feel like the world's against me.'

'Don't worry, honey. We all get in a pickle from time to time.'

Ruth lifts the bottle of milk from the water, checking the temperature before letting Bess latch on. The little girl chugs away at the milk, gulping with big eyes blinking up, and Ruth relaxes into a curve over her daughter. This is how it should work, Ruth thinks, sitting in a cafe with her quiet baby, having a heart-to-heart with a good friend, and she feels safe enough for once to go deeper. 'You know, I manage to worry about every little thing, and it's not just the illness that's brought it on, I've always been like this.' Her eyes trace a line of tiles along the wall; she knows full well she hasn't always been like this, that before she lost her sister her world had been as carefree as everyone else's in this cafe, but explaining that here and now would be too intense, too complex, so a little white lie to Sandra will do. 'I'm on my own so much with nothing to distract me apart from Bess that my fears have got nowhere else to go.' She rearranges herself on the seat. 'Do you ever have this thing . . . ? Well, it's something my sister and I used to talk about actually, but recently, I don't know why, I've been thinking about it again.'

'Okay . . .' Sandra stretches the vowels into apprehension.

'Sometimes, well, I get these ideas, sort of an impulse. Totally within my control, though. I mean, I know I'm not going to act on them, but I can feel the potential of what I could do, what I'm capable of.'

Sandra sits tall, blinking. 'Like what? Do you want to do something to Bess?'

'No, no, nothing like that. I don't want to *do* anything. That's not the point.' Heat creeps up Ruth's neck. 'I just get the sense sometimes of how close to the edge we all are. I'm terrified of anything and everything that could hurt Bess, including myself, even though I know I never would. I mean, like, how easy it would be to do something bad, because I have the power as well as the freedom. And of course I've thought about the crazy thing in the first place, so what's the significance of that? It's only good sense that stops me, stops all of us, in fact.'

Sandra stares hard into Ruth's eyes. 'Are you sure you don't need to see the doctor?'

Ruth's throat closes and she wishes she could put her words back where they came from. Sandra's not only misunderstood what Ruth's saying, she's running with it in the wrong direction, and that in turn makes Ruth feel culpable for the bad things she's attempting to push away. 'No. Look,' Ruth says, 'it was just a memory of something my sister, Tam, and I used to talk about. *L'appel du vide*. The call of the void. You know, like when you stand on a cliff edge and think how easy it would be to step off.'

'No, I don't think that's ever happened to me.' Sandra slowly forks in another mouthful, eyeing Ruth the whole time.

Ruth jiggles the bottle in Bess's mouth to get the bubbles from the milk. 'It's fine, I'm fine, really. Forget I said anything.' Her spare hand absently picks at the second muffin. 'Let's just move on. I'm not having problems with reality.' She forces a giggle. 'Really, I promise.'

'Right.' Sandra smiles weakly, looking as relieved as Ruth to have dropped the subject. Laughter bursts from the table behind them before Sandra says, 'Well, I've got some news.'

Ruth takes a big bite of the second cake. 'Really?'

'Yes, I'm starting back at work.'

'You going back to the dentist's?'

'Oh no, not that.' She whispers to Ruth with wide eyes. 'Don't know where my head was at when I did that.

Answering the phone and having to deal with those people and their problems all day long.' She screws up her smile and her nostrils flare. 'Having to pretend I cared about their aches and pains. I mean, life's too short. I've got my own family now and they come first, you know?' Sandra chuckles, nodding at Ruth like she's expecting her to join in.

'Um . . .'

Sandra stops laughing abruptly and sits firmly back in her chair. 'No, actually, Liam's bought me a business.'

'Oh, wow!' Crumbs fall from Ruth's mouth. 'That's great. What is it?'

'A hairdresser's. You know, one of those places where you walk in off the street without an appointment. "Speedy Cutz". You've probably seen them around. It's a franchise, so the one we're buying is already up and running. We're just taking it over. The turnover's OK, but after we improve it, we'll expand.'

'Right. You going to retrain as a hairdresser?'

'God, no! I'm going to manage the place, turn it into a unisex salon, hire new staff and get rid of those old dinosaurs who work there.' Sandra gesticulates with her cutlery, intermittently patting Ian's back with fork still in hand. 'Lots of lounging around looking at their phones and no one really cleaning up after a haircut. The place is filthy.' She peers into a high corner as if the scene is up there, and her smile is wide. 'I'll sort it out, get the business running smoothly, make some decent money.'

Ruth's eyes cloud with tears.

Sandra frowns and tips her head forward. 'You OK, honey?'

'Yes, fine. I'm sorry, it's great news.' Her breath stutters as she pulls back the sob, hating that she's making Sandra's news about herself, only she can't help it. 'It's just that something like that seems so far away for me. I can't even organize myself to get out of the house on time, let alone go to work.'

Sandra puts the salad box to one side. 'There's plenty of time for you, honey. Don't worry about it. I'm only telling you because I'm not going to be around so much any more.' Her voice is soft. 'Like recently when you called, I've just been so busy setting things up that I haven't had time to get back in touch. So I wanted to give you a heads-up to make other plans in the future. You know, get involved in a play-group or something. I care about you, Ruthie.'

'Oh right, thanks.' Ruth's teeth plough through the second muffin to keep her mouth busy, wishing Sandra could at least have texted back to say she was busy when Ruth left all those messages, rather than letting her fill the silence with an assumed inadequacy. When Ruth had worked at the office, there'd been the pressurized pitches and late-night drinking sessions that had forged a family of sorts, a temporary stand-in for the solid friends she was rarely able to make, didn't want to make after her sister, but all that support fell away when she stopped working. Older friends, who might be more forgiving, live far away and are as flummoxed as everyone else by the many needs of Ruth. She's just too big a project for anyone to take on. Her deep embarrassment is that she needs them at all. She searches for another subject to cover her shame. 'What about Ian?'

'I've sorted some childcare.'

'Whereabouts?'

'A local childminder. She's great, she can do breakfast as well as tea, so when I'm busy all I'll need to do is bath him and put him to bed. I'm so looking forward to being out the house for a bit, get my sanity back.' She bites her lip. 'Sorry, hun, that came out wrong.'

'It's OK, I know what you mean.'

'Anyway, once we're properly up and running with enough money coming in, me and Liam are going to try for another baby. You know what blokes are like, constantly pressurizing you to get on with it. Liam can't keep his hands off me!' She giggles. 'But it won't be such an ordeal next time 'cos I'll have everything in place from Ian.' Her tone brightens. 'It'll be the same for you too when you decide.'

'Yes,' is all Ruth can say. She swallows the last bite with a tight mouth, fighting to keep from polluting the air with envy and neediness. What she wants to tell Sandra is that the thought of another child terrifies her, repels her even. It's very possible that giving birth could trigger another psychotic episode, but even if it didn't, this hard, lonely road Ruth is currently on would then have no end in sight. Ruth's new normal is so far from her expectation that the only way to truly fix things would be to turn back time and carry on as childless, which Ruth had worked actively to change, calculating ovulation times and date nights with Giles – even in conception she'd wanted to be in charge. She misses her old life, her spacious and rambling interior world, the luxury of her and Giles being wrapped up in only each other. But that she even has these regrets crushes her with guilt. Mostly, though, she mourns the mother she thought she would be, and the now-broken myth that having a baby was going to complete her because, by her female design, it would come naturally and she'd enjoy it: the attachment, the love, the daily doings of childcare, all without stress or constant questioning that she was getting it right. She wants to be the kind of woman who could want another child. Yet again Ruth's getting left behind. The medication has made her functional, but only enough to be a witness to her failure.

Sandra chats on about future plans, how she and Liam are planning to move from the street and are close to completion on a house that needs loads doing. Ruth can't think of anything to say that's remotely civil, feeling betrayed too that Sandra has been house-hunting and Ruth never even knew she was thinking of moving, so she just listens as Sandra fills the gaps. The sadness Ruth wanted to leave at home snakes around her as if the roots of the horsetails have crept the miles from her street and are coiling up her legs.

'Right then,' Sandra says, checking her phone. 'I need to pop to the loo and then we should think about heading off.' She reaches across to Ruth, who recoils a little at her touch. 'I know we haven't been here that long, but are you all right to leave in a mo? I've got the crèche booked for Ian at the gym.'

Ruth uses her chirpiest tone. 'Of course.'

'Great.' Sandra gets up to go to the ladies'. 'And I'm really glad we've had this chat about how you're feeling. Promise me you'll go back to the doctor and get some more pills. You mustn't let yourself get unwell again.'

Ruth's chest sinks. 'Sure.'

The other table of mums is leaving too and a freight train of buggies steams towards the door. The women wave to Sandra and one holds up her phone. Sandra takes out her own handset and quickly types; a phone number probably or a date in the diary for a playgroup and coffee, events Sandra probably won't go to, but how lovely to be asked. The greatest tragedy of Ruth's illness is that it's made her weird and inaccessible, her loneliness like body odour, Sandra's odd tagalong friend. What Ruth would like most is to hang out with any one of those competent mums, be a silent onlooker to their days, with no pressure to perform or judgement from them returned, only to soak in their world so that one day she'll be able to return to that place as well. In all friendships there's a contract of give and take, and what people want most from each other is fun, but fun is the least thing Ruth is able to be; depressed people are depressing.

The cafe empties around her. She sips the dregs of her coffee, exhausted by the sudden hit of carbs and dreading going home. Her time ahead appears viscous, to be waded through. Aimless days, small insurmountable goals. She wishes she could live more like Bess, measuring time from one heartbeat to the next, alive to possibility without fear or the need for plans.

One last customer remains, an elderly woman sitting on the opposite side of the cafe, previously obscured by the crowd in between. The woman stands, gathers her bags and walks towards Ruth. She's wearing the beige uniform of late middle-age: slacks, a fleece, comfortable Velcro shoes – the kind of woman Ruth wouldn't normally notice. Her silver hair is tied in a frizzy bun at the base of her skull and she wears a funny little felt hat to keep the whole thing in place. So old-fashioned, even for her age.

The woman reaches Ruth's table and stops. 'I'm your neighbour,' she says. 'I live on the other side of the alley.' Her features rearrange themselves into Liam's mum, Sandra's mother-in-law, the person Ruth's been warned to avoid.

'Hello,' Ruth says too loudly, heart bouncing in her chest as she checks the toilet door for Sandra. 'I . . . I didn't recognize you. Out of context of the street, I mean.' She lifts Bess into the papoose, and sways back and forth to cover the awkwardness, finding extra buckles to fasten to occupy her jittery hands. Ruth expects the neighbour to stiffen and leave, but she remains still until Bess settles.

'I just wanted to say' – the woman speaks with the burr of a Scottish accent that's almost been weeded out – 'that I think you're doing a wonderful job. You're such a lovely mum and your wee girl is beautiful!'

Ruth's words are again stuck, this time behind emotions she's not experienced since leaving work: both gratitude and pride, fresh and unexpected. Ruth has never been told she's doing well.

The woman smiles. 'No one finds it easy. The ones that say they do are lying.' She pats Ruth on the arm. 'I'm right next door if you ever want to pop in for a cup of tea.'

Her small frame shuffles as she walks away, and before she exits, she turns to Ruth with a smile. A breath of something touches Ruth's cheek, as if a distant window's been opened.

4

Giles works on his laptop at the dining table in their open-plan living space. The table was a buy from a junk shop, and Ruth had begun to sand it down with the idea of painting it before the task became another victim of baby-overload. Giles sits at the smoother, still-varnished end, taking calls and typing emails, his concentration broken only by childcare and cups of tea. The dreamcatcher hanging in the window casts a wispy shadow over his hands on the keyboard.

It's a Tuesday and Giles has been home for the day. In their spirit of enforced transparency, Ruth's GP contacted them because of Ruth's calls to the surgery. Ruth bristled at the intrusion – from the doctor as well as from Giles – but this is how it's been since she became unwell, this is how it will remain, her illness catching everyone in its sticky thread, Ruth the most trapped of all, the life being sucked from her. She's better than she was, though not yet in the clear. Giles's eyes follow her around the room as she goes about the housework and tends to Bess, monitoring Ruth for any signs of the relapse they both fear. So much of family life is balanced on Ruth's mental health that no one can afford to be complacent. Accept the help, Ruth tells herself, enjoy the company. Be grateful he still cares enough to be present. Still, she's self-conscious in his spotlight, every shortcoming highlighted.

Ruth is busy in the kitchen as Bess begins to cry. She hears Giles's chair scrape back before he comes into view through the doorway, picking up their daughter and holding the little girl with the same concentration and love Ruth witnessed when their baby was born. Giles was the first to hold Bess while Ruth was stitched up, and he'd sobbed into the baby's swaddling, his connection pure and instant. The same moment, however, Ruth marked against herself as an error. Even though she'd had no choice by the time the caesarean became a necessity – legs still damp from the birthing pool as she was rushed towards surgery, her scented candles and intervention-free birth plan tracking out of sight – to this day she's still convinced she didn't try hard enough, that some weakness in her willpower meant her body lacked the fortitude to give birth naturally. In that instant she judged herself, and decided everyone else had done too, as a losing combatant in the mothering arena, and the pattern was set for all that followed.

Giles sings Bess his dad theme: 'You are my sunshine, my only sunshine . . .' The melody quickly settles their baby. Ruth watches with tight lips, her own inadequacy to love and be loved hopelessly in opposition to her husband's bottomless capacity.

*

That evening the house is messier than usual. Giles gives it a quick spruce, stuffing dried laundry in a basket, the unsmoothed crumples setting in the still-warm fabric, and stacking the dishwasher so densely that most of the plates and cutlery will need rewashing. Ruth settles Bess in her cot, and when she comes back down, she sneaks a bowl of leftovers outside for the fox while Giles is busy playing Tetris with saucepans in the machine.

The couple power up laptops and tablets, escaping from each other through the digital portal. Giles scrolls down his Twitter and Instagram feeds, clicking on film and music clips for seconds before getting bored and moving on. Ruth tries to guess what he's listening to from the snippets of audio chaos, but she's out of touch and too embarrassed to ask what they are.

She edits her day's photos, collating the good shots, tweaking their colour saturation and framing. The open lid of her laptop faces Giles so he can't see what she's doing; she's ashamed to admit her ambition, worried he'll find her foolish for thinking she could be good at anything ever again. Each time Ruth checks the clock, what she thought was only seconds passing has been minutes, her evening evaporating in the most pleasurable way. She puts the pictures that didn't make the grade into another folder, and as she drags the shots across, she accidentally pulls up a file of older photos taken when she'd been unwell. These pictures are full of shadows and flares, exposure anomalies Ruth had attempted to interpret as forms and faces, her mind making patterns out of the loosest connection until she'd convinced herself her sister really was in the background, having seeped out of the hole Ruth had made for her in the wall, to haunt Ruth or punish her, Ruth didn't care. Looking at these photos now, Ruth again experiences a twinge of empty hope, that even after all these years Tam might walk in the room, fresh-faced, laughing and saying, 'Had you going there!'

Before Ruth closes the photo folder, she comes across the shots of Sandra's house taken around the same time, when Ruth had sneaked down the back path with Bess in the buggy and held her phone over the trellis of the high wall to take pictures of where her eyes couldn't reach. Every aspect of Ruth's world then had been filtered through a bright paranoia and she'd become obsessed with what went on in Sandra's house and why she'd never been invited inside. Ruth squints at the image open on her laptop, picking out a shape in Sandra's lounge she'd once imagined was a figure behind Liam – a mottled, dense texture in the corner of the frame – but it's obvious now that there's nothing else in the blurry dark apart from walls and doors and furniture. She slams her computer shut, relieved she's no longer crazy enough to spy on her friends or give any significance to what she'd been convinced was real.

Giles's face is lit up by the aura from his laptop and he multi-screens with the TV on in the background, canned laughter plugging the spaces of the couple's lost conversation. Bess is restless and wakes intermittently, her cry fuzzing the baby monitor. Ruth waits for Giles to take his turn to go up to this tiny being they created with love, who now sets them so far apart – but he remains on the sofa, his shift over for the day, unlike Ruth's working day that never ends. After an hour of trudging up and down the stairs, Ruth shoves her computer on the coffee table.

'Think I'll go to bed,' she says.

'OK.' Giles's voice is directed towards the TV. He's added his phone into the mix now, computer still warming his lap while he half eyes the telly.

Ruth stands in front of him, blocking the TV. 'Night then.'

Giles glances up as an email whooshes to a more engaging part of the world. 'Yes, goodnight.' He stretches up to her, thumb still suspended over his phone's keypad. He's texting Faye, his office manager, with a line of *crying with laughter* emojis. Faye's a single mum with two kids. She juggles work, holidays, and still manages to keep fit. She has that *let's make it fun* way of getting the most from her workforce. Her life probably isn't easy, but Ruth envies her ability to come to the chaos with optimism, with lightness around imperfection. Ruth bends for Giles's peck on the cheek. No arguments, no passion, held together only by obligation. A text pings, his attention switches back to his phone, and the thread of a TV baking competition follows Ruth up the stairs as she thinks how lucky the contestants are to be losing their shit over mere eggs and flour.

Up in the bedroom, adrenaline motors through Ruth. She's scared of sleep, of the inertia and helplessness it brings, a hangover from when she'd been ill and had believed some unnamed terror could creep inside her room, breathe itself into her lungs and force her to do things she couldn't control. She lies under the duvet as a tingling panic crawls into her hands and up her arms. Her chest starts its flutter. Once, she'd googled palpitations and found a website called 'This Telling Muscle', an illustration on the home page of a heart torn in two, with the caption: 'What is the cost of your time unloved?'

Ruth counts backwards and forwards to a hundred, eventually falling into a shallow sleep. Sometime later, Giles comes to bed. The mattress shakes through her half-dream before finally she drops into a more solid sleep. Outside of all of their problems, Giles is still her force field of good, a metaphysical protection even if in reality they are strangers.

Bess wakes in the early hours. Ruth shuffles from under the duvet, toes curling on the cold dark floor, and she remains in this limbo, willing Bess to fall back to sleep. The little girl's cry grows insistent. Giles nudges his wife and grunts, 'Can you go? I've hardly slept at all.' Ruth only ever seems to snack on sleep – junk-sleep with little goodness – but there's no point trying to explain this to someone for whom eight hours are as expected as breathing.

She peels herself from the bed to warm a bottle and feeds Bess in the little girl's room. Still Bess won't settle. 'Poor lamb,' Ruth whispers, touching gently inside Bess's mouth. Hard bumps of teeth are trying to push through her gums. The baby clamps down on Ruth's finger. Ruth would take all the pain for her daughter if she could, but as she can't and nature's design is for her baby to *cut teeth*, wouldn't it be better for it to be over quickly, even brutally, then they could all get some sleep? With gritty eyes, Ruth paces in and out of the two bed-rooms, letting Bess's cries sound out, but Giles is hardened into his rock of sleep now. She takes her daughter downstairs and makes a cup of strong tea with three sugars. If Ruth can't rest, the least she owes herself is some comfort. Sweet caffeine buzzes through her, and she puts Bess over her shoulder, re-laxing on the sofa and kissing her baby's head. The soapy milk smell of Bess's hair is close to edible – if only she'd go to sleep. Ruth longs to put her baby in the pushchair and walk outside to settle her, but it's 3 a.m. When Giles was less busy with work, the three of them would drive around with a griz-zly Bess, and the vibrations of the engine would rock her to sleep. Perhaps tonight the cold air will rouse Ruth enough to guide the car in a straight line. Giles is fast asleep. He need never know.

Outside, the moon is as full as a pot of cream. Bess has a puffer jacket over her pyjamas, and her tiny limbs stick out at right angles from her body. With the baby clipped into the car seat and a blanket over her legs, Ruth guns the engine of their old Saab, bought in freer days, now wholly impractical for family life and planet-saving emissions. They should update to the obligatory four-door saloon, but it's been easier and cheaper to use public transport most of the time.

Ruth's not driven for months, and it takes several attempts to pull out of the hemmed-in space. She drives to the junction at the end of the road where a tumbleweed of litter blows across the forecourt of the empty petrol station, paintwork washed yellow by a street light. She takes a right and instantly her spirits lift, away from what she can only describe as a kind of miasma that overhangs the whole street. Three junctions later she's on the high road, pleasure in the simplicity of moving forward and making her own decisions. The shops, in an endless avenue, are mostly closed apart from a twenty-four-hour off-licence. A glow radiates from the door where fridge shelves are crammed with multicoloured bottles of liquid, and a man in a rumpled suit staggers onto the street. Further down she passes Liam's IT shop. Screen repairs, phone unlocking and laptop services are advertised in the window. The big fluorescent strip is on even though the shop is empty and the wiry guts of the machines he's working on are hanging out for all to see. Sandra's always going on about the order she likes at home, so it's interesting to witness the mayhem when it's down to Liam to do the tidying.

About fifteen minutes into the drive, Bess falls asleep. Ruth's eyes are growing heavy too and she steers a U-turn home. When she reaches her road, she cruises past her original parking spot, looking for a bigger space, but there's nothing, so she loops round at the top, ending up close to the main junction again. Tentatively she mutes the engine. Bess's seat faces backwards, but her face is framed in the headrest mirror Ruth's set up there. Ruth holds her breath in the fresh silence. The baby grumbles but remains asleep. Ruth exhales. There's little chance of carrying Bess the small distance to the house without waking her, and even if Ruth did get her inside, the chance of her remaining asleep after Ruth had peeled off the layers of clothes and put her in the cot is minute.

The caffeine's wearing off fast. Ruth's eyelids drift shut. She forces them open, the effort like winding an old clock. Why is it easier to sleep when it's forbidden? Outside, the hedgerow rustles in the wind. All the animals are asleep, and the rest of the street is in darkness. Ruth locks the doors, shunts her seat back to partway comfy and finally gives her eyes permission to close. The sensation is delicious. There is no plan, no seeing past the next few minutes, only the rest Ruth craves as her mind floats away in the simple bliss of effortless sleep.

She's underwater, swimming through a deep-green forest of kelp, the long stems swaying in the current like trees in a wind. Fronds lap her face as she passes through them. A shifting form in the darkness ahead, the shape indecipherable, then a shaft of sun illuminates a head of hair. Someone's moving away from Ruth, swimming fast. Ruth pushes hard through the water as she tries to grab the figure, but whoever it is remains always out of reach. The kelp opens onto a clearing. Light drops through the water into an underwater glade. Ruth floats in the centre, bereft, as the figure she was chasing has disappeared.

Bess's coughing breaks into Ruth's dream. She startles, wipes spit from the corner of her mouth, momentarily confused by her surroundings as she runs fingernails across her scalp to drag herself back to the present. The dashboard clock reads 4.06. Inside the car the temperature has dropped. Ruth lightly touches the cheek of her still-sleeping baby. Bess's skin is pale with cold, fingers chilled. Ruth warms the little hands in her own before sending a resigned huff to the ceiling – the sleep she was having was the best for days. She leans across the passenger seat to gather her bag and keys, and as she does so, a Transit van turns into the street then onto the forecourt of the petrol station. Headlights pool on the ground as the vehicle comes to a standstill. Ruth's a good distance away, but the clouds now covering the full moon act like a lantern, casting a sulphuric glow over the scene. A man jumps from the passenger side of the van to open up the back. Another man exits the driver's side. It's hard to see exactly what's happening, part of the action being hidden behind the van, but between the two men, they use what look like a couple of rods to lift a manhole cover on the forecourt.

Ruth's suspended across the gear stick, the stillness of the night so complete that any movement could ripple outwards and notify the men of her presence. They peer into the manhole and one of them crouches on his haunches. A shadow rises. Out of the ground. A figure. Whatever, whoever, drags themselves from the hole and up onto the tarmac. Seconds later another figure follows, then another – and another. One by one they clamber out and right themselves to standing. Four in total. Ruth's jaw shakes as she squints into the darkness. By their size and gait, she judges they are women. One carries a bag, another holds a bundle to her chest, and they stumble towards the windowless Transit. A step has been lowered halfway for easier access, but still the entrance is high. The women grip the sides of the vehicle to haul themselves inside as one of the drivers leans on the lamppost, cigarette smoke drifting up into the street light. A woman misses her footing, falls to her hands and knees directly in front of the smoking man. He remains stationary, like he's cut out of the night, smoke still billowing upwards. She picks herself up and disappears inside the van.

Ruth's hand searches blindly in her bag for her phone. She finds it, grabs it, powers it up and holds the camera app to the window. She presses the shutter. The flash is a lightning strike in the darkness. 'Shit.' Her teeth chatter. One of the men stares in her direction as the other hassles the last person into the van. The driver and his assistant hurriedly replace the man-hole cover, fold up the step and shut the doors before driving away. The engine's burr recedes into the night.

Ruth stares into the space left behind by the van. Only Bess waking jolts her into action. She fumbles with the door handle, dropping her keys on the pavement, quickly saving them before they fall down a drain. Her head bumps the door frame as she wrestles with the buckle to release Bess from her seat as all the while her baby's cry builds. With Bess held close, Ruth hurries up the street, scared she'll wake the neighbours or, worse still, Giles. She scans the houses. All the curtains are drawn, no lights have been switched on. She turns into her garden and glimpses the upstairs window of her next-door neighbour's house across the alley. The nets swing in a breeze, a window open perhaps, even in this chill. Ruth puts her keys in the front door, hands bumbling as each scrape and twist of metal is amplified in the silent night. The door opens. She trips into the kitchen.

Standing in the centre of the room is Giles in his dressing gown, hair spiky with sleep. 'Jesus, Ruth! Where've you been?'

'I . . . I just went out. I couldn't settle Bess.'

'You've been gone ages. I called you but it went straight to answerphone.'

'My phone was on silent. I think.' She scrabbles in her bag, remembering she'd switched it to airplane mode as she does every night when she goes to bed. 'I'm really sorry.'

'You totally freaked me out. I was so worried, I didn't know what to do.' His eyes are watery, face pale. 'I thought . . . I mean, I didn't know what to think.' He swallows the worst of his sob and presses fingers to closed eyes to push back the tears.

Bess is crying and Ruth puts the baby over her shoulder, attempting but not managing to soothe her. 'I'd been up for ages. I was only trying to get Bess to sleep, so I went for a drive. She was really upset.'

'There has to be a better reason for leaving the house in the middle of the night. If there's a problem with Bess, you need to wake me.'

'I tried.'

'Well, not bloody hard enough!' His shout cuts across Bess's tears and the little girl silences momentarily. Giles palms his face, wiping the sleep away. 'I'm exhausted from working as well as having to help with Bess, so shake me if you need to, I don't care, but you mustn't leave without telling me. My mind goes to all sorts of places.' He relaxes his shoulders and takes a breath before putting a hand out to Ruth. 'Have you been driving around this whole time?'

'I was parked up, just outside. I finally got Bess to sleep and I didn't want to wake her by bringing her in. I was just so tired, I fell asleep too.'

'Sleeping in the car? At four in the morning?'

'I only dozed for a few minutes. I mean, I was alert the whole time so you don't need to worry.' She steps towards him as he moves back, concern clouding his face. She continues, hoping to blindside him with a more urgent issue. 'I saw something, it was really strange. There was . . .' She can't find the right words, suddenly aware of how it's going to sound.

'What?' Ruth has to lean in to hear Giles's whisper. 'What did you see?'

She stammers. 'At the bottom of the road, there were some people.'

'People? At this time of night? Doing what?'

'Look, I know this sounds nuts, but this van drove onto the forecourt of the garage and some people climbed out of a manhole and into the back of a Transit.'

'Christ, Ruth!' Giles flings up his hands before placing them on his hips. 'Have you been taking your pills?'

'Yes, of course.'

'Really?' He leans his hip on the worktop, slumping a little. 'People under the ground, that's a new one. Shall we add that to the mind-control drugs in the contrails of planes and dirty electricity radiating from the wiring inside the walls?'

'It's not like that. Really. I saw it. Take a look for yourself, I've got a picture.' She holds up her phone and scrolls through to the last shot. 'Here.'

On the screen is a flare of white, the edges shaded by the outline of the windscreen. No detail in the photo, only the blinding glare of the flash as it bounced off the glass.

Giles crosses his arms. He peers at the floor and Ruth has

to strain to hear him. 'I thought you were doing so well. I just don't know how to help you get better any more.'

'This is different, Giles.'

'No, Ruth, it isn't. It's just more of the same, more of you seeing things that aren't there, believing things that aren't true. I've seen your photos before, remember? You used to show me them when you were ill. You said there were people in the house, in the wall, but there was never anyone or anything but shadows.'

Ruth shuts her eyes, her shame immense and all her own fault. Suspicion nips at her ankles, its constancy a reality she can never outrun. Why, she thinks, couldn't she just have been a normal mother and wife? She summons up the image of the forecourt with the figures climbing out of the manhole and already the scene appears distant, like the retelling of a story she once overheard. If the photo had worked, it would prove the existence, or not, of what she saw. To herself as well as to Giles.

'We'll have to go back to the psychiatrist,' Giles says. 'We have to stop this getting worse.'

Ruth's throat is sore. 'I . . .' She shakes her head. 'I just can't think how I imagined it. I must have been dreaming.'

'I'm exhausted by all this. Perhaps it's time to think of another option. Maybe, you know . . . maybe it's time to consider the mother-and-baby unit again.'

'No. Really, Giles. It's obvious what happened now. I thought I was awake, but I wasn't. It was just a dream, a bad dream, that's all. It was dark and I was cold and frightened. I'm so sorry. Honestly, I'm fine.'

Giles lifts Bess from his wife's arms and kisses the baby's teary face. He strokes Ruth's arm with his free hand. 'Come to bed, Ruth, you look shattered.' His palm is warm but shaking. Between the couple is a blink of what they once shared. Ruth leans into him and rests her head on his chest, her cheek fitting that familiar place they used to say was created just for her, back when they made promises never to argue over the washing-up or pick their toenails in bed. To fall out over such simple things now seems to Ruth a luxury.

'Please don't send me away. I'll try harder. I'm getting better, I promise.'

'You must never do that again.' Giles paces his words. 'I love you, Ruth, but you are ill, and you need to trust the process of getting better. Remember how the therapist compared your illness to an oil tanker at sea. You're making the turn towards health, but the curve is long.' He wraps an arm round her back. The three of them soften inside the huddle. 'And please, please promise me never to take Bess from the house again without me knowing.'

5

'She's OK for now.' Giles's voice floats up to the landing where Ruth has paused to listen. 'I can stay with her for a couple more days, but if you're able to fit in an appointment or a home visit as soon as possible, that would be great.'

Ruth treads carefully downstairs, Giles too engrossed in his call to notice her reaching the bottom step. To be under her husband's care is Ruth's ultimate humiliation; they've been paddling at the edges of their relationship for so long, it's yet to be revealed if there's still a *them;* the less he loves her, the more she retreats, becomes sullen, less loveable. And the longer Ruth takes to get well, the more likely Giles will give up on her or look for distraction.

'Bess is fine, thank God,' he continues into the phone, 'but there's another thing I wanted to discuss with you. A friend mentioned that Ruth's—' He glances up as Ruth crosses into the room. 'Yes, we're all absolutely fine.' He's flipped to toddler speak. 'We just need to pop in for a quick chat if that's OK.' He smiles widely at Ruth as he hurries a goodbye to the person on the other end of the line who Ruth assumes is the psychiatrist, the happy expression on Giles's face frozen for a few seconds after he's ended the call.

In the downstairs toilet, Ruth opens the cabinet and takes out her prescription. Last night's vision at the petrol station has shocked her. She thought she was better, or at least in control – people don't climb out of holes in the ground. Or do they? She pushes the thought away. It didn't happen, it's all in her mind. The foil packaging crinkles as she presses a pill from its cocoon and lays it in her open palm. The tablet appears innocuous: round, white and small enough to swallow with one gulp of water. It signifies wellness and assimilation, but it won't make her normal, only dampen her down, like poultice to a swelling. She puts the medication in her mouth and rolls it around with her tongue. Tang of chemicals to rein her in, that flatten her personality as well as her fears, though without this help she would be utterly lost.

Giles knocks on the door. 'Everything OK in there, Ruth?'

She chokes the tablet down with her spit. 'All fine.' A couple of tubes of hand cream and a liquid soap clatter to the floor. 'Just finishing up.' She shakes as she puts the containers back, covering the damage to the wall she made all those months ago.

'We've run out of bread,' Ruth tells Giles after lunch. 'I can pick some up at the end of the road to tide us over until the next shop.'

Giles glances up from his laptop. The light from the

screen drags his tired features. 'If you give me a minute, I'll just finish up this email.'

Ruth dresses herself and Bess for the cold and loads her daughter into the pushchair. She's been looking for an excuse to go to the petrol station, to witness first-hand that there isn't, and never was, a threat. Lance the paranoia before it grows any bigger.

Giles's phone rings and he checks the screen. 'Damn,' he says. 'Sorry, I need to take this. Be as quick as I can.'

It's stuffy inside the house in their outdoor clothes and Ruth pushes Bess into the front yard to wait while Giles paces on the other side of the window, holding up a *just be a moment* finger.

The shrubs in their garden have died back to skeletons. A few dead leaves hang on like wet feathers. Ruth touches a curled clematis stem, wondering if it will still be green inside. She pulls one of the outer tendrils and a whole length of the plant comes away in her hand. Last summer, towards the end of her pregnancy, she and Giles had spent a few days out here, weeding and planting. Giles had dug a hole for this climber and Ruth had pressed in the root ball before watering. Afterwards, they'd sat together on a low wall drinking tea, muddy handprints on mugs, shoulders touching with an absent familiarity. Ruth's belly was peeping out from her T-shirt like a ripe watermelon, stripy with stretch marks, and her tummy button had turned into an outie, the baby pushing with her foot to tell her mum she'd almost run out of space. Within the boundaries of this small yard, Ruth and Giles had experienced incalculable joy, over and above the planting of a clematis. They owned walls, they tilled earth, they trusted in nature. If some of the plants didn't flourish, they could be fed and watered. If parenting was hard, love would see them through. Their faith in the future at that moment was unbound.

A wind picks up. Ruth pushes the buggy back and forth to keep Bess quiet, the paving stones uneven as the fat white roots of horsetails regenerate and push up underneath. Ruth has the sense that if she stands still for long enough, the plants will curl round her legs and drag her into the ground.

Somewhere close and out of view, a power tool is being used, its drone invading Ruth's ears. Bess, too, grizzles at the noise – there'll be no settling her until Ruth can get out of range. Through the bare trellis, Ruth has a side view across the alley to where the adjacent row of terraces begins. The neighbour's galley kitchen stretches out from the main house into her yard, the same as Ruth's does, so that the two front doors that lead from the kitchens face each other. That opposite door now opens. Ruth's neighbour – the woman she met in the cafe, Liam's mum, Sandra's mother-in-law – shuffles out, head bowed, pulling her checked shopping trolley. Her hair is in the same scruffy bun and she's wearing that funny little hat, the sight of which roots Ruth in a quainter time, away from this place and all of her problems. She follows the woman with her eyes, wondering if she'll have to say 'hi' since they've already made introductions. The neighbour catches Ruth's stare and Ruth smiles a tentative 'hello'.

Liam's mum stops at Ruth's gate. She's speaking quietly. Ruth moves a little closer, heart quickening, hoping for another compliment or an invite for tea and a chat, even though she's been warned and knows it's forbidden. Perhaps she wouldn't need to tell Sandra, who's going back to work soon anyway. This could be Ruth's secret.

The neighbour speaks in a whisper, barely audible over the buzz of the chainsaw. 'I saw you out here last night.'

'Sorry?'

The woman speaks a little louder. 'Last night. I saw you come out of your car.'

Ruth strains to hear. 'Really?'

'Yes.' The neighbour's back straightens. 'Did you see them?'

'What?'

Opposite, a large tree in one of the gardens that backs onto the hedgerow shakes. A branch cracks and falls away, then the chainsaw revs up again.

'The people.'

'I . . . I don't . . .' A prickle rolls up Ruth's spine. 'What people?'

'At the petrol station.'

The ground underneath Ruth undulates as if a body of water has risen up, the culverted river that's rushing metres below, breaking through the surface.

The woman continues, her voice too low for comfort, Ruth catching only scraps of sentences. 'It's not right . . . petrol station shop . . . gave them a piece of my mind.' Her face comes close to the slats of the gate, lips pinched through the gap. Ruth leans a little closer. 'Up all hours . . . seen them coming out before.'

'I can't hear you properly,' Ruth says. 'I really don't understand what you're talking about.'

'God only knows where they take them.'

Ruth squeezes the handles of the buggy for stability, turning towards the house, willing Giles to come into the garden and save her. He has his back to her and is gesticulating wildly to whoever's on the other end of the phone.

The woman says, 'I'm going to sort it out . . . see what I've got . . . won't be able to deny it any more.'

The chainsaw is going full throttle now and people are shouting in the opposite garden as another branch crashes to the ground. Bess has started crying. Ruth's neighbour twitches her head, calling Ruth closer to the gate. Ruth's fear is directly matched by her need to know, and she slides the last few inches towards the woman, magnetized to the horror.

The neighbour's whisper is a loud scratch. 'There are tanks under the ground where they used to store the petrol. Now the garage is shut, they fill them with people.'

The front door opens and Giles steps briskly into the yard.

'Well, goodbye then,' the woman says. She grabs her trolley and breaks into a fast walk.

Giles comes level with Ruth. 'Was that our next-door neighbour?' He arches his eyebrows with a smile. 'What will Sandra say?'

Ruth takes a moment, tries to speak, but her words have cemented in her throat.

'Ruth?'

'Yes,' she says through tight breath. 'The neighbour.' The woman disappears from view.

'I've not seen you two speaking before. I didn't know you knew her.'

'I don't. I mean, I've only met her once.'

'What were you chatting about?'

'Nothing.' She braces her jaw to contain her shudder. 'She only said hello. That's all. Nothing else. You don't need to keep asking.'

Giles's eyes widen. 'Are you OK, darling?'

A goods train clatters past on the hidden side of the house; the double pitch of its horn is long and urgent, as if warning someone off the line. Ruth gathers herself before speaking again. 'I'm fine. It's just so bloody noisy here. I can't stand it.'

Giles frowns with a 'Huh' before saying, 'Well, it's nice you're making connections on the street.' He rubs her back, careful not to push too hard. 'I told you there are lots of nice people here, you just need to give them a chance to get to know you. Why don't you invite her over? I know Liam says she's a bit strange, but you never know, you might get on really well.'

'I don't want her in the house.'

Giles has his head to one side with a question on his lips. Then he straightens, appearing to choose the less fractious path. Ever the peacemaker, thank God for Giles. He kisses her cheek, 'OK then,' and shrugs his shoulders. 'Whatever works, it was only a suggestion.'

The couple leave their garden. Ahead, the neighbour takes a cut-through towards the main road, but before she's out of sight, she turns back to Ruth. Nausea sits in Ruth's throat. She looks the other way until the woman has disappeared as she and Giles continue down the road towards the petrol station.

The forecourt is empty, the steady drizzle hampering afternoon business. A couple of workers lean against a sheltered wall, one man on his mobile, the other with arms crossed, wet rag hanging from his belt. He's wearing a T-shirt printed with the car-wash logo, RAY'S HAND WASH AND VALET. The two Mercedes are parked to one side and Liam's big white car is next to them as usual. Giles takes the pushchair into the shop and Ruth lags behind, head bowed, legs feeble. If a strong wind were to blow, she'd topple over. A hum travels through the soles of her feet, like the tremble of a distant earthquake; hidden things, buried things, making themselves present, her illness a contagion drawing them close. Push the nonsense away, she tells herself, give the fear no space, stop airing the fantasy. She follows into the shop where Giles is rummaging through the bright-orange cheese selection, checking the sell-by dates on the sweaty packets. The man behind the counter stares at Ruth as she enters. He's the same man she thought talked about the scream. He checks Ruth up and down, speed-scanning her legs, breasts and face. Even here he does this, while Ruth is with her baby, her husband just out of sight. A second later his expression flips to neutral, verging on disdain. He's cast her aside, the act of dismissal an insult in itself, the message being *You're not good enough and I'm not even that fussy*. She's been rated and found lacking. His judgement repels her, but that it's been forced on her, and in the negative, shrinks Ruth. Whatever form her beauty used to take is now lost, another piece of her identity stripped away.

Outside a rubbish truck is collecting the waste. A mechanism on the back of the lorry lifts industrial black bins from the forecourt and tips their contents into the hopper. The winch whines as it levers each container up, then down. A man inspects a recently grounded bin and operates the lift again. Something must be stuck inside. He presses another button when the bin is poised overhead to make it shake. Whatever was lodged inside clatters into the back of the lorry and a few stray items spill onto the pavement. Scraps of paper swirl in the wind. One heavier object lands on the forecourt. Rubbish man picks it up and turns it over in his hands, calling to his mate to take a look.

With no consciousness of her decision to move, Ruth walks from the shop towards the man. As she gets close, she sees he's holding a patent pink shoe, platformed at the front and with a high spiky heel. The man says something to the van driver and the two of them laugh. They look up, see Ruth and stop. The man holding the shoe bows his head as if he's about to be told off, and he goes to throw the platform in the back of the truck when Ruth says, 'No.' She reaches for the shoe. 'It's mine.'

He hands it over with an embarrassed shrug before turning to continue with his work.

The shoe could have fallen from one of the cars while the

vehicle was being vacuumed, but why not give it back to its owner? It's not as if it would have been inconspicuous on the tarmac. Ruth checks the ground, her sightline tracing towards the centre of the forecourt and the manhole covers. The edges of the metal discs are silted with dirt, but one towards the back is clean round the rim, as if it's recently been lifted. A small piece of fabric pokes out, the material frayed, the remainder of the item trapped underground. Ruth scuffs the garment with her foot. It's dirty and wet, patterned with a tiny butterfly print. A delicate button at the cuff.

'There you are,' Giles calls to Ruth and she startles.

He's crossing the forecourt with a bulging plastic bag swinging from the handles of the pushchair. Behind him, Barry from next door enters the shop, his reptilian skulk marking his aversion to his neighbours. Once Barry had caught Ruth taking photos of his house, just like she had of Sandra's, sneaking her phone over his back wall, convinced he was making fox traps or laying down poison in his garden. He'd hammered his fist on his window that day, like he was scaring away a rabid dog, and even now Ruth crumples in humiliation at the memory.

'What've you got there?' Giles nods at the shoe as he draws up next to her.

'Nothing, it's nothing.' She hides the platform behind her back, her actions childish in panic as her elderly neighbour's words replay in her ears: *There are tanks under the ground. They fill them with people.*

'Come on,' says Giles. 'Let's have a look.' He tries to grab the shoe from her and she shifts this way and that to stop him. He's laughing, being playful. Ruth should join in but her breakfast is churning in her stomach. 'I didn't think you were that kind of girl.' Giles's eyes sparkle with fun.

'Please, don't.'

Finally he grabs the shoe from her and inspects the heel with an astonished whistle. Behind him, the man in the shop watches from the door.

'Give it back,' Ruth says, anxiety mounting. 'You don't understand.'

Giles is laughing out loud now. 'Where's your other slipper, Cinderella?'

Ruth's heartbeat scatters in panic. She checks up the road on the slim chance her neighbour might be coming this way, the same old woman Ruth couldn't wait to be shot of earlier, who she'd now openly hug if she turned up to ratify Ruth's story. Giles might just believe it if he heard it from someone else.

Giles's jokes die as Ruth isn't feeding him any lines. She tries to grab the shoe. It flies out of Giles's hands and lands near the bin, skittering on the tarmac before coming to a standstill. Giles shrugs and turns the buggy in the direction of home.

The shoe is tiny, about a size three, and would fit a child. Last night Ruth thought she saw a woman stumble across this forecourt, but perhaps she was younger. A girl taken somewhere in the back of a windowless van. Nobody knows about her apart from Ruth and her crazy neighbour.

The man from the shop has opened the door and he stands in the frame with his hands on his hips. Ruth crouches to the ground, keeping her eyes on him. She grabs the fabric that's caught in the manhole and tugs. The material is stuck fast.

'What are you doing?' Giles asks, looking back over his shoulder.

'I need to get this out.' The metal cover shifts a millimetre as she pulls, scraping with an empty echo. Ruth's courage accelerates as she pulls harder. The fabric begins to rip. 'Can you help me?'

'Ruth, leave it, it's filthy.'

Heat gathers under her thick coat and drizzle pastes her hair to her head. Without lifting the manhole, the material won't come loose in one piece, and she tries to fit her fingers round the edge of the metal disc to lever it up.

Giles is next to her now. He crouches at her level. 'What's going on?' His voice has reverted to toddler speak, but he's angry daddy, which fires Ruth up. She digs her fingers into the rim, bending one of her nails back, and she goes to put it in her mouth to take away the pain, but her hands are blackened with car-wash sludge. The two men who were standing on the forecourt march over to the shop owner, lips moving with messages Ruth can't read.

'This top belongs to someone,' Ruth says to Giles. 'A woman or perhaps a girl. She's been kidnapped. We need to help her.'

Giles's face is so close to Ruth's that she can smell the coffee on his breath. 'Ruth, we need to go home now.'

'Look.' She points to the manhole. 'The edge of this is clean, you can see it's been lifted recently.' She's on her hands and knees, hooking her fingers through the metal depressions in the middle of the cover, but it's way too heavy and she's instantly grimed. 'Help me, Giles. There are people down here. We've got to get them out.'

'For God's sake, not this again.'

From behind them comes shouting. The man from the shop charges across the forecourt, his rumpled suit flapping in the wind. He's followed by the other two in their grubby work tracksuits. 'What are you doing?' the man says. 'You cannot touch that. It is my property.'

Ruth looks up at him, still tugging. 'I know what's down here. I saw. You can't hide them from me any more. I heard screaming too, remember? You knew about it, but you lied.'

Giles puts his hand on Ruth's back. 'Get up, Ruth, please. Leave it.' He tries to ease her up.

'No,' she shouts, pushing him away and feeling round the edge of the manhole. 'I saw them coming out of here last night. We need to help them.' She points to the shop owner. 'What have you done with them? Where have you taken those girls?'

The man steps in front of Giles and grabs Ruth's arm. His lips are pinched white as if they've been pickled, and with an angry tug, he yanks Ruth to her feet. Her arm jolts in its socket. She yelps in pain. Giles jumps between them and pushes the owner, who staggers back across the forecourt.

'Get your hands off her.' Spit flies from Giles's mouth.

'You tell her to stop,' the man replies, pointing to Ruth and dusting imaginary dirt from his front. 'She is damaging my property.'

'I don't care what she's doing, you don't touch her.'

They shove each other, shouting and gesticulating. Bess's eyes are wide with fear and she starts to wail.

'Get off my land,' the man roars into Giles's face, 'or I will call the police.'

'You do that, mate,' Giles says, finally shrugging him off, his face glossed with sweat. 'I'm going to call them too. See what dodgy dealings you've been up to, shall we?'

'Leave.' The man points in the direction of their house. 'Never come here again. You are not welcome.'

'No fear.' Giles holds Ruth's arm, his grip firm but not hurting, and he guides her purposefully away. With his other hand he grabs the bag of nutrient-free food he's just bought and chucks it on the forecourt. 'There's nothing we need from you or your shitty shop.' Biscuits and chocolate bars roll out of the split carrier, Ruth's favourites that Giles bought for her, treats for them to share at home on this rainy afternoon. She loves him more in this moment than she can remember loving him in a long time.

The couple race along the road towards home. Behind them the men line the edge of the forecourt with arms crossed. A few people have come out of their houses and they stand in the way on the pavement, neighbours Ruth might recognize if she looked up, perhaps even Sandra or Liam, so she keeps her face tipped to the ground, only peeping occasionally at Giles. He's staring straight ahead, a muscle clenching and unclenching in his jaw, and the pushchair swerves as he steers with one hand. His other arm is firm round Ruth's shoulders. He squeezes and asks repeatedly if she's OK, saying he's going to report the man for assault.

'I'm fine, really.' Ruth worries about being the focus of Giles's call, in case any mention of her name might flash an alert on the call-handler's screen, meaning they'd dismiss what Giles was reporting immediately. 'Don't say it's got anything to do with me. We can tell them about my arm later. It's those girls who need our help. They're the priority.' She'd take over the buggy from Giles, but she's holding on tight with both hands to the pink platform shoe.

6

Giles dials 999 as soon as they walk through their front door. With his anger lit, Ruth convinced him on the walk home that there's more going on at the petrol station than meets the eye, and he recounts her story of the underground tank to the police, leaving out the part about the man pulling her arm, just as she pleaded with him to do. 'I'm fine,' she lied. 'Really, it hardly hurts at all.'

She hovers out of sight in the kitchen while Giles finishes on the phone, turning the shoe over in her hands, inspecting the indentations made by tiny toes and a grubby heel, unable to tame the panic that's running through her; is it that she's finally going to be believed or about to be found out?

'I know you're worried about those women,' Giles says after he's put down the phone. 'But you can't stop me telling the police the rest when they get here, about how that man grabbed you.' He places both hands on Ruth's shoulders and looks into her face. 'And you're sure about what you saw? You haven't missed any tablets?'

'I promise, Giles. Please, trust me.'

He circles her in his arms. Ruth relaxes into his chest, breathing his musky smell, her relief swelling after the weeks of waiting for genuine tenderness between them. She's missed this man, forgotten how good it feels to be his equal. The first steps back to the couple they used to be are so much less complicated than she'd imagined.

From outside comes the distant wail of a siren. The couple hold hands, sweaty palm to sweaty palm, and tiptoe as far as the front gate. The siren grows louder until a police car turns the corner and parks next to the forecourt at the end of the road. A few neighbours have come out onto the pavement to watch, heads bobbing in the way, blocking Ruth and Giles's view. Ruth guides her husband through their gate and they whisper to each other about what they can and can't see. The vehicle remains at the kerb. No one gets out.

Then another response car glides round the junction and points its nose up the road. A hush falls over the street as the residents' heads collectively follow the direction of the car. It closes in on Ruth and Giles's house, pulling up next to them on the pavement. Two officers are inside, a man and a woman. They climb out.

'Mr and Mrs Woodman?' the female officer asks.

'Yes,' Giles says. 'Please, come in.'

Giles holds the gate open as Ruth surveys the scatter of people up and down the road. A small group has assembled on the forecourt too, and they charge over to the parked police car, gesturing towards Ruth and Giles's house. Shouts carry through the air; impossible, though, to make out what's being said.

Giles leads the officers through the front door, gesturing to the sofa for them to sit. The seat is low and they strain in their bulky uniforms, tugging at padded, accessorized waistcoats. A laundry airer is next to the sofa, strung with baby clothes. Some of Ruth's baggy underwear is also looped over the rungs and she adjusts a towel to cover the items. It falls to the floor. Both officers stare into the middle distance as Ruth tries to re-hang the towel. If she'd left it in the first place, they might not have noticed her greying knickers and frayed bra. Instead she's pointed out these shamefully shabby garments that touch the most private parts of her body. Ruth offers tea; the officers decline. The policewoman's face is neutral, chiselled to a blank, and the man glances around the room, his gaze ending up on Bess asleep in the pushchair. Ruth wants to stand in front of her baby, block any judgement of her sweet little girl who in this stranger's eyes might not be thriving, but she holds steady, desperate to present as normal, not paranoid or unhinged. She eases herself into the armchair and Giles grabs a seat from the dining table.

'So,' the female officer asks. 'Was it yourself who reported the crime, Mr Woodman?'

'Yes,' says Giles. 'It was. I made the call.'

'And can you tell me what you saw last night? Can you give me the details of how many people were coming out of the manhole?'

The officer moves her foot and accidentally splays the pile of magazines at the side of the sofa. Copies of *Grazia* and *Elle* filled with gossip and horoscopes. Ruth bought them right before she had Bess, imagining the endless free time she'd have while her baby slept. She still hangs on to the possibility that she'll get round to reading them, along with the hope that one day she'll be a competent mother.

'It was my wife who saw,' Giles says. 'But by the reaction of the owner today, I'd say he has something to hide.'

The male officer interjects. 'And what was his reaction today? What happened to make you report this incident only now and not last night?'

Giles goes to speak, but Ruth jumps in. 'I was trying to get the manhole up.' Everyone in the room turns towards her in unison. 'To prove what I'd seen. You could tell it had been lifted recently, so I knew it was the one people had come out of.'

A crackle of voices spurts from the officer's walkie-talkie. He turns the volume down a fraction and asks, 'So perhaps you could tell me exactly what it was you think you saw.'

Ruth attempts to decipher the messages on the officer's radio. Among the jumbled voices, she thinks she picks up laughter. 'Well.' She blushes. The more she concentrates on trying to stop the heat from spreading up her neck, the redder her cheeks become. 'There were about four people. They looked like women, but could have been younger. Two men were driving. The women climbed out of the manhole and into the back of a Transit, then they drove off.'

'And what time was this?'

'About four in the morning.'

'So it was dark.'

'Yes.'

'And where were you when this happened?'

'I was in my car.'

The female officer huffs a little. 'Where was your car then?'

'On the road outside, parked up.'

'So you had a clear view?'

'Yes.'

'And what were you doing in the car at about four in the morning?'

'I was sleeping. I mean, my daughter was asleep and I didn't want to wake her. She's been teething, you see. Driving soothes her. When I parked up, I dozed a bit too, that's all.'

'Was it before or after you slept that you saw the incident?'

'After. It got cold and I was about to go back into the house.'

'So, you were fully awake?'

'Yes.' Ruth leans forward and makes fists of her hands. 'I know what I saw. There were people coming out of the ground. I didn't imagine it.'

The officers lean back on the sofa in a twin movement.

'Ask my neighbour,' Ruth continues. 'She saw too.'

'Which neighbour?' Giles says, his eyebrows shooting towards his hairline.

'Liam's mum, across the alley.'

The female officer turns to a new page in her pocket note-book. She scribbles without looking up at Ruth. 'Across the alley? Do you mean number forty?'

'Yes,' Ruth says. 'Number forty.'

Giles says, 'Why didn't you mention this to me before, Ruth?' His eyes are wide, his trust a hair from snapping.

'I did – I mean, I thought I had, at the petrol station. I . . . I don't remember.'

The officers exchange a look. The man gets up, unclips a smartphone from a pocket in his jacket and walks into the kitchen. He closes the door behind him, talking so softly it's not possible to hear what he's saying. Ruth tries to slow her breath, but her pulse only grows louder in her ears. Giles stares at her, the veins on his neck palpitating. Then the door to the kitchen opens. The officer crosses back to the sofa, shoes squeaking, and he sits. 'A Miss Cailleach lives at number forty,' he says, leaning forward. 'Is this the woman who witnessed the same events as yourself last night?'

'Yes, that's her name. Miss Cailleach. Ask her, she'll back me up.'

Giles knows as well as Ruth that they've not heard this name before, the packages delivered to their house always having been addressed to a Mr Smith, Liam and Sandra's surname. Ruth just assumed his mum would be called the same, probably Giles did too, but there's no one else who lives at number forty. She doesn't want to create any unnecessary confusion or doubt, and it must be the same woman. Perhaps Liam is named after his absent father and his mum never married, or she reverted to her maiden name in recent years. Ruth doesn't have the mental latitude now to unpick this anomaly, and she throws Giles a pleading look not to make a thing out of it. He returns a tight mouth.

Ruth continues. 'I wasn't sure if she was telling the truth

before . . . I mean, it was so noisy with the chainsaw and all, I thought I might have misheard her. But once I saw how agitated the man at the shop became, I knew she was right.'

The female officer says, 'So was it your own sighting of the events we're investigating or Miss Cailleach's?'

'Mine of course! But she saw as well.'

The female officer swivels to Giles. 'We have details here,' she says as her two-way radio fizzes with static, 'of previous calls made by your wife to the emergency services, about suspected criminals on the road.'

'What other calls?' Giles says, the beam of his attention firmly on Ruth, any faith he had in her burning out.

'We just need to get to the bottom of what your wife saw, Mr Woodman, and if it was a real or suspected event.'

The other officer clears his throat. 'A detective sergeant is currently attending the scene. I need to inform you that the owner of the premises is considering harassment charges against you and your wife.'

Giles opens his mouth to speak, and again Ruth cuts over him. 'Harassment! He's the one who was harassing me.'

The officer bows his head and looks at Ruth from beneath a frown. 'We need to warn you that going back to the car wash may result in an arrest. There must be no contact with the owner, from yourself on anyone acting on your behalf.'

'This is crazy.' Ruth jumps up, her voice high and loud. 'I mean, are you even listening to me? Has anyone looked inside the tank?'

A moped whines down the street, the local kids taking their chances while the police are occupied.

The woman closes the notebook. 'The petrol tanks have been decommissioned, Mrs Woodman. They're full of water, a health and safety requirement to contain any remaining fumes. It would be impossible for anyone to climb in or out without drowning.'

Ruth holds on to the back of the chair, last night's vision trembling in front of her like a heat haze. 'What about this then?' She holds up the tiny pink shoe. Both officers say nothing, then turn to Giles.

'Mr Woodman,' the policewoman says, 'at a recent strategy meeting, we were given information by the mental health team that your wife is under their supervision at present.'

Giles rests his elbows on splayed knees and places his bowed head in his hands. He stares at the floor, speaking softly. 'Yes, that's right.'

The officer tips up her nose, as if Ruth's illness were airborne and she's detecting spores. 'Two days ago, an officer visited this address to inform your wife that we can only respond to real incidents, and that suspicion is not grounds for an emergency call.'

Giles looks directly at the officer, blocking his wife from his sightline with his hand, but Ruth can still see through the cracks in his fingers that the colour is seeping from his complexion, and she knows she's lost him.

'Mr Woodman, if we receive any more spurious calls from this number, we will have to consider further action. Your wife has already been notified that a fixed penalty notice will be given in the event of more calls. The next stage after this is a prosecution. It is a very serious offence to waste police time.'

'But I saw them.' Tears stream down Ruth's cheeks. 'I did, I know I did.'

Giles sits upright in his chair, chin jutting out and neck stiff as he turns to Ruth. His mouth is open a crack. No breath comes out.

The male officer perches on the edge of the sofa as if ready to sprint. 'Are there any actual charges you wish to pursue? If so, I'll need to log the incident and take a full statement from both yourself and your wife and take witness statements from others who were present or who saw events this morning.'

Ruth remembers Barry going into the shop and she visualizes the houses closest to that end of the road, from where it would have been possible to see the station. Liam and Sandra have the best view from their bedroom. Their car was on the forecourt, so at least one of them was home and could have seen. If it was Liam, this would be the perfect opportunity for him to warn his wife away from her troubled friend. But Ruth and Sandra are best friends now. Ruth hopes that will be enough to secure Sandra's allegiance.

'Would you like to take any further action?' the officer continues as if reciting from a sheet, the inference being that Ruth is the twentieth time-waster he's seen today. 'If so, we will need to involve the mental health team in our inquiries.'

Ruth rubs her arm where the man had yanked her to standing. Her shoulder joint needles with pain. Giles's body is tight and upright as she begins to lift her sleeve to show where she was grabbed, where she's sure there'll be red marks left by the man's fingers, but before she can protest, Giles says, 'No.' His words are clipped. 'There's nothing else. I'm sorry, Officer. This won't happen again. I'll make sure of it.'

The police stand and wade through the room to the door, displacing two bodies' worth of air as they go. Giles shuts the door behind them, keeping his hand on the latch and staring at the doormat.

Ruth goes to him, touches his arm, her fingers barely making contact with his skin, afraid he might pop and disappear. 'Please, Giles,' she says. 'I was telling the truth.'

'It might have been your truth, but it's nobody else's.' He breathes hard through his nose. 'You know, when you get your teeth into something, you really go full tilt. Whether it's your illness or not, you create your own laws about all this nonsense, and nothing anyone says can convince you otherwise.' He brushes past her and up the stairs. Overhead, the floorboards give and the bedsprings wheeze as he flops down.

Ruth watches from the kitchen window as the officers call on her neighbour across the alley. Liam's mum is already back home, and from where Ruth stands, she has a clear sightline onto the woman's door as she opens it to the police.

'Tell them what you saw,' Ruth whispers at the window. 'Come on, back me up.' There's a brief exchange where Miss Cailleach shakes her head, and seconds later the officers leave. 'No,' Ruth says, leaning closer to the window. 'That's not right. She told me, I know she did.'

Ruth's neighbour stares ahead at Ruth as Ruth's teeth press together, fists at her sides, desperate to march over and demand what the old woman's playing at. But Giles is upstairs. If she leaves the house, he'll see from the window. He'll charge down to tell her to stop pursuing this fantasy and put an end to the continual embarrassment that lets them all down.

With every ounce of restraint she can muster, Ruth holds herself steady. 'You fucking bitch,' she mouths across the alley.

Opposite, Miss Cailleach closes the door of her house.

Ruth can't think where to sit and she flits around the lounge, unable to settle on any one thing. At the sink, she loads dishes into hot suds, leaving them unwashed to make food. Then she decides to clear a cupboard and restack all the plates and cups. The clanking wakes Bess in her pushchair. Upstairs, there's no movement from Giles, so Ruth sits with her daughter on the sofa. She should give her a bottle but can't think where to start, the order of the powder and the heating of the water jumbling in her mind. Her arm tightens round her little girl as she rocks, fear banging a rhythm in Ruth's ears: *Please don't let me be ill again.*

7

'Who is this?' Ruth says into her phone. 'What do you want?'

A breather on the other end of the line, another of the *No Caller ID* numbers Ruth's had in the last few days. A rasping noise as the caller's lips brush the mouthpiece.

Ruth says, 'I want you to leave me alone.'

Then, a voice so quiet it could be static, the faintest whisper in return: 'It's Tam,' before the line goes dead.

Ruth hurls her phone on the bed, steps away from the handset expecting it to combust.

'Ruth,' Giles calls up the stairs. She startles. 'We're going to be late.'

She looks around, trying to remember what she needs to do. Her hands shake as she finishes getting dressed, putting on odd socks and a T-shirt without a bra underneath.

It's Tam – she misheard, the voice can't have been real.

She should mention the call to Giles – he'll reassure her it was her imagination – but each step downstairs takes a little more of her courage until she arrives at the bottom in the certainty that her mind simply retuned the phone crackle into another sound entirely. Nothing more, nothing less than that. Plus, she absolutely cannot make any more fuss.

'I'll come into the appointment with you today,' Giles says, steering his arms through his coat sleeves and shrugging the bulky hood up his back, all while expertly avoiding his wife. Since yesterday's confrontation with the police, he's barely met her eyes, and the couple have only come close enough to pass each other Bess's food or nappies.

Ruth takes her own coat from the hook. 'Oh, OK . . . right.' It's been a while since Giles has sat in with her at the psychiatrist's, but yesterday's calamity bulges between them and he's fast-tracked her monthly session to today. She heats up under her coat – with embarrassment or anger, she can't tell any more. 'I don't mind if you've got work calls to catch up with after you've taken me there, or if you want to grab a coffee or something.' Her foot fiddles with the brake on the pushchair. She knows what Giles's answer will be, but even a facade of autonomy is better than none.

Bess waggles her favourite toy in the air. It's round, multi-coloured with a bell inside, and is one of the only things apart from milk that keeps her quiet. She loses her grip and the ball drops, bouncing off the buggy's wheels. Bacteria will be colonizing the toy. It will need to be washed and disinfected. Ruth's already late so she'll have to leave it behind. If Bess gets upset, Ruth will have fewer tools to soothe her and the doctor will mark it as an incompetence. When Ruth worked at the office, she'd dealt with complex, strategic problems, but this new world perspective that's been forced on her has shrunk her outlook to these four walls, as if the dark mouth of this house has swallowed her whole. And without a pay packet at the end of the month, Ruth struggles to attach real worth to what she does for Bess; no one's ever taught her to think differently, and certainly no one treats the constant, often menial tasks as having any value, so how can she? She holds tight to the earthing point of the buggy's handles and waits for the rage to pass.

'Righty-ho then,' Giles says, searching for his keys.

'There might be a wait at outpatients.' Ruth delivers her final attempt to keep Giles out of the appointment with the voice of a mouse. 'I'd sort of prefer going in on my own anyway.'

He places his hands on his wife's shoulders. She shrinks under the weight of his disappointment and the constancy of her failure. 'I'm here for you,' he says. 'I want to look after my girls.' He tries to make his hokey words palatable by giving her a slack hug, and when he lets go they both exhale as if the embrace was tighter than it was.

The perinatal outpatient unit is based at the hospital where parking is limited and expensive, so there's no point taking the car. But the walk to the bus stop entails passing the garage at the end of the road. In the distance, an asthma cloud of fumes from the queuing cars hangs over the forecourt. Pitted and rubbly tarmac, dusty manhole covers. Innocuous, grubby, humdrum. Nothing else, nothing to fear, only humiliation. Giles's hands are braced so tightly on the pushchair that Ruth imagines he could swing it above his head. Yesterday, he wrestled a man at the petrol station and his mad wife was laid bare for the whole street to see. Curtains twitch at the windows of a couple of neighbours' houses and Ruth ducks her head to plough on, remembering only now that, in her confusion this morning, she missed today's prescription. She'll take it as soon as she gets home. No need to worry Giles or turn back.

Ahead, at the end of the row of terraces, is Sandra and Liam's house. Their gate opens and Sandra backs out with her sleeping baby tucked inside his pushchair. Ruth stiffens. Sandra's wearing another new outfit, high-end high street, black and tailored. She's the only mum Ruth knows who wants to look like a woman instead of a girl. Sandra crouches to put something in the storage net under the seat. She's not seen Ruth yet, but in a few seconds their paths will cross with 'Hi's and kisses and questions. Fogging the space between them all is the possibility that Sandra witnessed yesterday's calamity or, worse still, that Liam's given her his version of events.

Giles veers sharply towards the cut-through, the longer walk to the bus stop by far, but this way they'll avoid Sandra, who's turned in the opposite direction now without seeing them. Ruth reaches out to link arms with Giles, to give back some of the support she receives, but he flinches, his body now electrified with tension, and her hand falls to her side.

The afternoon is sunny but chilly. Ruth is wrapped up well and Giles pushes the buggy fast. For once Bess isn't crying. With nothing to hold on to, Ruth chews the cuticles of her idle fingers, catching a strand of skin in her teeth and pulling a satisfying length. Now they're out of sight of the street, Giles's shoulders relax and he fills the airwaves with chatter about work, as he is able to do and she is not, the art of casual conversation lost to her months ago. A normality of sorts radiates from the front gardens they pass, the lawns mown and beds tidier the further they get from their house. The order makes Ruth feel safe, but there's less variety, less character here, almost a sterility; perhaps everyone is impelled to conform or outdo each other. Children shriek in the playground of the local school. Later on their parents will pick them up and take them back to warm, happy homes. The sun touches Ruth's face and with it comes a nod to better times, like the promise of a holiday at the end of a gruelling shift. The night before last, Ruth watched a line of people climb out of the ground, then her neighbour stirred up Ruth by talking about people in petrol tanks, but the only explanation can be that Ruth misheard her over the noise of the chainsaw. In this present moment, Ruth is secure enough to marvel at the creativity of her own imagination.

At the clinic, Ruth and Giles are ushered into the appointment without a wait. Dr Fraser and Giles exchange pleasantries – 'Good to see you,' 'Yes, great to see you too.' Giles puts out his hand for a handshake. The psychiatrist accepts. Giles is clearly relieved to see this professional, with all the assistance she'll be able to offer for his mad wife, but the enthusiastic pump of his handshake is a bit much. The doctor pulls away. Giles tries to cover his misstep by scratching his face, the gesture exaggerated, as if he's got a really bad itch and it had been his plan all along to scratch. It's not hard to see how he got it wrong, though; the familiarity of the people in the room has been brokered these last few months over a shared desire for Ruth's recovery. If it wasn't for the fact that Ruth continues to be the focus, along with all the shame and failure that her condition represents to her, she'd feel more sorry for Giles, who's now playing the don't-care card by sitting as far from Dr Fraser as possible. Maggie, Ruth's health visitor, turns up after a few minutes, along with Richard, the community psychiatric nurse.

'I hope you don't mind us popping in,' Maggie says, nodding towards Richard. 'We just wanted to see how things are going.'

Ruth fidgets inside her unease, a body memory of always being in the wrong. It's standard for Richard, her CPN, to be at these kind of appointments, but not her health visitor as well – she must have been specially invited – and even though Ruth appreciates the politeness of making out they were just passing by, it's annoying that her fragility requires the pretence. She lifts Bess from the buggy, taking the still-warm bottle from her bag. The little girl's not due a feed until later, but this way Ruth can occupy Bess before the baby even thinks about crying.

'How's it going with the solids?' the health visitor asks. 'Have you found the weaning diary I gave you useful?'

Ruth's face settles in a weak smile, refusing to let Maggie witness her true feelings. This woman is a master at leading Ruth into cul-de-sacs of emotional revelations, her highly tuned female intuition scanning Ruth's face for clues to failing health. Ruth used to glory in the fluidity of milk that streamed straight from her body into her baby, breastfeeding being one of the only things she actually did well, but she'd had to give it up when she started the medication. The dollops of processed powder she now has to mix with water to feed her daughter, to Ruth, symbolize defeat. And now there's this weaning sheet to factor in too, the basic kiddie fare of parboiled carrot sticks and banana porridge that Bess turns her nose up at, so Ruth can't even get that right. She opens her mouth to speak as Giles cuts across.

'Ruth's been doing her best, but Bess seems to know when she's around, and then she only wants a bottle.'

'Have you thought about Daddy doing some or perhaps all of the dinners for a while?' Maggie asks.

Ruth tucks Bess closer to her body. 'She's fine, she's just a really milky baby.'

'Well, we're a little worried about her size again,' the health visitor says. 'She's dropped down the weight percentile. Another pair of hands could help her get used to the new regime, give you the chance for a break, to get away for a bit.'

Ruth's voice raises a fraction. 'Where am I going?'

'Nowhere. I just meant that Daddy could feed her while you're in the other room perhaps.'

'But Giles needs to work. He hasn't got time to do everything. And I'm managing.'

Managing. Coping. How Ruth hates these mantras. And none of them are true. One day in the lifetime of her child was all Ruth was geared up for, a day of endurance with a prize at the end of a freshly minted, wholly dependent human. Ruth doesn't get invited to the NCT socials any more, the drinks and nibbles that rotate round the other group members' houses. Their husbands still play football together, and Giles was on the team before it became less embarrassing to leave them both out than admit that no one could cope with Ruth's condition. At first her seclusion felt like quarantine, but Ruth's come to understand it's not meant as unkindness. They're all rushing around trying to find time for their own vast and teetering to-do lists and simply don't have space in their lives to take on the responsibility of needy Ruth. How much can one person fix another anyway?

'Well, it would be good,' Maggie says, 'if we could perhaps try this routine for a couple of weeks. You know, every mealtime Daddy can take over. Just to get Baby into a routine. Is that possible, Mr Woodman?'

Giles fills his cheeks with air. He fought for his job at the charity against a hundred other applicants. His salary is the only thing keeping the family afloat. He's good at his job but no one is irreplaceable. He sighs. 'OK, I'll square it with the office.'

'Anyway, Ruth,' Dr Fraser says, 'I'm so glad you were able to come in today.' She glances at the CPN, who nods back with the same yoga-warm expression everyone's adopted since Ruth was first unwell. Earnest and sanctimonious. Steady, concerned eyebrows. 'We wanted to check how things are with you in general. How the medication is suiting you?'

Here it comes, Ruth thinks; even though she'd been expecting the cross-examination, it was comforting for a while to have the distraction – all that weaning stuff was just a warm-up. 'Fine,' she says. 'Absolutely fine.' How much do they know? When did Giles fill them in? She imagines his busy fingers detailing her failures in an email, like Morse code signalling the location of an enemy sub.

'You're not having any, um, issues?'

'Perhaps a couple. But it's all sorted now.' She squints at Giles, the lie atomized and floating between them. Ruth imagines she could sink her fist inside the untruth and pull out something yellow and stinking. Giles turns away.

'Maybe so,' Richard says. 'But Giles has been concerned about a few changes he's noticed recently. He mentioned you've seemed a little edgy, that you called your GP several times worrying about Bess.'

'I'm fine and Bess is fine.'

'Your daughter will only thrive if Mum's thriving,' the PCN says. 'And there's nothing to be ashamed of if you're struggling again.'

'She just doesn't like solids,' Ruth says. 'That's all. Lots of babies are the same.'

'Yes, we know,' Dr Fraser interjects, leaning forward and flicking a look at Giles, who's now staring at the floor. 'But we heard that there was an incident with the police, and we were concerned that you may be experiencing some confusion with what's real and what's not – that you might be seeing or hearing things again, things that perhaps other people can't.'

Ruth bites her bottom lip, tasting the blood that's millimetres from her tongue – of course they would know. Even if Giles hadn't told them, the police said they'd been in touch with the mental health team. As she'd been getting ready to come here today, Dr Fraser, Richard and Maggie were probably having an emergency meeting, discussing between them how to proceed, how they'd like to dissect her amorphous mind into neat little chunks and set it in aspic.

'If that is the case,' Dr Fraser continues, 'we need to give this some serious attention. You've been working with us long enough to understand that collectively we need to meet your changing needs, and those of your baby. It's all part of your care plan, the one we discussed and put together with you.'

'Perhaps it's time to try some antidepressants as well,' Giles says. 'Weren't you saying that was the next course of action for her, Doctor?'

Ruth swivels to Giles. 'I am in the room, you know.'

'Antidepressants have always been an option on the care plan, Ruth,' Dr Fraser says. 'If you or we decided they would help. And as the father of your child, it's useful for Giles to let us know how you're feeling sometimes. It's nothing more sinister than that.'

'Well, why don't you just ask me then? Instead of discussing me between yourselves.'

The landline bursts into life. Dr Fraser mutes the call without even turning to the phone, the sudden absence of noise leaving a rising silence in its wake. Giles gently opens the space. 'We have been asking you, but you won't admit there's a problem, so it's up to me to tell everyone what's going on.'

Ruth clenches Bess a little too hard and the baby jerks off the bottle.

'Let me have her for a minute.' Maggie stands and takes

the little girl from Ruth, rocking her gently. The baby settles within seconds. 'There's no set formula in these situations, Ruth. All we're doing is watching out for you and Bess. We want to work with you to find the best solution.'

Giles leans forward and rests his forearms on his thighs. 'I just want you to get better.' His hands are limp between his legs and he shakes his head as he mumbles. 'Some of the things you've been talking about recently, that stuff about people under the ground.'

His sagging back and bent head make a perfect arc, as if the weight of his worry is forcing him into a slow dive. How much this man has had to endure. All Giles's work colleagues are already moving on to their second and third children, those sunny, capable women who juggle budgets and meetings, complicated childcare and transatlantic flights. Giles has invested hugely in his family for such little return, and yet so has Ruth, the fault in her brain as much outside her control as his. Giles is the onlooker, but Ruth inhabits the horror.

'We'd like to encourage you to talk to us,' Dr Fraser says, 'let us know what's really going on with you.' Without Bess to hold on to, Ruth grips her elbows, forcing her shoulders close to her ears. Both Richard and Maggie's smiles are fixed. Only the psychiatrist's stare is serious as she continues. 'We have you on what is usually a pretty effective dose of medication, so we're a bit concerned if it's not doing its job. Perhaps the time has come to consider another avenue of help.'

'I'm not going on the psych ward.'

'It's highly unlikely you'd need to go to a hospital, Ruth.'

'I won't let you take Bess away.'

'No one's saying that, Mrs Woodman. We'd do everything in our power to find a bed at a mother-and-baby unit, even if it meant you going out of area. From your experience of spending time there before, I hope you can remember how supportive the staff were, and how they can assist you with any issues you might be having around medication or attachment.' She leans back in her chair, crossing her arms. 'When I visited you in the unit last time, it struck me as significant that you said you'd been terrified the place would be like some kind of Victorian asylum, but the reality was more like a hotel.'

'Look.' Ruth scans the faces in the room, her options falling away by the second as the likelihood of being sent away looms closer – whatever's going on with what she's been seeing and hearing, it's nothing like her illness was at the beginning, when the delusions had been her total world view. Her current state of mind is fixable by far simpler means than treatment at the mother-and-baby unit. Like sleep and logic, and avoiding neighbours who put ideas in her head. These things aside, she fears, however irrationally, that if the wheels were put in motion and there were no beds, there'd be no other option but to put her on a psychiatric ward where they have no facilities for babies. The chance is small, minute even, but it's still a possibility, and possibility is risk, a risk they'd take Bess away. Her voice falters. 'I've just had a couple of blips recently, just silly things bothering me. My sleep's been all over the place, but I'm totally back on track now.'

'If you're not sleeping, we need to know about it,' Richard

says. 'Insomnia and feelings of increased anxiety are in your care plan as early warning signs that might trigger a relapse. So being alert to these is part of the responsibility of looking after yourself, as well as your daughter, especially if there've been instances of hallucinating again.'

'I was just dreaming, OK? That stuff I said to Giles was nonsense, I know that now.'

'Well,' says Dr Fraser. 'A mother-and-baby unit might get you over this hump and help you find a better routine. We'd like to encourage you to consider this option very seriously. There's no shame in your illness, Ruth, but there's a possibility it might be growing bigger than you again, and none of us, yourself included, want to let it take any more control.'

'I told you, I had a bad dream.' A fleck of spit lands on her thigh as she speaks. 'If you want me to take the antidepressants, fine, but I'm not mad any more. I'm perfectly capable of looking after my baby.'

'No one's saying you're not, Ruth, but we do think it might be wise to adapt your care plan to incorporate another stay at the unit, before things escalate any further.'

'Right.' Ruth stands. 'I'm not staying here and listening to any more of this rubbish.' She grabs Bess from Maggie's arms and tries to strap her wriggling baby into the buggy. Bess hasn't had enough warning and she arches her back as Ruth wrestles the harness over her frantic little arms. One of the safety clips pinches the baby's skin and a scream bursts through the room. A blood blister inflates on Bess's hand. 'Oh God, oh no! Sorry, Bessie.' Ruth kisses the little girl's hand over and over, almost as if she could absorb the pain herself. She turns to the other four in the room. 'Look what you made me do!'

She wrenches open the door, the buggy too close, and the door jams on the front wheels before thumping shut again.

'Ruth, what are you doing?' Giles is at her side. He tries to take the handles. Ruth bumps him out of the way with her shoulder.

It takes several attempts to swing the door wide enough to get out. She turns briefly to see Maggie and Richard standing together, heads almost touching, frowning at each other across folded arms. Giles is speaking to the doctor. He grabs a prescription from her hand and breaks away to chase after Ruth as she speeds through the waiting room of judging eyes. She races down the road, trying to outrun Giles, who's drawn along by Bess's howl.

By the time they get off the bus, the school they passed earlier is emptying. A sea of parents and children surges towards Ruth. She struggles to get through the crowd without ramming the buggy into shins. The end-of-school bell is high and clear in the playground, and a backwash of memory hits Ruth: her sister waiting at the gates at the end of the summer term, Ruth fifteen, her sister sixteen, the two of them running to the park they used to play in as younger kids, grabbing the swings they'd grown too big for and swinging so high the chains went slack and their bodies became weightless. Tam's voice coming in and out of hearing as they passed mid-air, like opposing metronomes. 'When you reach the top,' she said, 'if you let go, you'd fly. Just for a few seconds before you hit the ground, you'd be totally free. What do you think? Shall we give it a try?'

When they finally get home, Bess has calmed a little, but she's still crying. Ruth focuses on this tiny machine of noise, her own hands frozen at her sides, overwhelmed by the multitude of things she needs to do in opposition to the one she wants, which is to cover her ears and block out the crying. The noise fills Ruth's brain, scouring her to the bone. There isn't enough room inside her head for all her fears as well as this shrieking.

Giles lifts his daughter from the pushchair and puts her over his shoulder. 'Hey, munchkin,' he says to the little girl. 'It's OK.' He kisses her as he goes to the downstairs loo. Bess's cry softens to a whimper.

Giles makes no attempt this time to disguise the creak and slam of the medicine cabinet door. He returns to Ruth with crackling foil and plastic, and as she turns he's standing next to her with a tablet in his open palm.

She says, 'But I've already—'

'No. You. Haven't.'

Her fingers falter over the pill without picking up, desperation propelling her into dead ends. 'I just forgot. It's not happened before. I was planning to take it, honestly.'

'This is how it's going to be from now on.' The whites of Giles's eyes are bloodshot. 'There are more people in this family than you, Ruth.' His voice grows louder as he spaces his words. 'I've done every bloody thing I can to help you get better at home, but I have no resources left.' Bess whimpers. 'Do you have any idea how hard these past months have been for me? Well, do you?' He's shouting now, face shimmering with a rage Ruth's not witnessed before. 'I'm at my wits' end, Ruth. I'm tired, I'm stretched at work, and worst of all, I don't know if I can trust you. So take the bloody pill or I will force it in your mouth. I've got the prescription for antidepressants as well. There'll be no arguments about taking any of them.' He shushes Bess with a kiss, holding her head gently towards him. 'Sorry, little one. Daddy's sorry.' He bobs up and down as the baby cuddles into his neck.

Giles hands Ruth a glass of water, and he watches as she swallows. The tablet sticks in her throat. She swigs again, the pill's impression remaining in her oesophagus. Giles waits until she's finished, then says, 'Open your mouth.' He peers inside and asks her to lift her tongue so he can check she hasn't hidden the tablet underneath, then he takes his daughter into the kitchen. With a confident flick of closure, he puts the kettle on to boil and pulls out a packet of processed baby cereal Ruth didn't even know they possessed.

For better or for worse, but how much worse can this get? An image of water comes to Ruth, of a vast black ocean through which no sound could travel. She helicopters above herself standing at a shoreline, fully clothed, wading into the waves, legs powering forward, not stopping until her head's totally submerged. The peace of letting go, of giving up.

'Go and read a book or something,' Giles calls to her.

'Take a nap. Do one of those things you're always complaining you never have time for.'

Ruth crosses to the back window. The sun is disappearing behind clouds and a feeble wind tugs the grass. Beyond their little garden is the back path that runs the length of all the terraces, and after this, the strip of land along the parallel railway fence. Several residents have taken over their share of this space that the street collectively refers to as the allotments, the plots well tended in the summer, their cottage gardens bursting with fat ripe veg, but the winter has stripped the raised beds and toppled the steeples of cane. Trampolines have been squeezed into other spaces and, elsewhere, plastic garden furniture has blown over, exposing black mouldy underbellies. Only Miss Cailleach next door takes care of her patch the whole year round, traipsing over to the rows of neatly planted vegetables come rain or shine, or digging over the bare earth in readiness for spring, refilling the multistorey bird feeder with seeds and fat balls. In these cold winter months, it sometimes seems to Ruth that her neighbour is tending the patch out of nothing better to do, collecting long spindly twigs from a couple of stubby trees near the fence. She winds string round the bunches of sticks to make ugly bouquets.

In Ruth's allotment, a homemade chicken shed has been left by the previous owner. It's about four feet tall, made of a collection of mismatched wood nailed together, with a part-felted, part-corrugated roof. The owner must have had a decent-sized chicken empire, perhaps even sold some eggs. When they first viewed the house, Ruth imagined herself taking over this cottage industry before it quickly became clear she wasn't the homesteader type. Chicken wire is buried deep in the ground to keep out foxes, so it will take more than Ruth and Giles's strength to dismantle the construction, and the task has slid to the bottom of their list of priorities to merely unsightly.

An intercity train streaks past. Carriages flash colour through the metres of trees on the sidings and the engine's *whoosh* reaches Ruth as an afterthought; it's a lonely echo, the sound of being left behind. A small group of railway workers in the distance move like shadows through the trees, barely visible without the reflective jackets they surely ought to be wearing. They beat the undergrowth with sticks, slashing at the grass and saplings. One of them picks up a piece of fabric and shows it to the others, who shake their heads. The fabric is tossed to one side and they continue through the scrub, shoulders broad, heads down, scanning the ground.

Ruth's skinny fox slopes along the path, his coat dull and mangy, absorbing the urban landscape he has no choice but to inhabit. He sniffs the entrance Ruth's made for him into the shed to keep warm, then lifts his head, and there's a moment when his eyes meet Ruth's before he wanders off unperturbed. She's no threat. No friend either. Ruth makes no impression on the world. She may as well not exist.

8

In this novel moment of daytime quiet, Ruth fidgets with what to do. She could use the time to edit her photos, but her laptop is downstairs on the coffee table and she can't bear to face Giles and be reminded so soon of his disappointment at having married the wrong woman. She turns on the bedroom TV, bringing her feet up from the floor where a draught lurks at her ankles. On the screen, a large dinghy is tossed by waves, then the image cuts to a hill of life jackets. People scramble on shingle, one sits at the water's edge holding a baby, another has a foil blanket over their back, head in hands. Ruth quickly switches to another channel: a couple relocating to the countryside with a toddler. They're smiling and walking through a summer field, the season as inconceivable to Ruth, here in the thick of winter, as an afterlife. Her chest constricts with something unreachable, from way back, before Giles, to the beginning of that summer with her sister, when the world had seemed safe because Ruth knew less, and her days had contained the binary simplicity of innocence. If it were possible to somehow transmogrify into her younger self and freeze in that moment, Ruth would clear every detail of here and now unquestionably.

She lies down, head submerged in the pillows. Sleep comes unexpectedly and fast – a fist of exhaustion after the past few days. Paranoia chatters through her dreams. She wakes sometime later to Bess's cry travelling up the stairs, followed by Giles's aeroplane noise. Ruth imagines him doing that expression, the way he pushes his lips to one side to make the sound, trying hard to get Bess to eat. Adrenaline kicks in – she knows Bess's scratchy cry, the baby's tired not hungry – and it takes all Ruth's willpower to trust Giles to get on with it and not go down and tell him what their daughter needs. She turns off the still-burbling TV, kicking her feet in a steady thump on the bed frame, cursing Giles's backhanded gift of an impromptu day off; if she'd had warning, she could have planned to do something concrete, perhaps even gone to the office to have lunch with her old friends. She holds the phone in her hand, wondering who'd be the best person to call, who might tolerate the interruption. Caroline or Sharon who she'd shared desk space with? She has no idea what's going on with either of them as she doesn't use Instagram any more – those quick scans of her friends' social media accounts used to be as good as a catch-up, so maybe they think she's being rude because she's no longer joining in – and no one bothers with phone calls these days, no one has the time or energy. But perhaps her old boss, Minnie, might be interested in a quick chat. She presses speed dial before she can change her mind and the call goes through to her boss's PA. 'I'll just check if she's in,' the intern says. A painful pause of muzak trickles into Ruth's ear before the PA comes back on. 'I'm sorry but she's in a meeting.' The assistant's new to the company, her position created as part of a budgetary and departmental shake-up, one that could see Ruth no longer needed. 'I'm afraid she'll be busy all day.' The young woman's still too fresh to the job to have learnt how to polish her lie. 'Can I take a message?' In Ruth's sightline, her wardrobe gapes open, spewing clothes like a wooden beast with its belly cut in two. Old work suits and smart jackets lie crumpled from the last time Ruth tried them on, when the pencil skirt had jammed at her chunky thighs and she'd flung it aside.

'Just tell her Ruth called and that I'm planning to come back to work very soon.'

The intern ends the call, accidentally leaving Ruth's line open to the office hubbub, as alive in its phone crackle as when Ruth had worked there. Like an interloper, Ruth listens in; impossible to believe this other world exists in parallel to her own, here at home, confined to her room with nowhere to go. She lifts out of herself and temporarily slides back inside the woman she used to be.

How efficient she'd been, how on the pulse and ready to respond to her clients' needs. 'You're so kind,' they'd said. 'You always go the extra mile. Promise you'll come back after your maternity leave.' Ruth laughed. 'Of course I will, what century do you think this is? Anyway, I'm only having a baby, not a heart bypass.'

At the beginning of each working day, Ruth would revise the to-do list on her computer, creating tallies of calls to make and schedules to pin down, knowing that all it took to finish those tasks was application and attention to detail. The completed and unnecessary were deleted, the digital rustle of her computer's trash basket one of Ruth's favourite sounds. Time to move on, it said, you've left nothing unfinished, no errors have been found. She'd attempted to translate that work ethic into looking after a tiny baby, but trying harder didn't correlate to more order at home, and Ruth's returns were insomnia and anxiety. Then, along with the chemical anomaly of her maternal hormones, the payoff was mental illness.

Ruth presses her ear to the handset. There are voices in the background, laughter too. It sounds like Minnie, who's supposed to be in a meeting. Ruth paces back and forth, unable to disconnect, guilty that she needs them more than they need her, tense in case something unkind is said about her. She wants to know the truth of what they think, but she's not sure she could cope with the honesty. The popular narrative for Ruth's condition is that it has gone from worse to better, though Ruth's molecular progress has at times been in reverse, the constancy of her needs exhausting everyone around her. Work friends are only good friends when you're at work, and it's unfair of Ruth to expect these busy women to be the rocks she needs them to be. She hangs up.

Like magic, the phone buzzes to life in her hand. Ruth's ready to have it out with the heavy breather once and for all, when the screen lights up with Sandra's name. Ruth answers immediately.

'Honey, you OK?' Sandra says, laughing. 'You robbed a bank this time?'

Even touching into lightness is a relief. 'Sandra.' Ruth relaxes back on the pillows. 'It's really good to hear from you.'

'C'mon then.' Sandra's ever gossip-ready, switching out problem for play. 'Spill the beans. What's going on?'

There's no pussyfooting around with Sandra and Ruth takes a heartbeat to summon up the same directness. 'I'm so embarrassed, but I really thought I saw something this time.'

'You sure? I mean, was it at night again?'

'Yes. Yes, it was. I know I need to be careful, but this felt different somehow. It was more crazy than anything I've seen before. I don't know how I could have dreamt it up.' The air thickens around Ruth, as if the heating's suddenly come on full blast. 'Consequently no one believes me.'

'Try me.'

'It's, well . . . It's just too weird. Giles is livid about the whole thing. He's had me up in front of the medical team this morning. I don't know how me and him will ever get back to normal.'

'It can't be that bad, can it?' Static down the line. 'Ruthie? You still there?'

Ruth sniffs up her tears. 'Yes, just a sec.'

'You can tell me anything you want, honey, and I won't laugh, OK? I'm here for you. Might help you to get it off your chest.'

Ruth breathes out long and hard. 'Well, yesterday Giles got into a bit of a fight for me with that bastard from the petrol station.' Sandra gasps and Ruth continues. 'I can't bear to show my face down there again – actually, I'm not allowed to – but it's not like it seems. That bloke was really aggressive. Giles was only protecting me.' Ruth pictures the first few houses on the street with their view of the forecourt and she bunches the duvet cover in her free hand. 'But then you might have seen anyway.'

'No, I didn't.' Sandra's voice booms down the phone. 'But more's the point, what did you see?'

Ruth pushes aside the too-plump pillows, cowed by Sandra's singularity. 'Well . . .' She runs her free hand up and down her thigh, palm heating on the denim. 'It was the night before last. There were some people, about four. Women, I think. A couple looked very young, like kids.' Silence on the other end of the phone, not even Sandra's breath. 'They were at the petrol station. It was night-time.' A streak of blood runs up Ruth's jeans. She must have torn a cuticle with her teeth without realizing. 'They climbed out of a manhole.'

'Bloody hell, Ruth.' Ian cries in the background, then the noise scissors off as if a door's been shut on him. 'That sounds really bonkers.'

'I just can't let it go. One minute the image of them climbing out seems so real and the next I wonder if my mind's playing tricks on me. But what if it is true? I mean, if they were children? Someone should do something.'

'Did Giles see? Was there anyone else around?'

Ruth recalls Liam's mum at her gate. *I'm up all hours and I've seen them coming out before.* Ruth's been consorting with her best friend's enemy, been taken in by the crazy talk she's been warned against, and if she admits this she suspects she'll lose these lifeline chats with Sandra, plus the nice little bags of gifts that demonstrate her friend's affection. 'No, no one else saw.'

'Listen, honey. Liam knows the blokes that run the car wash. They're OK, you know. They're nice.'

'I'm not so sure.'

'Look, you're a mate so I can say this.' Sandra's voice dips, like she's switching ears before she comes back, louder this time. 'But do you think you might be being a bit racialist?'

'What?' Ruth blinks away the tears. 'No, of course not.'

'Really? I mean, don't take this the wrong way or anything, but you do sometimes give the impression that you think you're better than the rest of us.'

Ruth opens her mouth to protest, aware of the hole she could dig herself if she protests too much, so her words simply evaporate in shock. Her bigger fear is that Sandra might have a point.

That night, as Giles and Ruth lie side by side, an invisible fence runs the length of the mattress, and Ruth doesn't dare move across the line. Giles's breathing slows into gentle puffs as he drifts quickly into sleep, never one to let stress interfere with his eight hours. His shape under the sheets reminds Ruth of a tomb she once saw, where man and wife lay chiselled side by side, together forever but never to touch, frozen under drapes of stone.

With all her unexpected free time today, Ruth's napped on and off, as a solo yachtsman would, banking an hour here and there in preparation for the bad weather that's sure to come, and the combination of the medication she's now taken isn't strong enough to knock her out. She tosses and turns with a growing thirst, her glass of water empty since she hadn't dared to go downstairs while Giles was still up. Her bag is downstairs too, and she never feels totally settled unless she has it with her, keys and money inside, in case she needs to run – to where she doesn't know, but the feeling that something's coming for her and her baby never goes away. Or perhaps whatever's coming is already here. Life was easier when she only had herself to think about. Now she's invested in Bess, she has everything to lose.

She takes the stairs quietly to the lounge where a half-light seeps through the uncurtained back window. At the sink, she fills a pint glass, gulps it down and refills before flopping on the sofa in the semi-darkness. The pills are beginning to soften her edges and she allows her eyes to close for a second before snapping them open – she mustn't fall asleep downstairs, what would that look like to Giles in the morning? Beer cans and Xbox controllers scatter the coffee table and she puts her feet up, careful not to knock anything over. Liam must have been over earlier when she'd been asleep, her snooze deeper than she thought as she didn't hear him. At least Giles has let off some steam, probably why he's sleeping so well now. Giles only ever plays his Xbox when Liam's around, goading the telly and sinking lagers, trying to be the kind of boy his brothers would have wanted to hang out with. She instantly forgives Giles the day's issues, wanting to cuddle into the back of this man who's still a hurt child, but she worries what Sandra might have passed on to Liam, and what Liam might have told Giles. A disquiet has stayed with Ruth since she spoke to Sandra earlier, that prejudice might be a preset, buried so deep inside she's not even aware it exists. The water she's drunk turns into a queasy pool in her stomach.

A snapping noise outside. Ruth sits tall and twists her head to look out of the window. The night is overcast, a city's worth of light pollution making dirty candyfloss of the clouds. Ahead is the solid block of the chicken shed and next to it a shaded area Ruth doesn't recognize. It could be her fox, finally finding his bed, but the shape is irregular and too dark to formalize. Then, a movement. From under the corrugated roof, a shadow unfolds, flexing tall into a dim outline. Legs, arms, head, just enough information in the darkness to make out the slender build and medium height of a young woman. Dressed in baggy clothes, a tracksuit perhaps, with hair hidden by a woolly hat. The figure climbs the small fence into Ruth's garden. On her feet are flip-flops – freezing in this weather – and she searches the ground, possibly for the toast crusts Ruth puts out for the fox, but Giles did the supper tonight, so the leftovers would have gone in the bin. Ruth kneels up on the sofa facing the garden, paralysed inside her fear and wonder as her skin prickles, like an electric current is surging into the room. She presses her face to the icy glass. The girl hugs her ribs and shivers. Ruth makes a fist, heart hammering, then taps her knuckles on the window. Outside, the young woman stops dead, checking side to side, then straight ahead at Ruth. She contracts into a crouch.

Ruth rests her palm on the pane, breath misting the window, and whispers, 'You're not real. You can't be real.'

The girl looks behind her, perhaps expecting others to arrive. Her breath makes clouds in the air. Nobody comes. Ruth rubs the mist from the window and smiles weakly. Frail and quivering, the girl uncurls in slow motion to stand tall before she inches forward. When she reaches the window, she flattens her palm to Ruth's on the opposite side of the glass.

'Please go away.' A sob pulls Ruth's chest. 'Please. No one will believe me.' Her voice is louder than she intended and the words startle the empty room. She raises herself higher on her knees, too fast, and the girl leaps back. In a flash, the skinny figure vaults the fence and darts up the path in the direction of the dead end. Ruth presses her cheek to the window as the young woman disappears from view.

There is no one for Ruth to turn to, no one to reassure her about what she might or might not have seen without setting off every alarm bell, and she's torn between the reality of this desperate girl and the fear that her illness is back, the latter possibility more attractive than accepting a desperate person is living in her chicken shed. The medication is finally fogging Ruth's brain and she settles on the plausible: the notion that again she's in a waking trance, that elastic zone between awake and asleep where nothing makes sense and everything is possible. All of it – the scream, the petrol station, now this girl – it has to be nonsense. She blames her elderly neighbour for stoking the embers of her own misfiring brain with talk of people under the ground, if Ruth even heard her correctly in the first place. All Ruth had to do was fill the gaps of suggestion, like some psychogenic illness passing between the two houses. A fold in Ruth's brain has created a friend to fill her lonely days, some warped magic of memory having stored and reprocessed her sister to come back when she needed her most.

Ruth puts a hand to the wall to steady her dizziness, the ground as buoyant as if she'd stepped off a boat, and she pauses for a moment as the bare plaster walls seem to ripple with her exhaustion. She turns and walks upstairs, her footsteps conceding the need for sleep, and an aching desire for the insanity to stop.

Bess is asleep in her cot. Ruth lifts out the sweaty little bundle to hug her close. The baby's translucent eyelids fidget with a dream. Languageless stories are playing out in her tiny mind after only a few months of life. Perhaps she's imagining the monster of her mother as a dark overbearing shape, a nucleus of mistrust that will grow and develop as she gets older. There's so much Ruth has to make up for, if the damage hasn't already been done. She kisses her daughter's tiny forehead, absorbing the little girl's perfection, the gratitude for this good sweet child both immense and perplexing, only to find that she herself cannot move. Effortlessly, at last, the connection Ruth's been longing for has come; she is incapacitated by love.

She cuddles her daughter, staring hard, reminding herself of every feature, finger and toe belonging to this immaculate being in her arms. Ruth can't bear to put Bess back in her cot and brings her into her own bedroom, switching on the lamp. The shadows instantly retreat into the comforting certainty of electricity and the girl outside is firmly consigned to

Ruth's imagination. Giles sleep-grumbles and turns from the light.

This room contains all of Ruth's hope. Without these solid people she owns nothing apart from fantasy. It is not possible to love and be loved when so full of error.

9

Ruth dreams of beaters, of men roaming the sidings, hacking shrubs with sticks to scare out animals for a hunt. In her dream she's at Bess's back window with her daughter in her arms. Ruth watches as the men gather in a small clearing of trees and one of them dives to the ground to grab something lithe and wriggling. He stands; Ruth recognizes him as Barry from next door. Triumphantly, he holds Ruth's fox by its tail, the animal bucking uselessly upside down and screaming like a baby. Another man has a wet rag in his hand and he snaps it at the fox's head. The sonic crack jolts Ruth awake. Sweat covers her body.

The clock on her bedside table reads 10 a.m. From downstairs, the baseline of Giles's voice filters through the floorboards, along with the higher pitch of Bess's chatter. Ruth wraps herself in her dressing gown and walks through to her daughter's room to peer at the sidings. She tucks the curtains to one side. Daylight overwhelms the darkness in the room and she hugs her robe tight, waiting for the residue of the dream to clear.

It's too soon for the antidepressants to be working, but with the benefit of a good night's sleep, a line is beginning to clear through Ruth's worry. Below in the garden is a sea of weathered plastic toys and, beyond that, the chicken shed is as solid and ugly as ever. Only wood and wire and junk. No one came out of it last night. People don't live in chicken sheds, the same as they don't climb out of holes in the ground or get bricked up in recesses under the stairs. She smacks her palms on her cheeks to scare the last of the night-time fears from her system, wishing she didn't have to work so hard to convince herself her nonsense was simply that and nothing else.

Ruth and Giles's home is in a single row of terraces with a hedgerow lining the opposite side of the street. The house numbers run consecutively to just past one hundred, and Ruth lives at number 39, situated about a third of the way up the street bordering one of the few alleyways to the back gardens. From the first floor of her house, Ruth has a good view onto the plots of her immediate neighbours, especially Liam's mum's in the next terrace on the other side of the alley. A waist-high fence squares off the woman's rear garden.

Since the police called round a couple of days ago, Ruth hasn't seen her neighbour, but this morning after Ruth gets dressed, she collects a bag of nappies from Bess's room and glances outside. The woman's garden is filled with laundry, pegged on the web of a spinning rack. Lines of beige slacks and fleeces flap in the weak sun. Yards of heavy-denier tights swing next to pale-green blouses. Miss Cailleach wears these same clothes as she walks past Ruth's house every day on her way to the shops, her hair in that wiry bun at the base of her funny felt hat. It's her uniform of timidity, a camouflage of mid-greeny browns. Most Fridays, the laundry's the same, as long as it's not raining, and the habit of a washday ages her beyond the years Ruth would have guessed at, like Ruth's grandma who used to set aside a day for chores – dusting on a Tuesday, baking on a Wednesday. Ruth too has been taken over by this domesticity, propelling her back to a time when women's work was dictated by the tiny universes they were permitted to inhabit.

A door slams and Miss Cailleach brings another load into her back garden. Today a brighter colour mixes with the usual beiges as she pegs out the clothes. She's wearing a red kimono, patterned with colourful flowers and birds, like she's emerged from a disguise. The material is ripped in a couple of places, but even from Ruth's distance she can tell the fabric is luxurious; the way the big sleeves swing and crease is heavy and authentic, not the usual knock-off item from some high-street chain. And the woman's hair is loose for once. Long grey strands fall down her back, puppeted by invisible strings of wind. She bends to collect another item of clothing, her movements jagging as if there's sand in her joints, and after she's hung the last garment on the line she takes her camera from the laundry basket and loops the strap round her neck. She walks across the path and over to her veg patch, checking the multi-pronged bird feeder for seeds and emptying one of the water trays to refill from a watering can. After this she puts the camera's viewfinder to her eye, pivoting the long lens round the trees on the sidings, perhaps searching for the birds she's scared away from her allotment. Her lips are moving; she's talking to herself. Cold air seeps into the bedroom where Ruth stands and a shiver speed-scans from her feet to her head. Then Miss Cailleach turns and points the camera directly at Bess's window. Ruth quickly steps back into the shade of the bedroom.

It would have been so comforting for Ruth to have had someone kind close by, but on top of the neighbour's crazy talk and her denial in front of the police – a betrayal Ruth would rage harder against if logic didn't tell her she must have misheard what was said – is Sandra and Liam's vehement dislike of the woman, warning enough, and who would know her better than family? Steer clear, nod a smile, and no more chats through the garden gate. Ruth's already learnt the hard way that no one in London expects you to be neighbourly.

Later that morning, Ruth's in her front yard cutting back the dead plants and pulling out armfuls of shaggy horsetails. Drizzle wets her face, but she refuses to give up, the fresh air a tonic. While Bess is asleep, she plans to stay outside for as long as possible with the baby monitor on her belt. Giles is expecting a conference call, and the less she has to lean on him for help, the more competent she feels.

A man walks up the pavement. From his purposeful

swagger, Ruth can tell it's Liam even before his face has come into view. He nods at Ruth as he closes in. She replies with a tentative 'Hi,' dropping the secateurs she's holding and fumbling to pick them up. She braces herself, for what she doesn't know. To her relief he moves swiftly past to his mother's gate without another glance. He's not in the mood for niceties or chit-chat today, but then he rarely is. Ruth almost admires his disregard for etiquette, to be so self-contained that he doesn't care what others think, though deep down his bad manners rankle – *probably his mum's fault*. She sheers off a gnarly twig, annoyed at herself for this knee-jerk finger-pointing that she too has been a victim of, but Liam's behaviour is the kind that's ingrained; what is or isn't put in at childhood recycles through everyone else, Ruth should know. Poor Sandra, having to manage that surliness, Liam keeping his little family tight and stopping anyone else from coming in.

Through the grid of bare trellis, Ruth watches as Liam strides into his mother's front garden. He knocks. The front door opens. Ruth prunes a bush closer to her gate where she has a diagonal view back to her neighbour's door. Liam's mother steps into her front yard, hair resecured in its bun, and dressed again in those neutral slacks and fleece. A heavy condensation has built up on her front window where the curtains have remained unopened. Usually Ruth can see right through to the neighbour's back window and she imagines the layers of drab clothes brought in from the rain, now steaming on radiators in the dark.

Miss Cailleach throws her arms round her son. It's a full

and strong embrace. Liam's arms lift a little to his mother's side before the smallest of struggles as he attempts to pull away and she holds fast. Liam steps to one side and her arms fall from him. He tries to enter the house, but his mum holds her palms up to his chest. Liam normally goes straight inside when he visits, and today he could easily push past, so he must have some respect for his mother, even if it's begrudged. A rumble of voices, Liam's a low thunder with the occasional flash of aggression, and the woman's a monotone patter. Ruth leans an ear in their direction, as if the few millimetres would help her hear what's being said.

She remembers thinking Liam's voice was attractively deep when she and Giles were first getting to know him and Sandra, when Ruth had cooked dinner for them all and the four friends had sat around her dining table, the two women heavily pregnant, the men tucking into a bottle of brandy. The rigidity of Liam's jaw, clean-shaven and angular like a model's, had relaxed as he'd turned a glass in his hand, losing his focus to the drink. 'We moved from Glasgow to this dump when I was about seven,' he'd said, when the conversation of childhood came up, his smile a resigned crease on one side of his face. 'It wouldn't have been so bad if Mum had let me keep in touch with my old man, but she cut us off from everyone. Anyway, he clearly wasn't in a hurry to stop me from leaving, the useless fucker.' He took a lug of his drink, wincing at the volume of the single hit, the pain seeming to serve a purpose. 'I've tried over the years to be good to her, but she's a cold fish. Got to have everything her way. All that mumbo jumbo in her house she think's gonna heal her. I'd like to sling the whole lot in the bin.' His knuckles whitened around the glass. 'San thinks it would do me good to cut Mum out of my life once and for all, but she's not well, so you know, someone's got to look out for her.' Sandra flicked him a look, her thick lashes accentuating the alarm in her eyes, and in an instant Liam shrugged his shoulders and leant back in the chair, crossing his arms and turning his gaze to the ceiling. He'd shared too much, gone too deep, and now he needed to make out he didn't care. Sandra scowled. 'Like you said, babe. She hasn't got your best interests at heart, just like she won't be good for our son either, if your upbringing's anything to go by.' She stroked Liam's arm. 'Me and junior are your family now, you don't need her. Anyway, now we're married, it's official.' She winked at him. 'You're all mine.' Ruth tensed for a possible backlash from Liam, but instead he leant across and kissed Sandra on the mouth. The couple's lips stayed together a beat too long, and Ruth and Giles had scanned the dirty dishes on the table, their focus ending up on each other in a shared grimace. Even in the awkwardness, Ruth had experienced an inadequacy close to jealousy that she herself was unable to inspire that total and unremitting passion in Giles. Giles loved her in a way that had always felt enough, only now she was faced with this new style of blind dedication, she couldn't help but compare. 'Soulmates we are,' Sandra said as the couple pulled apart, their lips making a wet noise. Her voice was high and wispy, lending it a fragility, and Ruth wondered if she was impelled to tell Liam these things to keep herself in his favour. 'Liam'd do anything for me, wouldn't you, babe?'

It was only the third time they'd all got together, and well before the slog of Ruth's illness. Those occasional socials before the babies were born acted as a form of speed-dating, each of them complicit in the silent understanding that making friends at that stage in life could be hard. That Liam had been open was a compliment and the rapport was infectious. Ruth shared in return, trusting them with parts of her story she wished they now didn't know, problems that could add ammunition to Liam's arsenal against her. In her teens she'd struggled with depression, and for a short period was hospitalized. 'It was just a glitch,' Ruth added quickly, noticing Liam's rigid posture. 'I lost my sister. Well, she died. I mean, we never found her body because she drowned, so it just took me ages to get my head round it. Sort of went to pieces for a bit. Did everything I could to numb the pain.' If Ruth hadn't been pregnant, she'd have taken a big swig of the cognac in Giles's glass. 'Tam had been such a big character, she was brilliant at everything – star pupil, footballer, loads of friends – she was destined to go really far. And my parents were so proud of her, they never got over losing her. Well, you don't, do you? I couldn't even begin to fill the hole she left.' Ruth was conscious of everyone watching, and she tried to even out her words. 'I wasn't jealous, though, I loved her as much as they did, was as distraught as they were. Without Tam around, we all kind of gave up on each other, lost the glue that made us strong.' Ruth took a gulp of ice-cold water. 'Mum and Dad all but said outright that they'd never forgive me for Tam going missing.' She stopped herself there, didn't want to go any further into the guilt that would always have its teeth in her. Under the table, she gripped Giles's hand, speaking more to the floor than anyone in the room. 'Mum died almost a year ago now. It was sad, of course, but then we weren't that close after everything that had happened. And Dad's remarried, he lives abroad.'

Giles squeezed her hand back even though she knew she was probably hurting him, and he saved her by jumping in with his own family saga, of being a late surprise for his parents, the willowy mistake at the wrong end of their child-bearing years. 'My brothers used to tease me,' he said. 'Called me arty-farty. Never let me hang out with them, said they didn't want the responsibility.' He scraped a knife across his dirty plate. 'After they left home it was like Mum and Dad were going through the motions. I guess you would be exhausted after four boys, wouldn't you!' He laughed. 'No one was cruel or anything, but looking back, my childhood was kind of joyless. I couldn't wait to leave.' There was a crack in his voice, perceptible probably only to Ruth, and Giles covered it up by clearing his throat. 'Mum and Dad are about a four-hour drive away and, well, you know, everyone seems happy enough with the card I send them at Christmas.' He turned to Ruth, eyes glinting as if he'd refreshed them with sea water. 'A couple of grown-up orphans, aren't we?' Sandra had leant into the table. 'Seems like we've all got a lot in common then.'

Ruth works on in the garden for a few minutes, eying the doorstep stand-off between Liam and his mum, attempting to interpret their body language. It's hard to imagine that same man all those months ago confiding some of his deepest

150

feelings at her dining table. Thinking about it now, Ruth realizes it was only Sandra who kept her secrets under wraps that day. Most likely, and very sensibly, Sandra intuited it wasn't the right environment to open up. Ruth already knew most of Sandra's secrets anyway, from their first couple of weeks of meeting, when it felt like Sandra was at a confessional, getting all her old shit out in the open in case Ruth had any doubts, and Ruth had felt instantly attached to this woman who, under her pristine surface, seemed vulnerable and in need of support – the irony being that it's Ruth who's ended up leaning heavily on Sandra. Once during that early time, Sandra had teared up recounting how her dad had passed away while serving a sentence. 'He used to call me his little princess, always looked out for me, especially when things got crazy with Mum at home.' This was the only time Ruth had ever seen Sandra's make-up smudge. 'Whatever bastard up above dishes out heart attacks, took the wrong parent if you ask me.' At the dining table in Ruth's house, however, Sandra had swapped-out sharing her own secrets for generosity, artfully pulling out the stories of her friends with sympathetic nods and gasps at the right moments of revelation, and Ruth had felt held. She wishes she could be more like Sandra, more like her old self: assured, less transparent.

Liam throws up his arms and again tries to pass into his mum's house. This time he's shouting and Ruth has no trouble hearing. 'Why can't I come in? You've never been like this before.' Miss Cailleach turns from him and goes inside, closing the door behind her. Liam stays put, staring at the shut door as if he could burn a hole in it with his eyes, hands on hips, widening his toned torso, the barrier a challenge rather than a denial. Then the door reopens and his mum steps into the yard with a couple of brown padded envelopes and a box or two – the computer parts he gets sent to hers as he's out most of the time fixing tech at his clients' houses. She hands them to him and strokes his arm before moving to hug him, stumbling a little as he brushes her off. Ruth witnesses less of the obstructive matriarch she's been led to believe and more of a lonely old woman who's spent years getting it wrong by her boy.

Wind sweeps through Ruth's hair. Without realizing, her hands have grown numb. Nails blue, skin puckered white and bloodless, feet like rocks in her boots. She packs up her tools as best as she can with her useless fingers as the baby monitor on her belt bleeps – *time's up*. Ruth retreats to the front door as Liam stomps from his mum's garden. No eye contact with Ruth this time.

Upstairs, Ruth lifts Bess from her cot. The baby's cheek has been tram-lined by the sheets and Ruth holds her daughter close, breathing her in as she takes her through to the front bedroom. Once, Liam's mum would have cared for her own son in this way, never imagining that one day he'd hold her in such contempt. Outside, Miss Cailleach is at her gate watching Liam walk away, clumps of hair coming loose from her bun, as if the style was put up in a hurry.

Giles is trying another weaning technique, letting Bess feed herself, and she's mashing batons of finger food into the tray of her high chair. The little girl's food interests are narrow – bland beige carbs: bread, pasta and potatoes – and the family tailor their appetite to its newest member, meaning lunch is drab and stodgy. Ruth will pile on the pounds this way, but as Giles is in charge, cooking another meal for herself is a hassle. Plus the extra medication seems to be making her care less. Their little girl takes ant-sized bites of food and spreads the rest over her face, throwing any stragglers on the floor. Giles sits with them to eat, forking in his food in silence, his mind located in work, breaking off occasionally to do aeroplanes with Bess's food to encourage her to eat anything at all. Her little mouth opens in obedience, as it rarely does with Ruth. As soon as Giles has finished, he takes his computer upstairs to the airlock of their bedroom, on hand if Ruth needs him and present to administer her medication.

A knock on the door, a courier with a package.

'Would you be able to take this in for your neighbour?' the man says. 'She's not at home.'

Ruth checks the address on the packet. It's for Miss Cailleach for once, not Mr Smith. Such a strange name, impossible not to take notice of, but Ruth wants as little to do with Liam's tricky mum as possible. She checks behind the delivery man to see if anyone's walking past. No one's around. 'Sorry,' she says, 'but I'm not really in touch with her. Is there another neighbour you can leave it with?'

The man tips his head back with a frown. He sighs. 'Right.'

'Who's at the door?' Giles calls down.

'No one,' Ruth's replies. The courier's eyes flash with

something hard. 'I . . . I mean, it's only a delivery.' She can't look at his face. 'No one we know, is what I meant, sorry.'

He begins to put the package in his satchel, but Ruth reaches to grab it from him. 'It's fine. I'm fine. I'll take it. I'm sorry.' He checks her with narrowed eyes as she stumbles on. 'I just thought I wouldn't have time. I've got a baby, you see, and I've not been well.' Too much information, she tells herself, and stop apologizing to strangers.

The courier hands her the package. Ruth backs into the house, squeezing the parcel between her fingers. It's an A5 padded envelope, lightweight and squidgy with intrigue. She puts it on her kitchen counter for Giles to take over later.

Ruth lays Bess on her play mat. The little girl's cheeks are rosy and shiny as she looks up at her mum. It's only been a couple of days but she seems to be filling out having Giles around to feed her. Ruth takes a few photos of Bess on her phone, planning to load them onto her laptop later and add to the folder marked 'Bessie', proof that mum and baby exist, confirmation too that's Ruth's progressing and will one day be fixed. She smiles hard at her bonny little baby, hoping to present a different mirror to the usual frowns and tears. The little girl returns a quizzical look, as if Ruth's expression is one she's never seen before.

'I'm so sorry, sweetie,' Ruth says, her heart aching with love, and she kisses her baby's soft face. 'You deserve so much better.'

What damage will an adult Bess display? Perhaps she'll find it hard to make friends or connect to joy. Ruth's baseline fear has always been that her poor parenting would result in having Bess taken away, but perhaps Bess and Giles actually would be better off without her, if she simply walked out of the door, caught a train to the end of the line, and from there made her way to the sea, pushing forward from the shore until the water was over her head, deeper and deeper until there was nothing but a big black ocean of beautiful silence. What's stopping her?

At the end of the winter day, when there's only an hour of light left in the sky, Ruth wraps up Bess ready to sit with her in the front garden while she continues to prune and weed their raised beds. Bess doesn't resist or cry, and Ruth's pleasure in these easy minutes is golden. She tips the wheels of the buggy over the threshold as Miss Cailleach passes on the pavement with her trolley. Ruth ducks back inside her house. In her rush to hide, she bumps the kitchen counter behind her, sending a dirty pan clattering to the ground.

Giles calls out from upstairs, 'Everything OK, Ruth?'

She attempts to shut the door in front of the pushchair, but the space is small and the door remains wide. Giles's feet clomp down the stairs.

'Ruth?'

The neighbour passes into her own front garden and stares at Ruth struggling in the kitchen.

'I'm fine, I just knocked over a pan, that's all.' She pivots the buggy inside and pushes the door shut.

'Where are you going?' Giles asks. 'Do you need something

from the shops? I'm just finishing up some calls. If you wait a bit, I'll come with you.'

'I was just . . .' Ruth stares at the cold, parched yard, her plan to clear their tiny patch pointless in this weather. With a baby, so many choices have been taken away, but in addition to her glacial days, she's under this house arrest. Everyone, including herself, is pussyfooting around her ability to be even remotely independent. All she needs is an excuse to feel the wind on her face. 'I've got a package.' She holds up the parcel the courier left, like she's won a prize. 'For the neighbour. I was going to take it round.'

Giles glances across the alley with a half-smile. Miss Cailleach has already gone inside. 'Who, Liam's mum?'

'I won't be long.'

'Okay.' Giles draws out the syllable with concern. Behind his eyes, invisible calculations whirr. 'Shall I come with you?'

'Giles! It's only next door.'

'But she's not really a safe contact for you. I mean, didn't she say stuff about the petrol station?'

Ruth lowers the package, her shoulder joint still a little painful from where the man yanked her arm two days ago. She mumbles to the floor. 'I misheard her, that's all, remember? The chainsaw was really loud.' Even the act of repeating this helps convince Ruth it's the truth.

'Really?' Ruth can see in the way he's leaning forward, almost rupturing with concern, that he wants to say no. 'Well . . . I'm not sure.' But he's trying to be fair, she knows he is. Her going out on her own will be breaking the rules.

'She's obviously a bit tricky. Remember what Liam's told us about her?'

Ruth exhales and shoves the package on the worktop. Her shoulders droop, head bowed.

A grumble deep in Giles's throat – 'Umm' – his vocal cords charging up. 'All right then. But don't get caught up in any nonsense. Perhaps leave Bess here? And come straight home?'

'Yes,' she replies, brighter than she intended. 'I will.'

Ruth grabs the parcel and bundles past her husband as he begins to unstrap Bess. She walks from her gate into the neighbour's garden with the small thrill of being out further than her gatepost, alone. Next door's yard is the mirror of her own, only with a different layout and plants, as if she's stepped through the looking glass. She marches to the neighbour's door, the top third of which is a glass panel like her own, only here it's screened by a heavy curtain made from the same fabric that's at the front window, still pooling on the damp sill.

Ruth knocks. On the other side of the door the neighbour pulls aside the drape and eyes Ruth, face lined with suspicion. The curtain drops, the door remains shut. Not sure whether to knock again or return home, Ruth shuffles against the embarrassment of being an unwanted caller. She holds her knuckles up to the glass one more time as a chain rattles and the door opens. The neighbour's hair is down from its bun. Silver and white strands fall across her shoulders.

A smile breaks on Miss Cailleach's face. 'Welcome.'

Ruth holds the package in her sightline to hide her sudden shyness. 'This came for you when you were out.'

The neighbour stands to one side. 'Thank you. Please, come in.'

'No, it's fine really, I'll just leave it with you.' She holds the parcel out at arm's' length.

Miss Cailleach takes the envelope and quickly inspects it. 'Aye, yes, this one's for me. Makes a change, eh?' She smiles and places it on the kitchen worktop next to her camera. Up close, the camera body is boxy and battered, and the long lens has a few dings too, like a reporter's souvenir from the frontline. Ruth inwardly scoffs at the archaic contraption; it would be so much easier to use a phone, but she imagines that kind of technology is beyond her neighbour's grasp. The woman's still smiling. 'Well, come on then,' she says with that creamy lilt of Scottish dialect, already at the sink filling the kettle, the door wide, heat pouring out. 'Born in a barn, were you?'

Ruth steps inside as her neighbour pushes the door closed behind her. Open shelves in the little galley kitchen are stacked with mismatched crockery, plus jars of pulses and spices. Well-thumbed cookery books take up most of the space on the worktop, and bunches of dried herbs tied with twine hang from the ceiling. The room reeks of vinegar, as if a bottle's been spilt. Without her baby, Ruth's hands feel twitchy at her sides.

'Can I get you a cuppa?' the woman asks.

'Oh, um, yes. Just ordinary builder's, please.'

'Make yourself comfy.' Miss Cailleach gestures towards the lounge. 'The brew won't take long.'

The heat in the front room is stifling. Ruth breaks into a

sweat under her layers of clothing and unbuttons her coat, but doesn't take it off. Hung on one wall are a few framed photos of birds, the shots amateur-looking, probably taken with that camera in the kitchen. The other three walls are crowded with mirrors, plus more standing on the sanded wooden floor, and the small amount of late-afternoon sun creeping through the back window bounces off the reflective surfaces, brightening the room and expanding the space beyond its meterage. A blond-wood sofa and two geometrically patterned chairs sit around a low glass coffee table, and the remaining floor area as well as the windowsill are filled with plants: succulents and cacti, plus a few taller ferns, their leaves glossed with health. A couple of star-shaped decorations made from twigs, probably the ones Miss Cailleach collects from her allotment, are placed on the mantelpiece, and what looks like a craft table with string, scissors and scalpel has been pushed into one corner. On top is another twiggy circle with a few feathers attached. A hot, herby smell catches in Ruth's throat, familiar and not unpleasant, like incense but more potent. Everything else, the configuration of the walls and doors, is the same as Ruth's house, only set out in opposite. Known but different, like returning to a holiday home. A stovetop kettle whistles, followed by the chink of a teaspoon on china. Homely noises that settle inside Ruth, taking her back to simpler times when she'd been small and looked after and only had to think about having fun with her sister: making dens in their bunk beds, talking in their own funny language that used to wind Mum up. Her legs weaken as she edges towards the sofa.

'Don't be shy,' the woman calls from the kitchen, 'sit yourself down.'

Ruth flops instantly, feeling guilty at her betrayal of Sandra, uneasy too that she's being so readily coerced by comfort. The muscles in Ruth's cheeks have relaxed into a smile, a pleasant suppleness, and she's filled with the memory of a different version of herself – calm with the space to be inquisitive, and that gentle confidence she used to possess – close but elusive. She shrugs off her coat as Miss Cailleach hands her a mug with leaves floating on the top.

'Sorry,' the woman says, 'I've run out of PG. Only got white tea left.' Her hands are patterned with the liver spots of the pre-sun-screened generation. She must have been an older mum when she had Liam. 'Anyway, you seem like you could do with some looking after.'

Liam's mother has off-white eyes and sunken cheeks, the skin loose at her jowls, but underneath, the structure of her face is pronounced. Here in her home where she can be herself, the lift of her head holds the grace of beauty, wholly at odds with the old lady Ruth had witnessed before. The woman takes the chair opposite and smiles at Ruth, who glows in this quick favour, tipping her face to the floor to hide her pleasure at the kind attention minus the usual concern. She reminds herself to stay alert, hasn't totally forgotten what might or might not have been said the other day, but of all the medicine Ruth's had, this is the most instant and gratifying she can remember. She blows steam from the too-hot tea, thinking that today is not the day to challenge this woman about what is very probably Ruth's mental health issue.

'My name's Frieda by the way. Nice to meet you properly at last.'

'Ah, right. Yes. I'm Ruth.'

'And your baby?'

'She's called Bess. Bessie. She's six months old.'

'Such a bonny wee thing. A sweetheart.' Frieda cups her scalding mug in both hands, like Ruth's mum used to. *Asbestos hands* she'd called it, toughened up from years of domestic work. 'It's not easy, though, is it?' Frieda continues. 'Especially when you're sensitive, like you are. No one understood it in my day either. Had them snooping around in my affairs all too often, telling me I wasn't the right kind of mum, but you learn after a while to stay under the radar.'

Ruth holds a confused smile, not sure of the correct reply to this woman's sudden and intimate revelation. 'Um . . .'

'Did you get the present I put through the letter box for your wee girl?'

Ruth glances over at the craft table and the half-made dreamcatcher. Of course. 'That was from you? I didn't realize. There was no card.'

'Gifts are better given without the need for thanks.'

'Right, yes. Well, thank you anyway.'

'You don't need to thank me, hen. It was a pleasure.'

Ruth swallows.

Frieda continues, 'So, how do you like living on the street?'

'It's OK, I guess. I'm getting used to it.' Ruth's so

accustomed to her anxiety getting the better of her that it's a surprise to find she's relatively settled, even with the strangeness of this new person and her odd manner. Perhaps the antidepressants are working already after all, they're certainly easing the chronic insomnia that's been messing with her head. The sofa cushions are fat and soft, and Ruth sinks backwards. Behind the double-glazing, street sounds are muffled and the gentle rhythm of a clock wraps Ruth in its hypnotic certainty. More than anything, she wants to lie down on the sofa and curl instantly into sleep. 'It's just that . . .' She fights the sudden heaviness in her body with a big sip of tea. The liquid burns her tongue.

Frieda's sitting to attention, waiting patiently for Ruth to continue. 'Yes?'

'Well, for a start no one can ever find the place when they come to visit. It's a bit out of the way, I suppose.'

'The energy can throw people off direction. The houses themselves are good, but not the land they're built on.'

'Really? How do you mean?'

The neighbour leans forward and speaks quietly. 'A lot's happened here over the years, right under our feet.' Her eyes don't leave Ruth's. 'And not all good.'

Ruth's seat tilts a fraction and she holds the cushion with her free hand before realizing the gravitational upset is in her head. It's the same unbalancing she experienced at the gate last time she talked to Frieda, but instead of heeding this warning, Ruth finds she's closing the space between herself and her neighbour, like a horror film she can't turn away from. She whispers, 'In what way?'

'Years ago, where we're sitting was woodland. Highway-men used to lie in wait for their victims.'

'My husband told me about that.'

'Can you feel them?' Miss Cailleach lowers her cup. 'That kind of evil gets stuck, like cold fat in a drain.'

Ruth sits upright. 'No, I don't . . . I can't.' Tea splashes on her knuckles, her calmness so easily undone. She bites down, jaw hurting.

The woman smiles weakly before looking away, as if she's marking Ruth off her team. 'Oh, don't mind me, I'm always getting ahead of myself. Telling people things they don't want to hear.' The edges of her mouth are turned down even though she's attempting to look happy, perhaps betraying the hardness Liam spoke of. 'Too much mumbo jumbo, that's what Rainbow tells me anyway.'

'Rainbow?'

'My son.'

Ruth suppresses a smirk. 'That's an unusual name. Does Liam have a brother?'

Frieda tuts. 'Oh sorry, of course you know him as Liam. He never did like the name I gave him.' Her fingers worry a thread on her trousers. 'As soon as Rainbow met *that woman*, things started to change. He wanted to fit in, I sup-pose, but seems she thought he needed a complete overhaul.' She talks quietly to her lap. 'Nothing wrong with him before, if you ask me, but then he probably had no choice but to follow through with whatever she wanted, otherwise she'd put the thumbscrews on.' Ruth's neighbour turns her face to the ceiling as if the answer's up there. 'Liam was his father's name, you see. I imagine Rainbow wanted something of his dad as he never got anything else out of the useless shite.' Ruth blinks and the woman sighs. 'And then when my boy got married, *she* got him to take her surname too, so now he totally belongs to her.' Frieda's eyes lock back on Ruth. 'He wasn't always ashamed of me, you know.'

Ruth grabs at anything that might get them back to a normal line of conversation. 'We're good friends, actually.'

'Yes, I've seen him round your place, with the lovely Sandra.'

Frieda holds on to the 's' in Sandra's name as if she's not sure where to spit it. Ruth can't help but be intrigued by this spiked perspective on her friend, and it's obvious now she thinks about it that the feeling would be mutual. Ruth's protective of Sandra, though, and she collects herself to stick up for her. If it wasn't for the fact that Liam is Frieda's son, Ruth would tell her it's him who's the problem. She swaps a look with Frieda, each of them silently evaluating their own version of events.

Perhaps sensing the need to justify herself, Frieda launches into more. 'Sandra has her own set of rules. Baffling to the rest of us, mind you, but we're still expected to follow them. One misstep and you'll be cast aside for something you'll never understand. You'll no' be the first and you'll no' be the last. She gets through people, that one.' Frieda gulps her tea, blinking the steam from her face. 'Rainbow – I mean Liam – well, we were very close. He used to be such a lovely boy, but you'd never know it now by the way Sandra talks about him. Puts the blame for everything at his feet, makes out he's fussy and greedy, but he never used to be until he met her. It's all lies, they're all her own demands.' Ruth's conscious that Frieda probably doesn't have many people to talk to, but she's still worried about her own duplicity in not defending her friend and she opens her mouth to butt in – just as Frieda takes a big breath and carries on. 'And now he spends more time chasing money than he cares to spend with me, so I never get the chance to make peace with him. He's got his fingers in so many pies, I've lost count.' A large leaf falls from a plant in the corner, hitting the floor with a surprisingly loud *thunk*. Frieda doesn't flinch. 'He's only interested in me now if I do what he says, but I won't bow to his idea of how I should live my life.'

The woman shuffles forward on her chair, closer to Ruth, who's stunned anew by being dropped so fast into this family dispute with its multitude of sharp angles. This sharing of secrets is now a recognizable Cailleach family trait, a trap Ruth doesn't want to get caught in again. For the first time she understands why people falter when she herself shares too quickly, when her neediness to be close takes her beyond the etiquette of gentle introductions; it's not rudeness, it's shock.

Frieda continues, 'I've told him he's no' welcome in my house any more unless I can see my grandson. It's a sad thing when your son takes the side of his wife against his own mother.'

Ruth's brain tries to catch up with all this information – perhaps the new medication's making her confused – and she chugs through a list of potential replies, searching for a way to console this woman who's been denied her grandchild, fearful too of being levered into a dispute beyond her sway.

'I'm sorry to hear that,' she says. 'They've always been very nice to me.'

Frieda huffs with a squint at Ruth, as if she's trying to read her small print. Ruth looks down to avoid the spotlight of her neighbour's gaze, scared it will reveal she already knows of Sandra's intent to keep Ian from Frieda. Glancing around, she tries to find the clock she can hear ticking, wanting confirmation of the time that seems to have rushed past, desperate for a reason to get away from this woman in whose issues she feels semi-culpable, too polite not to have a plausible excuse to leave.

Frieda pats Ruth's knee, the creases around her knuckles as defined as if they'd been drawn on with pen. 'Of course they have, hen, of course. Well, if you ever need me to help with your wee one, I'm right here. I've got all the time in the world, you just have to say.'

'Oh, OK. Thanks.'

'You and me are cut from the same cloth, hen. Sometimes we have to be brave to protect those less fortunate than ourselves.'

Ruth fidgets inside her unease, unable to connect the intensity of Frieda's statement with her preamble. The whole mystic shebang about the energy of this place and the way Frieda keeps digging into the nub of what she wants to say, all flare Ruth's neuroses, but since her illness, her people sensors have been screwed in sideways and it's difficult to tell what's normal any more. She glances at the door. It's close.

She could make it out of here in five seconds if she wanted. Fuck social niceties, any sensible person would get the hell out. She slides to the edge of the sofa. Momentarily and accidentally she's millimetres from Frieda's face. Even though the woman's eyes are dull, the dark of her irises is intense; persistent and demanding. What must it be like to be Frieda's age and so alone, having failed her only child who doesn't even want to be associated with her by name? Ruth understands only too well how rejection feeds crazy thinking, how the membrane between fiction and reality can be thinned by loneliness. It's no wonder fantasy fills in for company at Frieda's house. Perhaps Frieda's right, both she and Ruth are cut from the same cloth. Both are outsiders, and without a good friend it can be hard to break the cycle. Thank God for Sandra, Ruth thinks, she's lucky to have at least one close friend.

From above their heads comes a thump. Ruth's eyes jump to the ceiling.

'My cat,' the woman says quickly. 'She's very old, and not well. You won't have seen her because she doesn't go outside. Can't even handle the stairs any more, so she stays in my bedroom.'

'Really?' When Ruth was a toddler she'd been mauled by her auntie's semi-feral moggy, and since then she's never lost her fear of cats. Her eyes stay on the ceiling as she reaches to place her cup to the table, preparing her exit at last. The cup misses, tips over. Tea spills on the table. 'Oh no, I'm so sorry.' Pale dregs drip through the gaps of the glass table, pooling on the floor and sinking into the rug.

'Don't worry.' Frieda stands and shuffles to the kitchen surprisingly fast, as if her body-memory is still set to before she was old. 'Not a problem,' she says as she returns with a tea towel.

Ruth attempts to take the cloth to clean up for herself, and there's a miniature tug-of-war as the woman refuses to let go. Frieda dabs the rug with her face too close to Ruth, and Ruth leans back, chin compressing into a roll at her neck as she tries to disappear into the cushions.

Another bump from upstairs, bigger this time, and Ruth yelps. The floorboards creak as if something's travelling over them.

Frieda eases herself up from the floor, knees clicking. 'The cat has a litter tray up there. If I take her to the vet, they'll say I've got to have her put down.'

'Oh dear.' Ruth brings the empty cup back to her mouth where it clashes with her teeth. Without looking, she takes a sip, but there's only dregs left and a tea leaf catches in her throat. She coughs, searching the table for tissues.

Frieda says, 'I'm not sure what would happen to my cat if I wasn't around.' She snakes the damp tea towel through her hands as she sits on the sofa. Aside from the new tea stain, it's the whitest cloth Ruth's ever seen. 'If I ran into trouble, I'd need someone close by to look after her, someone who was kind.'

'Um, I'm sure nothing's going to happen to you.' Ruth's tone is faux-bright. 'I'm sure, you know, that Liam would step in if you . . . well, you don't need to worry.'

'He hates cats. Do you like cats? I've seen you putting out

food for that fox.' The woman's head shakes a little, and Ruth wonders if she's nervous, and what she has to fear from Ruth. 'I know you do what you think is right, and not what others want you to do, like that Barry. I saw him laying some contraption in his allotment. Probably a trap for the fox. I've half a mind to go over there and drop a rock on it.'

Ruth checks her wrist even though she doesn't wear a watch. 'I'm really sorry, but I have to go. Before it gets dark. My husband's waiting for me.'

Frieda clamps her mouth shut, eyes squinting. 'That's a shame, we were just getting started.' She pats her knees a couple of times before pressing her palms to her thighs and pushing herself to standing. 'I'm sorry, like I said before. I'm always getting ahead of myself.'

Ruth wrestles with the bulk of her coat, feigning a laugh. 'Don't worry about it. I just have to get home, that's all. I told Giles I was only dropping the package in to you.'

Frieda moves round to the back of Ruth to help guide her arms into her coat. She speaks quietly, as if someone might be listening. 'It's the same as that time we spoke at your gate. I said too much then as well.' She circles to Ruth's front and begins fastening her coat buttons from the bottom up. Ruth is frozen in the awkwardness of Frieda's hands so close. 'And I wanted to say I'm sorry I didn't support you with the police. It would only have made things worse.' Ruth balloons breath in her lungs in an attempt to keep herself steady as Frieda continues, 'When you've lived in the kind of places I have, you learn to keep your head low, to behave. Everyone here is the same. It'll take you some getting used to, I expect. Best keep the authorities out of it from now on. We don't need them snooping around, pointing fingers at the wrong people. Find our own way to sort out the problems.'

'I don't know what you're talking about.' Ruth moves fast towards the door.

Frieda raises a hand to stop her, as she did with Liam, her palm oddly commanding. Smoky breath drifts into Ruth's face. 'But you remember what I said and you know what you saw.'

'No, I don't. I didn't see anything. It was just a dream.'

Frieda pops in the last button at Ruth's neck, the one she always leaves undone, and it squashes her windpipe. 'Well,' Frieda says. 'If you ever want to discuss it or if you see anything else, no matter what time of day or night, I'm right here.'

'I won't need to, I'm fine. I'm getting better. There's nothing wrong with me.' On the kitchen counter the package she brought over has been opened and a sprinkle of dry leaves has spilt on the worktop. The smell clots the air, bringing with it a memory of teenage Ruth, getting stoned or high, attempting to blot out the pain of losing her sister with anything she could lay her hands on, messing with the chemistry of her already fragile brain and getting stuck in a loop of paranoia as her parents' frustration and anger mounted. To her mum and dad, Ruth was escalating the family's intolerable chaos, wilfully so, and the depression she subsequently fell into was deemed a kind of righteous penance for having brought the whole calamity upon them all. Ruth lunges towards the exit.

'I know it might not seem like it, hen,' Frieda says, 'but I am on your side.'

Ruth pulls the door wide and is winded by the cold air. 'I need to go.' She darts from the house.

The sun is dipping and a strong breeze blurs Ruth's vision. Getting the key in the lock takes several attempts because her hands are shaking so much. Once inside she bangs the entrance shut, standing with her back against it, half expecting the wind to blow it open and let in all the bad stuff. Giles is on the lounge floor, blowing raspberries into Bess's neck on her play mat. The little girl giggles and Giles holds his head above her and sings his dad song: 'You are my sunshine . . .' Bess is mesmerized.

Ruth grabs the dreamcatcher and yanks it from the window latch. The twiggy circle snaps and a feather falls to the floor. She hauls open the back door that's almost completely seized up with damp and marches across their garden and allotment towards the railway fence. With all her might, she hurls the dreamcatcher over the top, where it lands in the undergrowth, alongside all the sharp things Ruth used to own, items she didn't trust herself with when she'd been ill: the knives, the corkscrews, the broken mirror.

'Ruth?' Giles is stepping into the garden. 'Is everything OK?'

She pushes past him to go inside and catches sight of her reflection in the mirror over the mantelpiece, her complexion ghostly and the line of her jaw taut with fear. Huge quantities of her being have been lost these past six months, as if her core has been spooned out measure by measure, and she's been left with nothing to fall back on. This making of casual friends used to be relatively easy, but since her illness even that simple pleasure has become as loaded and frightening as every other choice Ruth has to make. She's never needed the care and company of women as much as now, yet everyone is in some way unavailable.

Giles crosses slowly towards her as she plants her legs wide to stop the floor from swaying; unmoored, all at sea.

'Is it time for my next dose?' she says. 'I need my medication, now.'

10

With her head below the fence line in her back garden, Ruth works quietly to avoid catching Frieda's eye. She scrapes over weeds to make space for plants to grow in the spring. Paper packets of seeds rattle with tiny hope in the pocket of her long, tatty cardigan. If Ruth can't walk or drive, then she will plant, the soil a balm to her anxiety, and taking control of this tiny patch of London is satisfying in a way that house-work can never be. She's completing tasks not instantly undone, creating life, improving her world.

Ruth thought she'd be safe out here today, that it would be too soon for Frieda's next washday, but her neighbour's out of sync, or perhaps she's finding extra things to do just to annoy Ruth. The gap between the houses is strung with tension as Frieda pegs out clothes in the thin sun, her shape bobbing in Ruth's peripheral vision. Ruth bows her head, framing the other day at Frieda's house inside the woman's instability. 'You and me are cut from the same cloth,' Frieda had said, but it's no cloth Ruth wants to be tangled in.

Whatever the woman wants from her, even if it's simply an outlet for her cryptic blather, Ruth needs to steer clear. She doesn't need another excuse to worry about things that don't exist. All roads lead Ruth to the psych unit.

She stands to go indoors only to find Frieda leaning at her fence as if she's been waiting there some time. 'Ruth!' The fence panel creaks with her weight.

'In a rush.' Ruth heaves open her back door. 'Can't talk.' The door is getting stiffer every day in the cold damp weather, and Ruth has to slam it behind her when she's inside. Breath wheezes in her tight throat.

From the glimpse Ruth caught of Frieda, her neighbour appeared gaunter than when Ruth was at her house, the circles under her eyes deeper. Today's winter sun could have accentuated her shadows or Frieda might have been wearing make-up before, though Ruth didn't notice it if so. Liam said his mum self-medicates for whatever's wrong with her, and Ruth wonders how much of the woman's illness is psychological and how much physical. And is anyone apart from Liam looking out for her? Ruth's never seen another visitor in the months she's lived here.

She peers from the window. Frieda's gone inside now and Ruth pulls back into the room with a sigh; the chance to make amends has been taken out of her hands.

The next day when Frieda walks past Ruth's gate, Ruth holds steady; her mood is brightening and Frieda will only take her down. Frieda knocks on Ruth's door when she returns from shopping and Ruth sneaks upstairs to Giles, whispering, 'I don't want to see her.' Giles is midway through a work call in their bedroom, annoyed at the interruption, but busy enough to wave the problem away, and neither of them answer the door. As Ruth peeps from the bedroom window, the woman shuffles from the garden with shopping trolley in tow.

'Faye, I have to go.' Giles ends his call and turns to Ruth.

'You should probably check with Liam,' Ruth says to him, 'that he's keeping an eye out for his mum.'

Giles leans back in his chair with arms crossed. 'I'm sure Liam's doing whatever needs to be done. I really don't want to get involved.' A text comes in and he checks it with a smile before laying his phone face down. 'Leave her to her bloody crystals, Ruth, and steer clear. She's not your problem, OK? Remember what the psychiatric nurse said when he came over yesterday? That woman lives in cloud-cuckoo land. Some people just keep butting up against the system. I can't see how someone like that would be allowed to keep a baby if she had one today. No wonder Sandra and Liam don't want her seeing Ian.'

Frieda's stoop as she walks to her front door reminds Ruth of her mother in those last months of illness, her mum shrinking as Ruth was beginning to expand into her pregnancy. They'd tried to make amends when they knew time was running out, each seemingly doing their best, but neither had their heart in it. Sitting at her mum's bedside as a grown woman with her own child on the way, Ruth could understand even less how her parents had shunned her when she'd needed them most. Tam had been everyone's shining star, with such high hopes for the future, and after they lost her, Ruth absorbed both the unspoken message that she was a poor substitute for Tam – her parents' preference only clear when it had nowhere to hide – as well as the idea, all too explicitly stated, that she was to blame for what had happened; this, with no one to tell her otherwise, she internalized as the truth. Ruth's mum on her sickbed that day had put her hand out to her only remaining daughter, and Ruth held on weakly, trying to remember the last time she'd had any kind of physical contact from her parents. 'We've never been very good at losing things, have we?' her mum said. 'But you should have told us, Ruth. You shouldn't have left her like you did. Your father and I had so many plans for her. Imagine how different all our lives would have been if you hadn't been so foolish.' Even then, halfway towards dying, her mum was still going over the same ground, but Ruth had even fewer answers after all the years, having examined her actions from so many different angles already it had sent her mad once. The best she could ever come up with was that she thought Tam would be OK, because nothing bad ever happened to Tam. Downstairs, Ruth's dad smashed a teacup, shouting 'Bugger!' before slamming the front door behind him. 'Women grieve, men replace,' her mum said, pressing her eyes shut, tears forming between the lids. 'Your father's not much use around the house, not like your Giles. He'll need all the help he can get and as soon as he can get it.' The subtext, Ruth thought, was that her dad was ready to move on, or would be soon; that wives were interchangeable – unlike daughters – and for such simple reasons. Ruth slid her hand from her mum's, clammy skin against skin accentuating her morning sickness, and she'd walked away grateful for having mourned her parents all those years ago, relieved also to be making a new family to replace these people she was connected to only through duty.

Bess settles into a groove of sorts; she's eating and sleeping better as Ruth's mood begins to lift everyone. The following day, after Giles gives Ruth her medication, he leaves to go to the office for a few hours, his time away to be extended each day. He was supposed to be home for at least two weeks, but Ruth's improving rapidly on the new concoction of meds and is being prepped for another return to independence, a possibility that both excites and terrifies her. She washes and dries the lunch things then organizes the food for supper, making a list of meals for the next few days – the tyranny of the pasta bake, the monotony of the jacket potato – and smiles into the tedium. If she was fit for work, she'd get a job, even if the wages only covered the nursery, but that sort of good health and confidence is still out of her reach. Her lack of financial independence ties her to the house, smack-bang in a gender stereotype she never imagined she'd accept, and yet she's powerless to change it. And the more that money comes to define her and Giles – who earns it and who doesn't – the less she is able to attach worth to what she's doing, even though if anyone else took on these hours, they would command a decent salary. But she skips over this annoyance; a semblance of order is better than obsessing over melting ice caps or people climbing out of petrol tanks. Richard, Ruth's CPN, told her to congratulate herself for small triumphs. 'Just let those negatives pop like bubbles,' he said. 'Don't dwell on them or they might take you backwards.' Ruth banks today's achievements as something to talk about next time they meet. Bess is asleep and Ruth picks up the book she's been attempting to read for a few days. So far she's two paragraphs in.

The light falling across the page flickers then darkens. Ruth glances up, looking for a dying light bulb, unsure what's changed. Nothing obvious. She carries on with the sentence before voices outside disturb her. She lays her book face down on the cushions and walks to the kitchen to pull back the nets at the window. An ambulance is parked outside Frieda's. Paramedics bustle in and out of the vehicle and her neighbour's front door, snapping on blue latex gloves and carrying bags of equipment. Ruth clasps a hand over her mouth, gripping the sink as she strains to see inside Frieda's door – impossible, though, from this angle. Seconds pass, then from Frieda's house comes a wheelchair. At first Ruth doesn't recognize the person underneath the blankets who's strapped in with chunky belts, like outsized luggage, but the wiry mess of hair gives Frieda away. Under the covers, the elderly woman's body is flattened, drained of substance. A cannula with tube is taped to her bony hand and she gestures to the paramedic, fingers battling the breeze. Ruth pulls her door open as the two paramedics manoeuvre the neighbour into the back of the ambulance. Before Ruth can reach her own gate, a third medic enters Ruth's front yard.

Ruth rushes towards her. 'What's happened?'

'Mrs Woodman?'

'Yes, that's me.'

'I'm sorry to let you know that Miss Cailleach collapsed earlier today. We're taking her in for observation.'

Ruth pushes towards the pavement. 'Can I see her?' She cranes her neck as the rear doors of the ambulance close. 'Which hospital is she going to?'

'We're taking her to the Royal Free. She's very agitated at the moment so it's best we keep her as calm as possible. Her son has been contacted and he'll be dealing with her immediate needs.'

The ambulance pulls away from the kerb and drives towards the turning point at the dead end of the road.

'Is she going to be OK? What's wrong with her?'

'I can't give details unless you're next of kin, I'm afraid.'

'But is there anything I can do?' Ruth asks.

The medic hands Ruth an envelope. 'Miss Cailleach asked me to give you this. She was very insistent you got it as soon as possible.'

Ruth holds the letter with shaking hands. All those times she's sidestepped Frieda when her neighbour must have been desperate for help. The medic watches Ruth with her head to one side, perhaps waiting for the tears she's expecting to come, the ones she doesn't have time for. She keeps one eye on the road for the ambulance's return.

Ruth sniffs and wipes her nose on her sleeve; she wasn't prepared to cry and she hasn't got tissues, though no one will care about decorum in the face of this greater emergency.

'Can you tell her I'm thinking of her? Can you say that I'm sorry?'

'Of course. We've given her something for the pain, but I'll make sure she gets your message when she's back with us.'

Bess is waking, her grizzle travelling through the window. The ambulance draws up by the gate, pointing in the right direction now, blue light flashing in silence. The gate shuts behind the paramedic and the vehicle streaks away.

Ruth returns to the sofa, turning the envelope in her hands, its contents crunching. Inside is a letter plus something hard and loose. Bess will be OK for a few more minutes in her cot. Ruth shoves the book she was reading to one side, the cover closing over the saved page, and slides her finger under the gummed flap of the envelope to rip it open. Frieda's writing is shaky and in large letters:

Dear Ruth,

I'm sorry for our misunderstanding, but I trusted you were the right person when I met you – there's no such thing as coincidence. Please look after my cat, she is very precious. Do not let my son in, whatever he says, and do not tell your husband. They might call the vet!!!

A package is coming for me. You will know it when you see it. Keep it safe until I get home. Remember, it belongs to me and to no one else. Thank you.

Your friend, Frieda

Inside the envelope is a set of keys. One fob on the key ring is a leather angel's wing, another a clear resin disk with a baby cannabis leaf embedded in the plastic. Ruth rereads Frieda's note, hoping more will be revealed, but what's being asked seems a huge rigmarole for one small animal. The cat must have become the focus of Frieda's lonely days, filled with nothing other than smoking drugs delivered by the postman.

Bess's call echoes into the lounge. Ruth shoves the letter and keys in her pocket and goes upstairs, the thought of dealing with a sick animal and cleaning its litter tray making her hands tacky with imagined germs.

An hour goes by feeding and changing Bess in Ruth's bedroom, by which time dusk is coming in. The baby is a warm cuddle in Ruth's arms and she sways from side to side patting the little girl's back, not wanting this precious moment to end – and not wanting to think about the poor animal next door who has no one else to give it food.

A white car draws up outside, the flashy engineering shouting for attention. Ruth's heart skips in the millisecond it takes to realize that it's Liam. He strides from the car into his mother's front garden and rattles the door, peering through the window even though the curtains are still drawn. Ruth's legs stiffen as she strokes Bess's downy head, shushing her gently. Liam disappears from view. Ruth holds Bess tighter, unsure which impulse to obey: to hide or hand over responsibility.

From the back of the house comes the sound of scraping, something falling. Ruth tiptoes to the rear window where she spies Liam in Frieda's back yard. He's stooping under the laundry and turning up bricks and flowerpots. His thick dark hair has been recently clipped round the sides and the full-ness of the curls left on his crown have been oiled into submission. Ruth bunches her knuckles close to the window to knock, but she can't formulate the lie she's been asked to tell. She curses her own indecision, annoyed too at being put in this situation in the first place. But Frieda is ill and perhaps if Ruth had been more considerate she could have warded off this emergency. Liam rattles his mother's back door, then disappears under the line of the fence. He's out of sight for several seconds before reappearing with a brick in hand. He holds it behind him and is about to smash it into the pane of the back door when Ruth pushes the window open.

'No.' She shouts through the gap in the window. 'Don't.'

Bess strains in Ruth's arms and Ruth holds her away from the opening. Liam turns his head.

'I'm up here.'

His face pivots to Ruth at the window, cheeks glossy, eyes asquint. She steps back, imagining the brick being hurled in her direction. Liam drops it with a thump. Ruth puts Bess in her cot with a toy before returning to the window. Liam's in the same spot, tension concentrated on his face as he stares up at her.

'My mother needs some things,' he says. 'I need to get in.'

Ruth leans further out. 'How is she?'

'Not well, not well at all. By the time I got to her she was unconscious again.' His voice is contained considering this huge piece of news. Perhaps he's trying not to cry. 'We're not sure of the prognosis at the moment.'

The Frieda who Ruth saw earlier was still attempting orders, her hand directing the medics, unaware of the sinkhole that lay ahead. 'God! I'm so sorry. Is there anything I—'

'Do you know if she's left a key?' Liam's feeling around the window frame, working his fingers into a gap. 'She needs some home comforts.' *Home comforts.* The words sound wooden in Liam's mouth, as if it's the first time he's said them, and what would she need if she's unconscious? 'Has anyone got a spare?'

Ruth's fingers creep into her pocket, the envelope crackling against the hard nubs of keys. A cat springs across the fence and into the allotments. 'The cat!' Ruth shouts. 'She must've got out.' She fishes out the keys and holds them up, but Liam's still focused on trying to prise open the window frame.

He says, still concentrating on the window, 'What cat?'

'Your mum's cat.'

He laughs. 'Thought that mangy old thing died months ago.'

'She said it was unwell and mustn't leave the house.'

'Huh, she's full of surprises. Shows how good she is at keeping secrets from me. She knows I'd only tell her to have it put down.' Liam leans his whole body away from the window to wrench the catch, but the double glazing won't budge. The cat hurtles up the path and out of sight; no evidence of being old or ill, so it can't be Frieda's. 'God, she's irritating,' Liam says. 'Bloody woman.' He smacks the wall with his palm, then picks up a plant pot and hurls it to the ground, where it breaks. Ruth flinches, thinking of Sandra's airiness and how much of her day must be spent trying to float above Liam's wants and needs: buy the latest gadget, make yourself attractive, be sexually available – as well as all his other weird character tics Sandra's always complaining about. Liam shouts at the ground, 'Why does she always get in my way?'

No wonder Frieda doesn't want her son in her house, this man who makes a big deal out of everything, who's so blinded by whatever it is he wants that he's willing to break her window just to get inside. And for what? Some *home comforts*? He probably wouldn't even bother with the vet; he'd simply turf his mum's only companion onto the street. Ruth makes a fist of the keys and closes ranks round her neighbour's secret. Again Liam attempts the window, the frame finally shuddering in his hands.

'I wouldn't do that.' Ruth takes on the same tone the doctor uses with her, sensing she's not dealing with a rational person. 'It'll cost a fortune to get mended. Plus, it's not safe to leave the place open. You know what it's like round here. Those kids on mopeds. They'll probably burn the place down.'

Liam grunts and steps away. He lifts the back doormat and kicks about on the ground, mumbling. Ruth buries the keys deep in her pocket.

'When you see your mother,' she calls, 'please send her my love. Tell her . . .' Liam stares. 'Tell her I'll look after her packages.'

'Sorry?'

'From the postman. Or the courier. You know. They deliver here when she's not in. I'll keep her stuff safe until she gets home.'

He squints at Ruth, then leaps over the fence. She takes a step back into the room as if she's expecting Liam to launch himself through the window, wishing she could swallow the words that were meant as code for Frieda, to show that she's understood what's being asked of her, and how difficult it must be to have a son like Liam. He disappears. Seconds later there's thumping on her front door. Ruth's heart jolts to the beat. She waits. Knocking again, softer this time. Ruth pulls the window shut, hides the keys in her bedside table and goes downstairs.

'I need you to give me a call,' Liam says as she opens the door to him, his jeans tight and tailored, trainers so new and white they almost sparkle; the same outfit he always wears, everything so clean he must have duplicates, like he's found or been given a formula of how to look and doesn't have the imagination to try anything new. 'If something turns up. You know, for my shop.'

'Of course. Yes, I will.'

'Or anything else that comes for her for that matter.'

'Oh, right.' She shuffles from one foot to the other. 'But I don't mind hanging on to it, I mean, if it's something for your mum.'

'Yeah, like some weird potion or something illegal.' His eyes widen, trying to draw Ruth into his pact by playing on her good citizenship. 'I'll get rid of it for her, along with the rest of that stuff in her house. All that crap's got her into this mess in the first place, and I've got her very best interests at heart.' Again, Liam's words have the hokey tone of being performed in a school play.

'But it's no problem. I mean, perhaps I could visit her when she's up to it, take whatever comes for her to the hospital so she can open it herself.'

'That's really not necessary.' Some innate compactness in Liam's body begins to uncoil. 'But it's very kind of you anyway.' His shoulders soften. One arm rests at his side, and he raises the other, elbow against the doorframe: the embodiment of chilled. He directs a full smile at Ruth.

She falters in the sudden and surprising glare of his attention, wholly unused to anyone, even Giles, looking at her this way. Liam is ultra groomed and classically good-looking, nothing like her type at all, but he's switched something on that's almost magnetic and a forgotten excitement pings in her chest. He looks deep into her eyes. Ruth flushes as if he's seen a secret piece of her. Momentarily, she's struck by the possibility of being desirable, and it disarms her. She runs a hand through the mess of her hair and pulls her cardigan tight round her waist, annoyed at herself for caring what Liam thinks, while also being unable to stop. He continues to lean against the doorframe, muscles straining at the crisp white T-shirt he wears even in the winter, as if the cold's not going to tell him what to do. She can't help but take him in, in the way that Barry would look at her breasts, and she's shocked at herself. Not for the first time, Ruth imagines how it might be for Sandra to be the focus of his devotion, and if it wasn't for Liam's possessiveness, she'd be a tiny bit envious.

His smile is lopsided, boyish. 'And you're right, of course. I'll make sure she gets her stuff in hospital. I don't think she'll be well enough for visitors for a while, but I'd be really grateful if you could let me know if anything turns up.'

Ruth's flustered by his continued attention and too shocked by his directness to deny him what he wants. 'OK, sure, I'll give you a call.'

'Good.' His smile drops. 'Just call Sandra. She can come and get it from you.' Ruth receives the reminder of Liam's loyalty like a punch. He's telling Ruth not to raise her hopes, as if she would, as if she even wanted to, but she's been tricked by his flattery that played on her very obvious desire to be vital, attractive, human even, and she's furious with herself for letting him think he's got her gagging. He walks away without saying goodbye, back to same old rude Liam.

'Send my love to your mum,' she calls. 'I hope she gets better soon.'

As Liam's car door shuts, Ruth notices that Sandra's in the passenger seat. Ruth waves brightly, but Sandra's head is turned away, the moment too slight to tell if Sandra witnessed Ruth and Liam's weird flirtation on the doorstep. Her friend's face is in profile: high, proud and serious with the effortless-ness of one born into beauty, who never expects that advantage to be taken away. Ruth pushes against the small fear of having betrayed her friend, ashamed by how openly she received Liam and how blatant were her needs. The ribbon of her vanity unravelled with the gentlest tug, and Sandra probably witnessed the lot. The car zooms away.

Steam pumps into the alleyway from the boiler vent on Frieda's exterior wall. These are Ruth's last moments of freedom for the day as Giles could be home any minute. The keys to Frieda's house are at only a staircase's distance, though surely the cat would have been fed this morning and the plants won't die from one afternoon without water. Ruth closes her front door and makes a cup of super-sweet tea to settle her nerves, her concern for Frieda again tempered by annoyance at this huge imposition from a woman she barely knows, let alone all the trouble it might stir up with Giles. But Frieda's ill, perhaps high on whatever drug she's been self-prescribing, and Ruth more than anyone should understand the woman's desire for some control over her health. Maybe it would be best to confess to Frieda's letter when Giles gets home, but then he'll want to know why she didn't simply give Liam the keys in the first place, and whatever just occurred between the two of them feels somehow tainted with disloyalty. If she does tell Giles, he'll give Liam the keys for sure, then Liam will know she lied. And how will that sit with Sandra?

Ruth slurps her tea, savouring the dregs at the bottom that are thickened with undissolved sugar. The prospect of a small break from her own space by entering the comforting secret of next door is not unattractive. She imagines herself alone there, the change of scenery like a mini holiday, where no one would judge or expect anything from her, not even Frieda with her mad ideas. If Ruth is careful about when she goes into her neighbour's house – *if* she goes – she could stay a while, perhaps even read her book while Bess lies on the fluffy rug. Ruth's back softens with the memory of the doughy sofa cushions and she wipes a finger round the inside of the cup, scooping the last of the tea-stained sugar into her mouth.

11

As night comes in, the weather turns from winter-lite to hard winter, and the sky bulges with the threat of cold. Ruth shivers as she puts out the rubbish and tidies gardening tools into the shed.

'Why don't you leave it till the morning?' Giles calls from the lounge.

Ruth moves slowly, eking out the time. 'It might rain.' The front door is ajar, and she pushes it onto its latch to muffle Giles's concern.

She's alert to any movement on the pavement, anyone who might be turning into Frieda's front yard, and the possibility that Liam has secured a set of keys. Ruth's wheelie bin is out front. She decants the couple of rubbish sacks into Monica and Barry's bin, then pulls her own bin down the side alley and into the back garden under the pretence of keeping it from the street's junior arsonists. She parks it against the back wall. The plant pot Liam smashed earlier lies where it was dropped in Frieda's yard, leaking earth, but the rest of the house is as secure as before. Anticipation rises in Ruth, as does dread. Only she has been invited inside.

She dusts off her hands as she comes back up the alley. A car passes, headlights flashing on the glass of Frieda's upstairs window, and for a second it appears as if a curtain is tweaked to one side. Ruth freezes, staring at Frieda's first floor. She recalls the noise of the cat creeping across the floorboards. Perhaps the animal is scrabbling at the window, desperate for food, medicine or the company it's used to. She thinks of its nails and teeth sinking into her skin, her fear compounded by the likelihood of the cat's mange and fetid litter tray. But what if Frieda were to return from hospital and find her beloved pet had died because Ruth didn't get to it soon enough? If Ruth confesses everything to Giles now, she could go next door immediately and get it over with, or perhaps Giles could deal with the cat himself. She pauses inside her options, only to return to the lies she's already told and how the deception could wound her. With her sights trained on the window, she wills an absence of movement to prove the cat's OK and can wait one more night. Nothing moves, nothing changes. The twitching curtain was all in her mind's eye.

Giles pokes his head out of the door. 'Ruth, it's freezing!' She drops a gardening fork with a clatter and leaves it where it fell to go inside.

Bess wakes in the night for her bottle. For once, Giles gets up to feed her, then Ruth takes over as she knows he needs to be fresh for a big work meeting tomorrow.

'Thanks anyway,' she says as she brushes past him in the darkness. The backs of their hands connect by accident.

He stops, turns to her, kisses her forehead – 'You're welcome' – before returning to bed.

Ruth's dozing on the chair in her daughter's room after the bottle's been emptied when a scraping noise outside disturbs her. Her eyes are gritty with sleep as she puts Bess in her cot. She opens the window and calls into the back garden. 'Is someone there?' A couple of thuds, then silence. She squints into the black night. Nothing. She's banned from calling the police, and there's no point saying anything to Giles; he'll only dismiss what she's heard or log it as her slipping back into illness. It's probably Ruth's fox anyway, looking for the food she didn't put out earlier because she forgot, because she was preoccupied with worries about another animal. The chicken shed is open. The fox will be warm at least.

A moped buzzes past and further up the road a bright patch flares the night sky. Smoke fills the glow of a distant street light. A wheelie bin's on fire, the pyrotechnics of bored kids. She waits for the siren before taking herself back to bed, relieved now the emergency services are involved, happier still that the problem has nothing to do with her. She falls into a luscious sleep, and in the night, she and Giles make love for the first time in a long time. Through the mud of her half-dream, Ruth has a moment when she's not sure if it's Giles or Liam's hands she pulls towards her. She quickly banishes the thought.

*

The alarm clock of Bess wakes Ruth with the dawn. Even in the semi-darkness there's a subtle change to the bedroom, a dampening of sound and an alien glow through the curtains. Ruth peers outside to be met by a world in opposite. The bins, weeds and plastic furniture are all blanketed white, their imperfections smoothed to a collection of humps, freshened by the buff of snow.

Giles wakes, blinking into the bright morning as he checks news outlets for weather updates. Most transport links are closed and there are warnings to travel only in an emergency. He makes a few calls but everyone's phones are off, all probably taking the opportunity to lie low. If no one else is working, then neither can Giles. Without the routine rush to deal with business, the little family is more relaxed than usual. The weather's given them a sick note, a gratis day, and they indulge themselves by eating a slow breakfast and brewing tea in a pot rather than mugs, going back for second and third pourings. In the background, the TV updates them with stories of milkmen delivering against the odds and farm animals stuck in knee-deep snow. Somewhere on the planet, wars are still being fought and sea levels continue to rise, but if the news is giving everyone a break, Ruth is content to pretend they're safe too, even if only in this moment. Bess is on the floor on her play mat, and after weeks of practising she finally turns herself from her back onto her tummy, lifting up her head in triumph, eyelashes curling in a perfect fringe towards her forehead. The little girl's excitement flutters around the room, gathering them close, and if Ruth were to be granted one wish now, it would be for the snow to never melt.

In this small holiday of family cohesion, Frieda's chaos is too close to home. Ruth washes up at the kitchen sink, concentrating on the sudsy plates to avoid looking at her neighbour's house. She works at baked-on cheese on a casserole dish as the opposite wall radiates its displeasure across the alley. Ruth feels a headache coming on and goes upstairs to search for paracetamol in her bedside table, fumbling through junk in the drawer. Frieda's keys scrape to one side, reminding Ruth of what needs to be done, what cannot be avoided forever. She stuffs her cardigan with the letter still in its pocket into the wardrobe, aware of what those few words could detonate if Giles were to read them. With the benefit of another good sleep last night, Ruth can't get her head around why she didn't give Liam the keys in the first place. If she'd stopped overthinking when he'd asked, the problem of going into Frieda's house would now be gone, the responsibility handed over to a son who has more rights than her. Ruth's been taken hostage by a woman she barely knows, and lurking in the shadows is the knowledge that Liam lit something grubby inside her, but which had nothing to do with what she and Giles came together for last night. Her judgement was coloured by her vanity, and now she's thick in the mess of her lie, all her own fault.

By late morning, a few cars venture along the street clearing a grey gully through the snow. Giles's phone rings as opening rail lines and buses pave the way for the city's return to work. His missed meeting has been rescheduled for later this afternoon. Husband and wife kiss at the door. Giles hugs

Ruth for longer than usual, whispering close to her ear, as if too much volume might unbalance them.

'It hasn't gone, Ruth.' He holds her tight round the waist, the press of his body against hers a tempting memory of last night. 'We just forgot how to look.'

She puts both arms round his neck and buries her head in his shoulder, terrified her face might scare the good stuff away.

'Hey,' he says, gently pulling himself from her grip. 'I'm sorry, but I've really got to go.' He kisses her lips. 'We can continue this later.'

Ruth remains in the doorway as Giles cycles down the street, her thoughts whirling back to last night, the long wait having made their love as intense as when they were first together; they'd become strangers again and were able to put their best and boldest selves forward. But with daylight has come the reality that the tiniest error, the minutest of slip-ups on Ruth's part, will bring the whole lot crashing back down.

Fat feathers of snow fall into the alleyway and Frieda's front yard as the weather regains its bluster. The postman's footprints mark a path to Miss Cailleach's front door where a few pieces of junk mail stick out of the letter box. The regimen of the house continues while Frieda lies in hospital; for whatever reason, she's entrusted Ruth with her most valuable possession, and Ruth needs to repay her ill neighbour by feeding her cat, for today at least. By tomorrow Ruth will have had time to think of another plan, perhaps tell Liam she went searching under plant pots and found keys after all.

Ruth puts Bess in her cot for a sleep. It'll be an hour before the baby wakes again. Ruth sways anxiously, passing Frieda's keys from one hand to the other; if she leaves Bess at home, the visit next door will be quicker, plus she'll be close enough to get back if her daughter wakes. Ruth loads her pockets with latex gloves and hand sanitizer, clips the baby monitor to the waist of her jeans with her coat over the top and Chubbs the front door, trying the lock several times to check it's secure.

Tyre skids on the road are refreezing and a fresh deposit of dog mess has melted a hole in the snow. As Ruth steps out of her gate, Monica from next door is loading another sack in her uncollected bin.

'Ruth!' she says, smiling widely. 'How about this weather, eh!'

Ruth stiffens. 'I know.' She waits for Barry to step out of the gate as well, but he doesn't.

'We should have a coffee sometime.' Monica rubs her hands against the cold. 'You know, get Bess to meet Danny properly. There's only a couple months between them.'

'Yes.' Ruth should be being more friendly, but she really doesn't have the time or patience. Monica mustn't see her going through Frieda's gate either. She'll want to know why and might tell Barry, who'll probably tell Liam. But if Ruth goes back home now, her courage will disappear. She stamps her boots on the ground, compressing the snow to ice.

The pause lengthens until Monica says, 'Well, anyway, things are calming down a bit for me now I've got Danny into a routine, so I'm around a bit more if you need anything.

196

I know how tough it can be with your first baby.' She laughs. It's gentle, reassuring. 'Wait till you have four, like me!'

Ruth tips her head up in a weak smile as Monica pulls her gate closed behind her. People are nice, Ruth thinks; it's her who makes the judgements, who is inaccessible.

She checks up and down the road before entering Frieda's yard, immaculate save for the postman's footprints, now dusting over with fresh powder. Frieda's lock is stiff and it takes a hefty rattle to get the door to open. Ruth walks inside to a pocket of warm air, the kitchen more ordered than last time she was here, as if Frieda had the foresight to tidy up. She flicks through the junk mail stuck in the letter box and, when she finds nothing of consequence, leaves the post where it is so Liam won't notice the change. In fact, if she hadn't have been so flustered, she would have thought to use Frieda's back door instead. Next time – if there is a next time – she'll use the other entrance so her footprints won't show.

She heads further into the kitchen, building up the courage to deal with the cat. A few padded envelopes are on the worktop, all addressed to Mr Smith like the ones Ruth's taken in for Liam before. They're unopened and Ruth decides it's best to leave them where they are. Next to the packages is Frieda's camera, back open and empty of film canister. Ruth closes the compartment to lift the heavy machine to her face, so much less portable than her phone, and she again wonders why Frieda bothers with this archaic contraption when digital is infinitely easier. With her eye to the viewfinder, Ruth adjusts the focus on the long lens. Even at its shortest focal point, the room is still a blur. She puts the camera to one side and checks in the fridge. A near-empty milk carton is in the door, but hardly any other food. Frieda's daily trips to the shops must have been to stock up with only what was needed for the day, only what could be carried, a leftover habit from the pre-refrigeration generation perhaps, though she doesn't seem that old, just old-fashioned.

Ruth rinses and refills the milk container with water, which she then pours over the plants arranged around the floor and on the windowsill in the lounge; a few stems have wilted in the sauna of the room, not helped by the fact that all the curtains are shut, even at the back where they'd been open last time Ruth was here. Every light is on, though, and a halogen glow of fake sun glosses the leaves. Ruth unzips her coat to hold the baby monitor up to her ear. Behind the static is the faint in and out of Bess's sleepy breath. Ruth sweats under the layers of clothing, but to take her coat off would imply permanence, which in turn would mean she's comfortable having this chore expected of her. A voice comes close to the house. Ruth freezes, terrified that Liam's about to march through the door. A baby's cry starts up too – not Bess's, though, Ruth would recognize that anywhere, and not Ian's either; he only ever whimpers. The scream passes into the distance, before another noise thumps over the top, this time from inside Frieda's wall – a loud *thunk* and grinding. Ruth holds a hand over her mouth to keep her shriek inside. The banging repeats then speeds up as, in the kitchen, the boiler on the wall whomps into life, radiators joining in the chorus. Ruth bends forward to regain her balance, her breath as choppy as her heart. The decrepit boiler is almost as old as Frieda, and it clangs and bangs like a one-man band, pushing hot water through creaking pipes buried inside walls and floorboards. In the lounge ceiling, another pipe clanks as it expands, making the same noise Ruth heard the day she had tea with Frieda.

With the plants all watered, Ruth creeps up the stairs. 'OK, let's get this over with, puss-cat.' She listens for meows or scratching, but there's only silence; perhaps the cat's already dead. Ruth imagines having to explain to Frieda that she didn't get here in time, and it motivates her to press on. She turns into the front bedroom with the odd acclimatization of turning right rather than left to access this duplicate of her own room, though inside it couldn't be more different. Walls are painted a deep red and taking up much of the space is a four-poster bed with patterned woodwork. The piece is worn and must have been an ordeal to get upstairs into this tiny room. No one would have bothered if it wasn't loved; perhaps the bed was inherited from a mother or a grandmother. Generations of Frieda's family have probably been conceived and born in this bed, maybe even Liam.

The mattress is heaped with patchwork bedspreads and cushions. Ruth lifts the dangling covers to check underneath the bed. There, sleeping on a tatty blanket, is an ancient black cat. It leisurely opens one eye and takes Ruth in before resetting its head on its paws. Ruth leans back on her haunches, let's out the breath she hadn't been aware she was holding and looks around the room. In the corner there are a couple of bowls, one with water and one with biscuits. Both are full to the brim. She drags the food towards the bed and slides it underneath, careful not to get her hand too close to the cat. The animal briefly sniffs the dry biscuits, then returns to its snooze. 'C'mon, eat,' Ruth says, prodding the bowl slightly closer. 'You've not touched your food since yesterday.' The cat remains asleep. A dusty metal box is also under the bed and Ruth nudges it into the cat's blanket to try to get it to move. This time the animal cracks open both eyes and hisses. Ruth snatches her hand away, noticing the initials F. C. etched on the side of the box – they must stand for Frieda Cailleach. The container is full and the lid won't shut over the stash of envelopes inside. One has fallen to the floor. 'Express Photos' is printed on the side and a couple of grainy shots of trees poke out from the sleeve.

Ruth stands, dusts her knees, as the skinny cat ambles out from under the bed. A cushion on the floor holds the ghost of its shape. The animal settles into the round depression, neither too ill to move, nor too feeble from lack of food, and Ruth's relieved that her not getting here sooner hasn't resulted in the animal dying on her watch.

She turns a circle in the room. On the walls, paintings of flowers and landscapes ping with colour, not the usual beiges Frieda chooses for her clothes. One bird in foliage is faintly cubist; another has a Mexican feel. A couple of photos of birds too, like the ones on the walls downstairs, fairly amateur and most probably taken by Frieda with her long lens. In one picture Ruth recognizes the streak of a train in the background; perhaps the shot was taken from Frieda's allotment. Another image is of a kestrel hovering above the trees, taken from a different perspective, looking the other way, with the chimney pots of the terraces as its backdrop. Frieda could only have got this shot if she was on the other side of the fence, standing on the sidings, so there must be an entrance, which would explain the fires Ruth sees occasionally, the local kids getting their fix of wilderness; an antidote to the tarmac and bricks of their usual stomping ground.

Two baby plants on the bedroom sill have the telltale feathery leaves of cannabis, and Ruth glows a little at this frisson of illegality as she waters them, though she has no desire to ever smoke again and return to that brand of paranoia. She makes a small gap in the drawn curtain to put the plants on the daylight side. Hanging from the window latch is a dreamcatcher, the same kind that was posted through Ruth's door when Bess was born, the one she threw on the sidings only a few days ago.

On Frieda's bedside table is a photo of a much younger looking Miss Cailleach with a little boy at her side. He looks about seven, is chubby and cute and hugs into his mum, giving the camera a big smile. Frieda has an arm round him and she radiates happiness. Ruth picks up the picture frame. Underneath the boy's puppy fat she recognizes a young Liam – or Rainbow as he would have been then. He and Frieda are on the allotment at the back with the railway fence behind them, the space overgrown with brambles and nettles, totally different to how it looks today; they must have just moved in. Liam has an earnest face, open and kind, and Ruth thinks she'd like to have a conversation with that little boy who seems innocent enough to have been unselfconscious about his name. She could ask him where it went wrong, and why, of all the paths he could have taken, he chose to reinvent himself into such a difficult man.

Ruth puts the frame down, impatient to find and clean the litter tray so she can finally get home. She pulls on the latex gloves and steps onto the small landing where two other doors lead off the top of the stairs. She opens the door to the bathroom. Towels and flannels are stacked neatly in a cupboard. Dusty plastic flowers in a vase on the windowsill, and a strong smell of old-lady carbolic over a background of drain. No litter tray here. Ruth runs the hot tap and water steams into the plughole, taking some of the smell with it. Next off the landing, the final door is a mirror of Bess's bedroom, the room that must have been Liam's when he lived at home. Ruth tries to imagine a young Liam inside; even though she's seen the photo of him, he's the sort of man who seems forever grown, with no soft edges left over from childhood.

She turns the handle, worried about where the cat's been going to the toilet since it hasn't been able to get inside this room. Her hands are wet from the bathroom and the knob slips in her latexed palm. The door shifts millimetres but no further. From across the baby monitor comes a grumble. Ruth turns up the volume to full, the reception poor this far from her house, but it's still possible to pick out Bess's movements. A rustle as the little girl fidgets on the sheets, then a grizzle as she resettles. Ruth waits to be certain she's gone back to sleep, though it won't be long until Bess is fully awake. She pulls off the gloves and dries her palms on her jeans to get a better grip on the handle, then with a shoulder to the door, Ruth pushes hard. The door is set fast. Now more than anything she wants to get inside and get it over with, and she shoves her full weight into the barrier. With one last bash, the door bursts open.

A chair that was blocking her entrance splays on the floor. Ruth lurches into the small room. On the bed, directly in front of her, is a skinny girl with wide tear-filled eyes.

Ruth screams and leaps back onto the landing. 'Jesus!' Her thoughts jump to Bess, home alone in bed. If this girl attacks, Ruth won't get back to her baby. 'What the hell?' She presses herself to the wall, attempting if she could to push the space back a few millimetres.

'Please.' The girl is bunched up, arms tight round her knees. 'She told me you would come.'

'Who? Does Frieda know you're here?'

The girl dips her head into the well of her legs, voice muffled. 'Yes.'

'I don't understand.'

Slowly, the stranger brings her mouth level with her knees. 'Please, I am a secret.'

Ruth is panting. She's been tricked into Frieda's house with this dangerous person. 'This is nuts.' She glances towards the stairs, her exit clear. Now is the time to run, to leave and never come back.

As if sensing Ruth is about to bolt, the girl shouts, 'No, don't. I only need food.'

'I'm not . . .' Ruth edges towards the staircase. 'I can't do this.'

The girl leaps forward and grabs Ruth's sleeve. 'You must help.'

Ruth wrenches her coat away. 'Get off or I'll call the police.'

With this, the girl lets go. Ruth bounds down the stairs, two at a time, feet scuffing the skirting as she grabs the hand-rail to right herself. The girl follows close behind. Through the lounge and towards the front door. Ruth seizes the latch, but the girl springs forward, leaning her weight against the barrier. Small grunts of determination bridge the air between them, each aware that no one outside must know they're here. Ruth tries to pull the girl out of the way and drags a ragged nail down her forearm in the process. A line of blood springs up on the stranger's skin.

'Please,' the girl says. 'Just until Mrs Frieda gets home.'

'No way, I am not getting involved.'

'I beg you.' She grips Ruth's hand, her tremble running into Ruth. 'There is no one else.'

Ruth steadies, panting now, the boiler still grumbling behind. Tentatively, the girl takes a step away from the door. As she does so, Ruth lunges at the latch, and with her other arm she pushes the girl with full force, flinging her to the opposite wall where her head cracks against the architrave of the lounge door. The girl yelps and wraps two hands over her skull, curving her chest and shoulders inwards as if she's attempting to shrink, to disappear if she could.

Ruth pauses, flattens herself to the door. 'My God.' She did this, she is capable of this force. 'I'm so sorry. Are you OK?'

The girl is rigid, waiting to deflect more of what Ruth might send. Ruth's fingers loosen round the door handle as she takes her first proper look at the young woman: a teenager, barely eighteen, possibly younger, dressed in Frieda's clothes; bony shoulders under the green fleece, legs disappearing inside voluminous slacks.

A whisper from the girl. 'You saw me before.' Her words are muffled behind her arms. 'And you didn't tell.'

'When? When did I see you?'

'Before, when it was dark. I was in your garden.'

Ruth clasps her stomach over the invisible punch as the girl slowly removes her hands from her head to reveal her slender neck. Possibilities hurtle towards Ruth and she speeds through them, arriving in the twisted logic of being well enough to consider her illness. Even in the familiar terrain of her psychosis, could her mind be capable of such fantastical leaps, of summoning up a three-dimensional being who feels pain? A girl she imagined all those months ago living in a wall of her house, who's now demanding to be fed. With what? With Ruth's sanity? It can't be possible.

Bess grumbles over the monitor. Ruth's baby is at home. She's alone. Ruth needs to do the fastest thing to get out of here. She summons up words. 'What do you want?'

The girl hugs her arms round her waist. Tears collect at her chin and drop to the floor. She makes no sound.

Again Ruth speaks, more forcefully this time. 'How do I make you go away?'

She won't look at Ruth. 'After you saw me, Mrs Frieda found me.' Blood has trickled down her arm and blots her sleeve. 'She said you were kind.'

The sensation of raking a nail across the girl's skin is still fresh in Ruth's fingertip. An impulse had unlocked in her, giving her permission to do what was necessary, to create pain if need be, and the rush of it was barely within her control. She'd been hot with fear, of needing to win.

She reaches out to the girl, whose skinny body is still compacted in terror. 'Does it hurt?'

The girl flinches from Ruth's hand. 'I only need food.' She rocks back and forth, holding on to herself. 'Frieda did not know the hospital would be so soon.'

Noise bursts over the baby monitor. Bess is building up to a cry.

The girl shakes, knees hard points under her trousers, words almost inaudible. 'Soon I will go back.'

'Back where? Into the wall?' Even as Ruth says this, it sounds ridiculous, but the act of speaking the worst helps dismiss some of her fear.

The young woman holds her bottom lip with her teeth, skin blanching with the pressure. 'Are you mad?'

Bess is crying hard now, anxiety tugging at Ruth to get home. 'Yes,' she says quietly. 'I'm afraid I am.'

There is no more space in Ruth's life to absorb this new problem, and there's not a single soul she can ask for help, her own fallible judgement all she has to rely on. She's trapped between two people she's responsible for, only one of whom she fully trusts is real. She needs to be well, to prioritize herself and her baby.

Slowly, she turns, leaving this world in opposite, aware also that she'll need to do more to make it disappear. Who would ever believe this girl is hiding at Frieda's, and how can

Ruth be sure, if she brought Giles or the police here, that the girl wouldn't disappear? Either from Ruth's imagination or by darting through the back door. Giles must never find out. If he does, what they rediscovered last night will evaporate. Wife and husband will again become patient and carer.

She opens the door. The young woman's mouth hangs open, palm pressed over the cut on her arm, eyes rimmed red. Ruth takes a last hard look.

The girl says, 'My name is Leila.'

Ruth shuts the door behind her.

12

Ruth is stiff with tension as she lifts Bess from her cot. 'I'm so sorry, sweetie.' She kisses her baby's head and hugs her close. 'Mummy didn't mean to leave you for so long, I'm really sorry.' The little girl's cheeks are slippery with tears. She calms a little in Ruth's arms, but milk is what she needs.

Downstairs, Ruth paces the room while the bottle warms, footsteps driving her thoughts as she goes over and again what's next door and what is possible to believe. Ruth is getting better, is currently too healthy to have dreamt up another apparition, yet her mind hasn't always been her own and she can't completely discount the possibility of it running on auto again. There have, after all, been other hallucinations recently. But those times she'd been barely awake, and none of the visions had been like this: a talking, bleeding human. As soon as Ruth sits she stands again, legs jumpy with the energy of needing absolute surety.

Bess cries and stretches for the floor. Ruth holds on tight to this living, squirming nugget of normality, the only creature she's wholly confident is of this world. One-handed, she searches her wallet for the non-emergency number the PCSO gave her, and she seesaws the battered card in her fingers, pressing two digits on the phone, finger hovering to continue as she anticipates the irreversible connection she's about to make. Would the police even register her concern if she rang? And if she insisted they come, those officers whose presence still lingers at the edges of her ineptitude, they'd sink into her sofa, watching, judging, waiting for the silence to be filled with Ruth's stammer: 'I found a girl in the house next door. The owner knows she's there, so I'm not even sure it's an issue. But the bigger problem is, I may have made her up.' She cancels the call.

Bess wriggles to one side. Ruth slides the baby into her bouncy chair and gives her the bottle. Chubby little hands grasp the milk and the baby gulps through sighs of satisfaction, eyes following Ruth with a knowing luminosity; a barometer on reality, more sane than the adult in the room.

Ruth smooths her daughter's damp hair and with her other hand she scrolls through her phone contacts to Giles's number. She practises what to say: 'I went out without you knowing and got caught up in something that might be dangerous.' Or: 'Will you help me untangle my most vivid hallucination and still trust me to look after our daughter?' The words sit on her tongue, poised to roll out to the ether and into Giles's ear, where he'll use them to calculate the fastest way to get her back to the mother-and-baby unit. Ruth lays her phone face down.

On the dining table is an envelope Giles left earlier, his handwriting scribbled on the front: 'Don't forget to take.' Inside is her antidepressant. This is how he leaves the medication now he's spending time away from the house. He used to at least sweeten the command by planting a kiss on her forehead, or console her with a joke – 'you're my favourite patient' – but in only a few days the message has become perfunctory, another chore inspired by his wife's difficulties. In an hour or two he'll be home. After that Ruth won't be able to leave the house and the question of the girl will stretch into another day. And if the snow thickens and Giles can't get to work again tomorrow, a young person will be trapped and hungry, waiting for Ruth, the only one who can help.

No wonder Frieda didn't want Liam in her house and the curtains have been drawn for several days against prying eyes. Even though Ruth's mystified about what she should do, she's also strangely honoured at having been the one tasked with looking after Leila – no one else has trusted Ruth with much for months. And she feels wretched for Frieda too, that the little boy Ruth saw in a photograph just minutes ago has grown into such an ogre that his mother is certain of the unkindness he'd show the girl she's harbouring in her house. Perhaps, if food is all that Leila needs, Ruth can manage that until Frieda comes out of hospital – *if* she comes out of hospital. Only one thing's for sure: Ruth is stronger, physically at least, than whatever is next door.

She swallows her tablet and grabs a plastic bag, putting in bread and a few old cans of food. Some cheese, milk and butter from the fridge, not enough to empty the shelves, and she avoids the pâté and ripe cheese Giles loves and would know were missing in an instant. With Bess in her arms, Ruth puts a blanket round the little girl and leaves from the front, her back door now swollen shut with damp. She takes the alley to the rear of Frieda's house, opening the door there as she would a gate to a bull, holding Bess away from the opening as Leila rushes forward. Ruth takes two rapid steps backwards into the yard, putting up a hand to a bewildered Leila, who daren't move into the garden where she might be seen. Bess blinks, tucking her head into her mum's neck, then peeps out, fingers scrunching Ruth's jumper. Ruth looks between the two girls. There's a sweaty caution in her baby's breath. Leila's face is shadowed in the doorway, but her eyes are fixed on the baby. Bess curls further into shyness, keeping this new person at the edge of her vision.

The baby is fresh to the world, so closed to suggestion it would be impossible for her to pretend or disguise her reaction. Ruth points at Leila, saying, 'Who's that?' Bess smiles and kicks her legs, like a rider on a pony. She wants to be closer. Ruth takes tentative steps towards the house and, as they come level with Leila, Bess stretches out an arm and the young woman on the doorstep touches her own fingers to the little girl's. Bess giggles excitedly into her mum's neck, strangely warmed by this stranger, and the radiance that breaks on Leila's face at once tells Ruth that Leila is no threat to her or her daughter. Nor an illusion. Now Ruth's sure, she realizes she never really believed otherwise, it was only her crushing self-doubt that refused to let her listen to good sense. With this answer, though, has come a different set of problems, ones that belong to a hidden and desperate young woman.

Ruth steps inside to the fruity kick of hot, unaired rooms. Leila's face is wide with anticipation and fear, a question balanced on her barely open mouth. She'll want to know if Ruth has told.

Ruth closes the door behind her and gives Leila the bag of food. 'You're safe, don't worry.'

The carrier shakes as Leila opens it to look inside. 'Thank you.'

'It's not much, but it should last a couple of days.'

The girl swerves past Ruth towards the kitchen, hurriedly opening one of the cans and spreading butter on bread.

Ruth's redundant hand pats her daughter's back, and Bess's head turns left and right to explore this new environment. The stark lighting is accentuated by the many mirrors and a green hue refracts from an infinity of plants. Ruth puts a hand to the curtain at the back window to let in some daylight, when Leila shouts, 'No.' Ruth freezes, turns. The girl says, more quietly, 'It is enough that you come. If anything else is different, they will see.'

'Who? Frieda's son? Has he been here today?'

'No one has been.'

'Who then?'

The girl mumbles. 'From the car wash.'

Ruth tightens her arm round Bess. 'Are they looking for you?' She imagines the road blocked by the small army that circled the manhole, vengeance for the scene she caused on the forecourt.

Leila brings a plate of food into the lounge and sits at the coffee table, hunched over bread and cold beans, attacking them with her cutlery. Ruth perches opposite in an armchair.

Leila says through a full mouth, 'If they knew I was here, they would come.'

'Why?'

She swallows. 'Because I would not do what they wanted.'

Ruth shuffles her words, trying to find the best way to ask even though she already knows the answer. 'And what was that?'

The girl sits tall, rigid. Ruth is pinned to her chair, cursing herself for having asked the obvious and putting this girl through further humiliation. Leila says, 'I am for sale.'

Ruth gulps, can't muster a suitable reply, and chooses, 'I see,' the phrase overly formal, but it's all she has at her disposal to keep the fear from her voice. 'And you wanted to stop?'

Leila shovels in more food. 'Of course.'

'Were you working on this street?'

'No, there is a flat with other women. But when we arrive in this country, we come here.'

'Why?'

Her fork wavers above the plate. 'Because of the police, of immigration. We have to hide.'

'Do you stay at the petrol station?'

'No.' Leila blinks fast. 'We go under the ground.'

A prickle runs across Ruth's scalp. 'I saw people, at night. They were climbing out of a petrol tank.'

'No one will look there.' The girl mashes what's left of the beans. 'They keep us inside until it is safe, then they take us to work.'

'But the police said it's not possible. They said the tanks were full of water.'

'They are wrong.'

'How, I don't understand?'

'Maybe they lie. I do not know.' She looks at the floor. 'After we come out, no one talks, we are happy only for fresh air.'

'How long did you stay down there?'

'Some hours, maybe a day. We have no light, no place for toilet, we cannot even stand.' Her knife clatters to the ground. 'It is like death.'

Ruth leans closer to Leila. 'Is that where you escaped from? From the tank?'

'Ray tried to make me go down again, but I ran.'

'Ray?'

'The man who keeps us.' She picks up the knife and jabs it into her food. Ruth strains to hear Leila's whisper. 'They separate me from my sister because we help each other, we plan to run away. I did not know where they took her, so I fight for Ray to tell me, but he would not. I am angry all the time, make it difficult to work, so no one will pay for me.'

The air closes in on Ruth, her altitude dropping.

'Ray wants to put me under the ground to punish me, to break me, like an animal. He thinks it will make me do what he wants, work better, but I only want to find my sister. I scream and run when he tried to put me there.'

'Jesus.'

Bess smiles at Leila, who reaches over to stroke the little girl's cheek. 'My sister was like my baby. I try to protect her, I promise I would look after her.'

Ruth puts her daughter on the floor between them and crosses to sit next to Leila. 'I'm so sorry.'

'I do not know how to find her. My only chance is here, outside, but there is no one to help.'

'What's the address of the flat where you worked?'

'We were always locked inside. I never see the street. Once I asked one of men who pay to help, but he was scared of the police. He had a wife and children, he did not want them to find out.' Leila loses her focus to the curtained window in the distance. 'My sister and me had school once, I learnt science and English, a good home too. My parents had money, but they use everything to help me and Farah leave, to keep us safe.' A deep intake of breath. 'But the men trick us. We pay all the way from leaving home. Is a long way, sometimes in a car, or walking, sometimes hiding. Soon after, the boat is dangerous. Maybe on purpose it sinks so the lifeguards will come, but no one did. They are not allowed to help any more.' Her head drops. 'Is lucky we can swim because the life jackets are bad. I saw people under the water.' Bess stares quietly at Leila as if she too has sensed the intensity of the girl's story. Leila's shoulders heave, then she looks up at Ruth, speaking soft and fast. 'When we try for the tunnel our money has run out, so we have to work to pay back, and now the men never let us stop.' Panic swells in the girl's tears. 'My sister only wanted to go home. I have to find her, she won't be safe without me. She will think I

215

have left her. I have been in this house one week. Is too long doing nothing, without helping.'

'Do you have any idea where they've taken her?'

Leila shakes her head. 'Another flat to work, maybe? But I do not know where.'

Ruth gently puts a hand to the girl's back. 'Have you spoken to the police?'

Leila pulls away from Ruth. 'No, no police. They are bad.'

'They're not. Really, they can help you.'

The girl tips her head back to make more distance between them. 'Maybe they help you, but for me it would be different.'

Ruth shifts about in her seat, tugging her too-hot jumper, unable to find a comfortable position, aware she doesn't fully believe what she's saying, nor understand the ramifications of getting the police involved for Leila. 'I'm sure they'd listen if you told them your story. I mean, your sister is missing.'

Leila's breath is sweet from the food. 'But I am illegal. They will arrest me. I will go to detention centre, then I will never find Farah.'

'Can you call someone at home? Your mum or dad? A friend?'

'There is no one left. Everything is gone.'

'But where are you from?'

Leila jerks her chin at Ruth. 'What is the difference? You will only help people like you? Same money, same skin?'

'Of course not.' Bess is trying to push herself onto her knees, and the effort of holding up her head is tiring. She looks to her mum with a cry. Ruth lifts the little girl into her arms and hugs her close. The baby's features are a template of her adult self: almond-shaped eyes, full mouth, dot of a nose. Ruth and Giles had no conscious design over where Bess was born, it was simply chance that they had been born in this corner of the world and could offer that same safety to their child, but if that advantage was taken away, who would Bess be able to trust, who would value her like their own child if Ruth and Giles weren't around?

'What if you paid the men what they say you owe?' Ruth asks. 'How much do you need, for you and your sister? I don't know if it's possible, but maybe I can get some cash.'

Leila sinks back, gravity pulling her into the cushions. 'You do not understand. The men say they want money but really they only want more work.'

Sweat glows on the girl's face and her hair is shiny with grease. Ruth hot-wires back to her teenage self: the bitten nails, refusing to wash, a limbo of questions over Tam, uncertainty whipping up anger, tipping Ruth over the edge; and her parents, too exhausted by their own grief to know how to handle this new assault, choosing to lose both daughters rather than cope with the defective one, the one they believed was to blame for leaving Tam in danger. Ruth remembers them pacing the shoreline the day Tam went missing, spitting anger – 'Why didn't you tell us sooner? How could you be so wicked?' – as the lifeguard went back into the waves one more time, even though it was getting dark and he was weeping with exhaustion and only really a boy himself. Ruth's startled by her uninvited tears in the face of Leila's desperation, and she covers her face with a hand. She's not cried this hard in years.

Leila takes Ruth in, probably thinking the tears are for her, which they are, but also for so much more. Then the girl says, 'Where can I go, what can I do? I have no passport, no friends. My English is not enough, so everyone will know I am not from here.' She leans away. 'But maybe,' her words gather speed, 'maybe the men will listen to you? You are a citizen. Ray cannot hurt you.'

Through sniffs, Ruth says, 'Ray?' She thinks for a moment. 'I mean, what could I do? I don't think . . .' She stands, collects Bess in her arms. Voices outside, car doors slamming, people coming home from work. Ruth checks the clock in the kitchen. 'God, I have to go.' Her teeth chatter as she shuffles her guilt from one foot to the other, eyes on the door that's only feet away, though it may as well be a mile. 'I'll come back to-morrow, OK? I can bring more food.'

Leila stares at the floor, her body so thin she's almost translucent in this light-filled room, armed with no other weapon than a safe place to stay; rootless and powerless, all for the want of a better life. 'Then I have to go back to work, for Farah. Is the only way.'

Ruth hoists Bess higher on her hip and moves to the back door. 'Look, I'm sorry, I didn't realize how late it was. We'll talk about this again tomorrow.'

'My sister is fifteen.'

Pins and needles travel up Ruth's arm and her fingers cramp on the latch, the effort to leave counterintuitive to the pull of this girl who has only Ruth to help.

Leila says, 'My baby sister.'

Options fly at Ruth: all the things she needs to do, and everything she mustn't. She palms the door to steady herself against a sway under her feet. That day at the beach, she and Tam so far from the shore that they were beyond the surf, watching the people-coloured dots against a band of yellow shingle. 'How long do you think before anyone notices we're gone?' Tam had said as Ruth paddled the deep black water, imagining the forest of seaweed below that could wrap round her legs and drag her under. 'I'm really tired,' Ruth said through salty coughs. 'They'll be worried. Please, Tam, come on. I want to go back.' Tam, the stronger swimmer by far, glided close to Ruth. 'You're such a goodie two shoes, Ruthie.' Then she dived under the surface and bobbed up like a beautiful mermaid. 'You go back if you want to, but promise me you won't tell Mum and Dad where I am. They never stop fussing over me.'

Ruth lets her hand fall from the door and faces Leila. 'I'm going to have to speak to my husband.'

'Do not tell him. Please, I beg you.' Leila smudges the tears from her cheeks, shutting away the vulnerable child she'd briefly allowed herself to become.

'Why?'

'Because Mrs Frieda said only to trust you. If he comes, I will run.'

'But . . .' Ruth turns her face to Bess so Leila can't read the treachery she's considering.

'I will watch for you.' Leila's knuckles are bloodless on

the couch, holding on as if the whole thing might go under. 'I will disappear if you bring him.'

Ruth recognizes every atom of Leila's fear as if it were her own. Bess is nearly seven months old, and in that time Ruth's world has flipped from magnetic north to south – there's not a single part of her old self she recognizes any more. All Ruth ever needed was one good person, without their judgement.

'OK,' Ruth says. 'I won't tell.'

Leila nods, a contract blazing on her face. Ruth nods back, though she has no idea to what she's agreeing.

She opens the door. Cold air streams into the house. She skids on the icy path, grabbing the fence to steady herself. 'Shit,' she mumbles. 'Bloody shit.' *I'm the one who can't be trusted, I'm the one who's dangerous.* Chaos is a place Ruth once inhabited, bedding in with the worst of the dirt, and now she's inviting it in again. Giles wants to protect their baby, and if he knew about this girl, or whatever it is Ruth's about to get involved in, it would be the final straw.

Dusk is moving in as she crosses the alley towards her house. She rehearses what she'll tell Giles about her afternoon, picking out trivialities at odds with the enormity of the truth. On the railway sidings, saplings lean in the wind, and through the trees she sees a small gathering of figures in a clearing. Their footprints have broken the pristine surface of the snow.

13

By the time Ruth and Giles have finished eating and putting Bess to bed, it's time to turn in themselves. On the other side of the alley, condensation from Frieda's boiler has formed a tear shape on the exterior wall. At least Leila will be warm. At least she has some food.

In bed, Ruth can't settle; questions and anxiety churn up her thoughts until about 3 a.m. when she thinks she hears Bess. She climbs from her sweat-damp sheets only to find her baby is fast asleep. Ruth grinds her jaw, frustrated by the false alarm, grateful, though, that she's alert to any comings or goings next door, because who else knows to be on guard? In her own room, she pulls the curtain aside as her fox skulks along the road, tail and nose to the ground, as if he's been told off. Again Ruth forgot to put out food, the Leila-sized problem occupying all her time and energy. She hopes the animal will find an easy bin to raid.

Next to Frieda's gate, a large evergreen shrub has collected clouds of snow in its leaves. On the ground, a fresh

221

line of footprints make a trail between the bush and the front door.

A movement next to the plant. Then a shadow leans from the leaves. A figure emerges, opens the gate and walks out onto the pavement. Ruth's temperature plummets – it's Leila. The girl sets off at a pace down the road. Ruth grabs a jumper and socks, stumbling to put them on, bumping into the chest of drawers in her panic to leave the room. A picture of her sister topples from the dresser onto the floor, glass cracking.

Giles stirs. 'Ruth?' He sits up and blinks. 'Where are you going?'

She freezes on the landing, one foot still inside the bedroom. 'Just going downstairs. Can't sleep.'

'Really? Did you take your medication on time?'

'Yes, of course, I always do.'

'Then come back to bed, you'll drop off again if you give yourself a chance.'

'I was going to make a hot milk.'

Giles pushes the bedcovers back. His feet *plonk plonk* on the floor. 'I'll do it. You go back to bed. Try and rest.'

'But—'

'Ruth.' He's next to her now, holding her arm and guiding her back into the room. 'Let me help. You need your sleep too.'

She takes a last peek from the window but Leila's gone.

Back in bed, Ruth shivers under her big jumper, her body boiling and freezing at the same time as a tide of sweat runs down her back. She takes off the extra layer and her pyjama bottoms, kicking the covers aside. Downstairs, a pan clanks. Cups chink as they're taken from the cupboard.

Leila will be close to the end of the road by now. Ruth's nails make tiny crescents of pain on her thighs. She shouldn't have left the girl alone today, she should have found a way to help there and then, or been brave enough to tell Giles, perhaps even call the police. But what can she do now? There's no one next door any more, and even if she did take Giles out with her to look for Leila, the girl would hide. Whichever way Ruth comes at the problem, there's only ever one outcome, and that's confirmation to Giles that she's ill.

Ruth's husband's feet are a sturdy trudge on the stairs. He puts a cup at her bedside, another over his side for himself, and props up pillows to rest his back against the headboard. The light stays off.

'Drink,' he says. 'I'll wait with you till you go back to sleep.'

'I'm fine, really. You'll be tired for work tomorrow.'

'It's OK. I want you to be rested.' He turns to her. Light from the street sparkles in his watery eyes. He takes a big breath as if he's about to sing, but only a whisper comes out. 'I'm sorry if you being ill is my fault in any way, for leaving it all to you when Bess was first born.' He strokes her hair, palm warm on her head. 'I took it for granted you'd just get on with it. You were always so capable, so adamant you didn't want help. I simply assumed it would be the same with a baby.' She knows his words are heartfelt because he's waited until dark to say the things he really means. 'And I guess that assumption was convenient for me. It made me

223

lazy, a little selfish. But if we had our time again, I'd be more present. I realize now it was all a shock to your system.' His voice cracks. 'I want us to be back to how we were. I miss you, Ruth.'

She holds his hand across the covers. Both of them are shaking. How good this man is, Ruth thinks; she chose well in marrying Giles, did one thing right at least. These long-awaited intimacies need to be shared if there's any chance of being a couple again, and Ruth wants to leap into the space being opened up for her with her own apologies and failings, of which there are many and mounting, but all she can think is that Leila will have reached the petrol station by now. A young woman is out alone in the night, and no one cares apart from Ruth. And if Leila's discovered by the wrong people, she'll be snatched back, then Ruth will have no chance of reaching her ever again.

Scraps of sleep until morning finally arrives. Ruth is down-stairs making Giles a packed lunch, tidying the kitchen, and has Bess dressed and fed before her husband is even out of bed. She fidgets with any extras he might find to help with, kindnesses she's normally grateful for but will get in her way this morning. A fat black spider lurks in the sink. The drain is partially blocked so the creature must have come up the eggy pipes. Usually, Ruth would cover the spider with a glass, put a card underneath to take it outside, but she hasn't the patience today and runs the hot water hard until the last of the creature's legs has disappeared down the plug. From the cabinet in the downstairs toilet, Ruth takes out her pills, pressing one dose into her palm and, with lips to the tap, swallows it with a gulp of warm water. Now there's nothing Giles needs to stay home for.

He comes down into the lounge, rubbing the sleep from his eyes and faltering in the dawn of the immaculate room. 'Wow!' Ruth is on the floor finishing changing Bess's nappy. Giles bends to kiss her neck. 'Those extra hours last night obviously did you good.'

'Yes, thanks for that. Thought I'd return the favour and help get you to work. For once you could be early, imagine that? And you're going to the pub tonight, aren't you? Isn't it Faye's leaving do?'

'Oh yeah, I forgot about that.' He stretches and yawns, flicking on the kettle. 'It seems a bit soon to be leaving you on your own for that long. I'm not sure I'll go – I mean, I don't have to.'

'Of course you do,' Ruth says loudly. 'It will be good for you. And I'll be fine.'

'Really?' His inflection is tinged with relief, and he hugs her, breathing her in as if smelling her for the first time. He moves his arm round her waist, their intimacy fully unlocked by last night's words, and they can touch again without permission. Giles whispers, 'In fact, I'm sure I could swing it with work to stay home today.'

Ruth slides from his grip and lifts their daughter from the floor. 'Bessie's not due her sleep for another hour.'

Giles follows Ruth with his hands. 'You could put her down, perhaps with some toys in her cot?' He wraps his wife in both arms, seemingly less scared of her breaking. 'We could give it a try.'

Ruth is unwashed, with bed-breath and grey underwear. Not an inch of her feels sexy while she's preoccupied with Leila, and she's flummoxed too that Giles can so quickly revert to fixing all the broken parts of them with the physical – but the regaining of what's been lost warms a point inside her. Husband and wife kiss. In spite of herself, she slides her hips into his, and is moments from accepting what they both want when her mind forces her back to a desperate girl who needs her help.

'I'm sorry,' she says, shaking a little with the effort of pulling away. 'I'm just not in the mood.'

Giles's resentment is plain, his rejection harder to bear because she too needs to continue what they started only the other night. The choice to be a couple has been taken away and there's no way to explain the real reason, so all fault lies with Ruth.

'If I mess up Bess's routine,' Ruth mumbles at the floor so Giles can't see the tears in her eyes, remembering Sandra's edict too, that men need sex or they'll look elsewhere, 'the day will be chaos.'

Giles slumps away, grumpy and resigned. He gathers his things to go, sending a few texts before he leaves, his phone pinging with replies, then he cycles off without turning to wave as usual. Ruth rubs her eyes with the heel of her hand, so hard it hurts, as the urgency of Leila quickly overtakes her sadness. She collects Bess in her arms and leaves the house, checking down the road to be sure Giles has turned the corner before striding round the back of Frieda's. Fresh snow has fallen in the night and her footsteps leave a trail on the path behind her. She slides the key into the lock and shoves open the back door, the force of her entrance slamming it against the wall. Bess startles as Ruth charges through to the lounge.

'Leila?' she calls into the empty space. 'Leila, are you here?' No response. She shouts up the stairs. 'Leila.' Silence rolls through the rooms. 'Please, answer me.'

A scrape of furniture from above. Ruth's relief is brief; it's a heavier noise than she remembers from before. One of the men from the petrol station could have forced Leila to bring him back here, and now Ruth is unprotected in this house with her daughter. She curves herself round Bess, clutching the baby close with a full palm over her little head. Footsteps across the floorboards, slower than Ruth remembers. Her legs shake – they wouldn't hurt a woman with a baby, would they? She remains by the exit, hand on the latch and ready to run if she needs to, but if she leaves now she'll never know if Leila is safe. Feet clomp down the stairs. Ruth opens the back door an inch in readiness as Leila appears, limping.

'Leila, thank God!' Ruth bangs the door shut, relief switching to anger. 'Where did you go last night? I saw you. It was so late, you left the house.'

'Is crazy doing nothing.' Leila's chin crumples and tears spring into her eyes. 'I have to try to help. Is the first time I go.'

Ruth moves closer, a hand on the girl. 'I was worried about you. You mustn't leave without telling me.'

Behind Leila's vulnerability is a simmering rage. She shucks off Ruth's hand. 'I can do what I like.'

Ruth doesn't react; Leila is a girl struggling with a woman's problems, a state Ruth recognizes only too well.

Leila continues, 'I did not know if you would come back.'

'Of course I was going to. I said I was, didn't I?'

'How can I trust?'

Ruth says gently, 'Well, I'm here, aren't I?'

Leila's shoulders soften and Ruth guides her to the sofa where they sit. A scummy tide mark circles the bottom of the girl's trousers, the material having soaked up the snow, and her clothes smell musty. The overhead lights have been turned off, leaving only a couple of standard lamps in the corners of the room, and in the twilight of the curtained lounge, Leila's complexion is as dull and dry as old cloth. It must be weeks since she's been out in real sunlight.

Ruth says, 'Why did you leave? Do you need more food?'

'I went for Farah. I told you, I am too long here and I have to find her.'

'But I thought you didn't know where she is?'

'I don't.' A tiny shake through the sofa, Leila's fear running into the seat. 'But I cannot wait any more, so last night I try to find a clue.' She pulls a white silk scarf with black spots from the pocket of her fleece.

'What's this? Where did you get it from?'

'Is Farah's. I found it at the petrol station.'

'You did? How?'

'I broke a window. The room behind the shop is an office.'

Ruth's memory spools back to that day when she'd asked about the scream, a group of men in the back room with food on their laps, Katty eating Haribos and putting her finger in Bess's mouth. A pretty silk scarf hanging from the door handle. 'God, Leila, what if someone had been there?'

'I had to chance. I was lucky.'

Outside, barking and growls. A man shouts, then a squeal and yelp, like someone's kicked a dog. Angry voices trail into the distance.

'But why was the scarf there? Do you think that means Farah's in the tank?'

'She is not.'

'How do you know?'

'Because I looked.'

'Jesus, Leila. How did you even get the manhole up?'

'In the shop is the tool.' The girl pushes out her bottom lip and shrugs her shoulders. 'And I am strong when it is for my sister.'

'But what about what the police said? That the tanks are filled with water?' Ruth thinks back to that night she saw figures emerging from the ground.

'Is no water. I think you call it a sewer? A ladder in the wall to go down. Blocked off at the bottom and dry at least.'

'Huh.' Ruth slumps back on the sofa, running a hand through her hair. 'Well, that makes more sense.' Not a petrol tank at all, but a sewer. She'd be relieved to know she hadn't imagined people climbing out of the ground if it didn't make the reality so terrifying. The nails on her scalp hone her focus. 'So what now then?'

'There is nowhere else to look. Only thing now is to ask Ray.'

'But that's not possible.'

'Later, I am going to the petrol station. They can take me back, take me to Ray.'

'Leila, that's crazy.'

The boiler in the kitchen fires up with a clank and both women jump. Leila leans forward and says more quietly, 'Is for my sister.'

'I don't want you to go, Leila. You need to find another way.'

The girl's expression blackens. 'It is not up to you. This I do because there is nothing else.'

'But—'

'I do not know what they have done to Farah.' Leila tips her chin up to Ruth. 'I was stupid, I should not have left, but I thought I could find help outside.' Bess tucks into her mother's neck with an anxious cry and Ruth strokes her daughter's soft head. Leila continues, lips twitching with anger, 'Now Mrs Frieda has gone, I have only you.' She blinks rapidly, keeping her tears inside. 'And you can do nothing.' Then she jumps up and limps into the downstairs toilet. The door slams behind her.

Ruth stands and flattens her ear to the door, knocking gently. 'Leila?' No answer. Inside, the trickle of a running tap.

She uses the pause to fill the kettle, putting teabags and sugar in cups, the familiarity of the ritual giving her space to think. Ruth was only supposed to be feeding Leila, but now she's giving advice too, actively deepening her involvement and widening her own problems, the repercussions of which could swallow her whole. But it's nothing compared to what Leila's going through. Even taking into account Ruth's illness, Leila's experienced more hardship in her few years than Ruth ever will; Ruth's multiple safety nets – family, money, healthcare, citizenship – catch her whenever she falls. She returns to the empty lounge with two mugs in hand, imagining the young woman on the other side of the door, repacking her emotions, weaknesses impractical for both herself and the clients she once had.

Minutes pass. Steam blows out of the teacups. Ruth changes Bess and feeds her with a pouch of food she keeps in her bag for emergencies. On the wall next to the toilet door is another of Frieda's photos of the kestrel, perhaps taken on the same day as the picture in the woman's bedroom. The kestrel is hovering over trees, the chimney pots of the terraces and petrol station roof in the background, the perspective only possible if Frieda had been standing on the sidings looking back towards the street.

Ruth knocks again on the door. 'Leila? I've made you a drink.' Silence. Outside, the wheels of a car hiss through slushy snow. 'Leila!' No sound from the toilet. Fear rises in Ruth. She thumps the door with her fist and pushes down on the handle, expecting it to be locked, but it bursts open. Leila is standing in the middle of the small room, stripped down to her T-shirt and pants, skinny body lithe with muscle; a street cat honed for battle. Down her arms are bruises, like stains, like hung meat. Ruth puts her hand to her mouth. Leila's foot is immersed in a shallow tub of water that's pink with blood.

'Who did this?' Ruth says.

The girl's face is sullen. 'Last night I cut my foot on glass from the window.'

'Why didn't you say? Are you OK?'

Leila's stooping, so slim it's like she's bent over the hollow of her stomach. Wads of bloodied tissues lie on the floor. 'Maybe I need a bandage.'

'I'll see if Frieda's got one.' She leans in for a closer look. 'But I think that'll need stitches.'

'No.' The girl gently pushes Ruth away. 'The hospital will ask questions, then I will be sent to detention centre.'

Ruth measures out her words. 'And what about the rest?' She nods at the girl's arms, lifting the corner of her short sleeve. The bruises continue across Leila's shoulders. 'Where did these come from?'

Leila pulls away from Ruth, shrugging as if it's nothing, but her scowl could boil the water. 'Sometimes Ray, sometimes one of the men who pay.' She turns bloodshot eyes up to Ruth, challenging her with the same stare she gave before, refusing sympathy, urging action. 'Farah did not want to work, so she stopped eating, stopped talking. The customers complained she was no good. They did not want to pay if she was difficult, not sexy.' She stands a little straighter, pained effort in her face. 'Ray did not hurt her because she was popular, the men pay less for bruises, so he punish me instead to make Farah change.' Her face is sweating and she tries to rebalance her weight, wincing as she leans too hard on her bad foot. 'Ray think when Farah sees my pain, will force her to work to make him stop. But I did not tell her what he was doing to me. I was happy for him to hurt me as long as she was safe. Then he sent her away from me. Is why I need to find her. She has no help without me.'

'Jesus.' Ruth puts a hand to the wall, the totality of Leila's predicament sweeping under her feet, like the river underneath has scooped out the earth and opened up a sinkhole. She used to think that threats were from aliens or storms, floods and famine, biblical catastrophes that seemed remotely tangible. And whatever energy she had left over she'd used to carry on with her tiny life, fear circling her lovability and the minutiae of childcare, when all around was this other darkness, real and urgent and foul. She's always known it exists – everyone knows – but there was only so much she could do when all she had was suspicion.

Leila speaks as if she's talking to the water. 'I have only Farah, and Farah have only me.'

'Then they'll be expecting you to go back for her. It'll be even more dangerous for you.'

The gate bangs. Footsteps and a voice at the front door. 'Yeah, mate, it's a Yale and a Chubb, just standard, I think.' Liam's on the other side of the shut curtain. A pause before he shouts. 'Can't you do it any sooner? I thought you locksmiths were supposed to be an emergency service?' Ruth and Leila hold their breath, both creeping to the toilet door to locate Bess. The little girl is on the rug playing with something she's found in the thick pile. The object is tiny and round, the size of a bead or small battery, and she rolls it in her fingers before putting it in her mouth. Ruth hyperventilates into the silence. Liam continues, 'What, three this afternoon? You're mugging me off!' Bess's gums work the object. It's keeping her quiet, but at a choking distance. Ruth crawls towards her daughter as Liam carries on. 'Nah, it's me mum's house. I live down the road.' He kicks the door with a steady *thump thump* and Bess's eyes widen in alarm. 'It's a fucking joke, mate.' Liam's voice is as loud as if he were in the room with them, and Bess is suspended in the seconds of shock before she'll start to wail. Ruth reaches out to her daughter. Liam again: 'If that's the best you can do, I've got no bloody choice, have I?' Then his footsteps stomp into the distance and the gate bangs shut. Ruth launches at Bess, digging a finger into the little girl's mouth and pulling out a large seed covered in spit, aware only then of Leila's sweaty palms squeezing her own arm. The girl's nails have left dents on Ruth's skin.

Ruth pushes her away. 'I can't do this any more.' Her words spurt out before her thinking's even caught up. 'I mean, what do you bloody expect from me? I'm just a woman with a baby. Bess, she nearly . . . she could have choked.' She gathers her few things as Leila watches, chest sunk, head bowed in glowering defeat. Ruth opens the back door. 'I'm sorry. You'll have to find another way. Call the police or call home. There must be someone. Frieda has a phone. You need to do it before Liam comes back, and you need to get out of here quick. It's not safe.' She closes the door behind her.

At home Ruth grabs the landline, the call less traceable this way if Giles were ever inclined, although there's nothing she needs to hide, not yet. The dialling tone burrs and the receiver squeaks in her damp palm. With the handset sandwiched between ear and shoulder, Ruth scrolls through her mobile contacts to find the number of the hospital where she had Bess. She dials and gets patched through.

'Miss Cailleach hasn't long woken up,' the nurse tells Ruth. 'She's still quite frail, but I'll see if she can take your call. Did you say you're her daughter-in-law?'

'Yes.' Ruth's heart skips with tiny treachery. 'My name's Sandra, Sandra Smith.' The line is paused as Ruth is connected to her neighbour's bedside.

Shuffling noises. 'Just a moment, please.' The mouthpiece sounds like it's being stuffed with cotton wool.

'Are you OK?' Ruth asks.

Frieda comes back on the line, clearer now. 'Ruth? Thank God, they told me it was Sandra.'

'Yes, sorry about that.' She swaps the phone to her other ear. 'How are you?'

'Been better. I'll be here for a while yet.' A phlegmy crackle. 'They've got me on God knows what. I'm so groggy I don't know if it's night or day.' Another long pause as Frieda catches her breath. 'Are you taking care of my cat? Is there a problem?'

'Yes.' Ruth grits her teeth. It's not possible to shout at an old ill woman, but Frieda's big ask that was never a question is made worse by the silly school-girl code. 'There is a huge problem. You have no right to put this on me.'

The woman slurs a little. 'But is my cat still in the house?'

'If you're referring to Leila, of course she is, but Liam's coming over with a locksmith today.'

'My son mustn't get in.' Frieda coughs. 'He won't understand. You mustn't let him find her there.'

Ruth works hard to control her voice. 'I know, which is why I'm calling you.'

Clanging metal travels down the line, mixed with a clinical echo of hospital chatter. 'I'm sorry, I know it's a lot to expect of you, but it's very important we keep Leila safe.'

'We? There is no we. You're in hospital, so this problem is now mine.'

'It's bad luck it's turned out this way.' Frieda makes tiny grunts as if she's rearranging herself in the bed. 'I wasn't expecting to be here, not so soon anyway. I was trying to stay well, but the universe had other ideas.'

Ruth turns her face to the ceiling at this esoteric nonsense, unable to control herself any longer. 'Fat lot of use your home remedies were then.'

Frieda's replies comes fast, like she's rehearsed what to say. 'I'd have been in hospital much sooner if I'd done nothing at all.' Her voice grows distant. 'It's just that all my mistakes caught up with me at the same time . . . it's my reckoning.' Heavy breathing. 'Please, just a minute.'

'Frieda?' A long pause with knocking and clanking. 'What's happening, what's the matter?'

'I'm all right, just needed some water.' The woman speaks so softly that Ruth has to press her ear flat to the receiver. 'There are some things you need to understand. About Rainbow – I mean Liam – when he was a boy.' Her breath is asthmatic and slow. 'I . . . well, I did things differently. Didn't think he needed school for a start, not the rubbish they wanted to teach him anyway.' Her words gather pace, the memories gifting her a little energy. 'We were doing fine, doing things our own way, but the social worker didn't think so.' Her cough rattles in Ruth's ear. 'Thought I was being negligent, that my flat wasn't the right environment to bring up a child.'

Ruth itches with frustration. 'I don't follow.'

'If I'd had a nice husband and a posh house, they wouldn't have batted an eye, but money's got nothing to do with love, and I didn't need a man around, certainly not someone like Rainbow's father.' Frieda's words are sticky. 'I could see what was coming, it'd happened to other people on the scheme – you know, the estate. They'd have my boy off me. So I came to London for a fresh start, tried to stay under the radar, but they found me anyway. Then I had to behave all over again.'

'Look, I'm sorry for whatever's happened, but what has this got to do with now, with Leila?'

'I'm just trying to explain about me and Rainbow. People can be cruel, they don't want to let you in. It was like I had a smell about me and, no matter what I did, they sniffed me out. Even my own son turned his nose up at me in the end. But he was just a lonely boy. All he ever wanted was some-one to help him belong.'

'Frieda, none of this is making sense.'

'My son's not perfect, and he's got himself in over his head this time, but I love him, no matter what. I can't let him down again, can't let them take him off me. As a mother you must understand that.'

'So, because you and Liam have got issues, I'm suddenly

involved in this total mess?' Her voice rises, politeness bypassed, landing the two women in this candid exchange, as if they are family. 'Leila is not my responsibility. It's dangerous. Where the hell is she going to go if she can't stay at your house?'

Frieda's voice is soft and muffled, like she's got the mouthpiece up against her face, her energy fading fast. 'I believe in you, Ruth. You remind me of myself when I was your age. A lot of people were against me too.' Ruth strains to hear. 'I sense you're the right person to help, I've always felt that about you. You know what it is to be alone in the world.'

'I've got enough going on without all of this.'

'With someone like you on her side, Leila might have a chance.'

Ruth growls. 'Why is any of this my problem?'

'Because it is your time. Please, it will all make sense. Something's coming for me. Keep it safe, don't let anyone else get hold of it.'

'What? What's coming?'

'I know you will do the right thing. I've seen all this in a dream.'

'For fuck's sake.'

'Ruth . . .' Frieda's voice trails off, and the handset clatters.

A distant squeak of rubber-soled shoes on clean floors, then another person in the background, the nurse. 'Miss Cailleach?' He comes on the line, panic in his voice. 'I'm sorry but your mum needs to rest now. No more phone calls today, I'm afraid. Best speak to the doctor later after her rounds.'

The line is disconnected.

Ruth slams down the receiver, her anger high-pitched. It would be possible to leave Leila to sort it out for herself, but the likelihood is the girl will end up back where she began, and allowing that to happen would be as wilful as getting involved. Now that Ruth's hardwired into the truth, she can no longer turn away; she has responsibility, and at least the choice between right and wrong, whereas Leila can only hover around Ruth's kindness, hoping not to frighten off her one and only ally, herself and her sister dispensable through the misfortune of being poor and from far enough away to be judged by many as *other*. But every turn Ruth can think of, every possible course of action, is connected to someone or something that could weaponize Ruth's choices, and she will end up as collateral damage. If Ruth could exist in the parallel universe where she'd handed the keys to Liam when he first asked, she'd have no idea Leila even existed. Her days would now be brightening and her marriage continuing to heal. But she'd also be back to pat-a-cake with Bess, meal planning her life away, and pretending those tiny steps weren't like trying to damn a river with only handfuls of twigs.

She moves to the kitchen window, her heart fluttering so fast it's coming up her throat. Across the alley, Ruth trains her eyes on Frieda's front door. Any moment Liam might turn up with the locksmith, or Leila could fly out in a panic and run back to the petrol station. The opportunities for Ruth to act are ticking away with the speed of a countdown, only now that her rage is subsiding, the walls of her house for once seem less confining and the outside world draws close. It is possible to have purpose and do good. Ruth no longer needs to be invisible, shut away caring for a small child.

14

Leila remains stock-still in the centre of Ruth's lounge, clothes sagging like old skin from her tiny frame. They fled from Frieda's, the mess left behind more reflective of the house's owner having been unexpectedly whisked away than the neat and ordered home that met Ruth when she first discovered Leila. The girl unwinds the scarf Ruth wrapped round her head and shrugs off the old-lady mac; a double agent removing her disguise. On her feet are a pair of Frieda's Velcro granny shoes, too small for Leila, but the only other option were the flip-flops she'd arrived in. Leila scans her new surroundings, and Ruth watches as the girl logs the electronics – the big TV with its multiverse of remotes, Ruth's laptop, an archaic music system with turntable and speakers. Ruth in turn eyes her possessions that only seconds ago had seemed shabby. Through this stranger's filter, they have become riches.

She bolts the front door. Giles isn't due home until after his post-work drink, but still she's jittery in case he changes his mind and turns up unannounced. Bess cries for food and it settles Ruth to focus on this immediacy rather than the chaos gathering on the horizon. She warms Bess's bottle and takes a Tupperware of yesterday's stew from the fridge, leaving the food to simmer in a pan. The meaty smell takes the chill from the atmosphere.

Leila pulls what looks like a photo from under her fleece and T-shirt – she must have been hiding it in her bra for safety. She stares at the well-thumbed picture, holding tight to what Ruth realizes must be her one true possession, the moment intensely personal. Ruth wants to honour the girl's privacy by not asking to see unless she's offered, though she's itching for a look. She pretends she needs something from her bag, putting Bess's bottle on the coffee table as she passes, and catches a glimpse over Leila's shoulder. The shot is of Leila and another girl, the picture still too distant to make out details. Bess stretches for the bottle from her bouncy chair and before Ruth can get to her, Leila has lifted the baby onto her lap. The young woman tests the temperature of the milk by shaking a drop on her hand, then she offers the teat to Bess, rocking the baby gently from side to side, as if feeding her is the most natural thing to do, as if she's done this a thousand times before. Bess calms instantly and guzzles the milk, big eyes locked on Leila, free hand exploring the older girl's chin. Ruth hovers close, wanting to take Bess and feed her herself, experiencing an inadequacy close to jealousy, that she's not the natural Leila is, that this relative stranger has found ease with her daughter after only a short time – and Leila didn't even think to ask permission.

Ruth suspects Leila's from a place where less is demanded of children, and where mums and dads don't pressure themselves to be perfect. She looks up at Ruth and smiles, and the open joy in her face is instantly reassuring. Even Ruth's nervy attention to her daughter doesn't faze Leila; there's no judgement. Bess plays with Leila's hair, the bottle half finished, and Ruth wants to gift-wrap the moment with Leila here to help and her own sense of purpose growing, reconnecting her to the person she used to be.

The photo has dropped to the floor. Ruth picks it up. Leila doesn't object or try to take it back. The picture is of Leila with a younger girl whose similar features – deep-brown eyes, high forehead, straight, attractive nose – tell Ruth it's Farah. The younger sister's cheeks are fuller than Leila's, her smile more shy, and she's tucking herself behind Leila as if the camera is too revealing, her vulnerability a birthmark she can't disguise. Leila's shoulders are pushed back, head high, attempting to fill the frame for them both if she could. And Farah's wearing that same spotty silk scarf Leila brought back from the petrol station, knotted slightly too high at her neck, perhaps in an attempt to look more adult, alluring even, and Ruth wonders how long into Farah's journey it took for that innocent act to become more sinisterly realized.

Ruth sits next to Leila on the sofa as the girl bends her head. Tears fall in circles on her trousers. Ruth gently slides her daughter into her own arms as Leila makes fists in her lap, Farah's absence a tangible presence in the room.

'She is only a year younger than me,' Leila says. 'But it seems more. She won't be safe without me.'

'I'm so sorry.' Ruth puts a hand on Leila's arm and rubs. 'Listen.' Her shoulders rise and fall with a big sigh. 'I really think we have to call the police now. It's time. I can't see any other option.'

'No.' Leila's volume bounces off the walls. 'Even if they help, it will take too long, and Farah might be hurt.'

'But there are refuges for women like you, organizations who can look after you, who'll know what to do.' Ruth reaches over to her laptop, animated with this new idea. 'We can do a search.'

Leila puts out an arm to block Ruth's way. 'If these people come, they will ask questions. It will only make trouble.'

'But they're set up to help women in your situation.'

'See?' Leila pulls up her top, face shining with anger. Her bruises seem to have deepened in colour; old blood under thin skin. 'This Ray does when he is a little angry. Only a little. If they think the police are coming or if the people you say try to help, then with Farah it will be more.' Fear radiates as a heat off Leila. She pulls down the layers of clothing and sinks backwards, defeated by this wave of emotion. Her eyes glaze. 'Last night I had a dream. I was under the ground. It was cold and dark. My hands found Farah, but I could not wake her.'

Ruth stands and straightens her little girl's clothes to give her own pulse a chance to even out. She moves to the window to reassure herself the world's still turning. Two dog walkers pass each other from opposite directions with a cursory nod and no smile, perhaps smarting from the earlier dog fight. The pavements are still grimed with snow, but the weather's ceased to be a novelty, the white slush now merely a bother. All it took for the blitz spirit to die was a small rise in temperature. Perhaps even Monica wouldn't give Ruth the time of day now. Ruth draws the curtains and busies herself by dishing up the stew, a small offering in the face of Leila's huge need. The food's caught on the bottom of the pan and Leila adds handfuls of Cheddar that Ruth's grated to cover the charred taste. Strings of cheese drip from the girl's spoon as she shovels in the food, wiping the spills on her sleeve. Ruth watches with a satisfaction denied by her own daughter's picky eating. In the safety of this house, Leila's dropped the illusion of adulthood that's enabled her to survive for so long, and there's a childish quality to her lack of table manners. Her sleeve skims the surface of the stew. Ruth pulls it out of the way and tucks a stray clump of hair behind Leila's ear, keeping her hand on the girl's head a beat too long. Leila tweaks a smile. Somehow, being here among the mountain of Leila's problems is more fulfilling for Ruth than the daily demands of being at home with her daughter. But this strange little unit, camped out in a darkened house, can only last so long.

'I've messaged Giles,' Ruth says, extending her arm across Leila's back, the girl's vertebrae a hard line under her top. 'He's not getting home until later, but if we can't call the police then we need to make a plan about what you're going to do next.' Giles's reply to Ruth's text was curt, obviously still smarting from this morning's rejection. *Don't wait up*, he wrote. *And I'd appreciate no baby duty tonight.* She read the message several times, willing the words to reveal more, but there was nothing cryptic, no underlying softness. No smiley faces or kisses at the end.

Leila puts down her bowl. 'I will go soon.' Her foot accidentally kicks the empty bowl on the floor and the spoon jangles against the china.

'You're not serious about just turning up at the petrol station, are you?'

'It is the only way. I must, for Farah.'

'I really don't want you to do that.'

'What else is there?' Leila runs her nails along the seams of her trousers. 'Tell me? What?'

'But it's not safe.'

'Safe? I can never be safe.' The girl jumps up, face scrunched in pain as she puts pressure on her foot. 'You do not know what it is to always be afraid, to have no country, no choice.'

'Leila, please, someone might hear.'

Leila whispers, 'You think I want to leave home? No one goes unless to stay is death.'

Ruth opens her mouth to reply, but there are no words. Leila crosses her arms over her stomach as alarm breaks on her face. She runs to the toilet. Behind the closed door comes the sound of retching followed by a vomiting echo. Panic is bringing up the food Leila's just eaten. The stew was the only protection Ruth had to offer, and now even that's gone. Bess clings to her mum as Ruth picks up one of the baby's picture books to calm her. The board-thick pages open on an illustration of a smiling girl dressed in red, basket in arms, stepping into the woods. How ancient and universal these myths are,

Ruth thinks, the warnings, even in childhood, not to stray off the path to where wolves lie in wait. Where those who can will do what they please. Leila comes back into the room and sits stiffly, as if she's preparing to sprint, as if the cut on her foot wouldn't stop her, as if she had somewhere to escape to.

Footsteps outside and Liam's voice. He passes Ruth's house, and there's the swing and bang of the gate as he enters Frieda's front yard. Ruth tiptoes to the window, peeping from the curtain. Liam is pacing his mum's garden, talking loudly on his phone.

'I'm here, mate,' he says. 'I'm waiting, so look lively.' He's early for the locksmith, keen to get inside his mother's house and rifle through her things, itching to take advantage while Frieda's absent, while she has no say.

Ruth lets the curtain drop and turns back to the room. She had no concrete plan in bringing Leila to her own house other than sidestepping immediate danger, and what little safety she is able to offer is quickly being superseded. She urgently needs all these problems gone, and the only way for that to happen is to make it personal. Ruth says quietly, as if to herself, 'You can't go back.' She moves towards Leila – mad enough to make this mess hers, sane enough to know there's no other option – and speaks louder. 'I'm going to get you a phone and some money.' Her nerves settle in the relief of forward motion, the endless preparation for disaster and building anxiety finally finding an outlet. 'Then we'll set you up in a B & B. Frieda has some plan or other, something she's expecting to arrive. I need to speak to her again, but I won't be able to until tomorrow.'

Leila's fingers tremble over her eyes. 'You would do this for me? Why would you do this?'

'It's the only practical way.' Bess is scratchy with tears. Ruth puts a hand to the baby's forehead; she's teething-hot and desperately needs to be put in her cot. Ruth hasn't got time to factor in a sleep, though. She remembers her promise to Giles after she drove around with Bess in the car that night, and the terror on his face when he thought something had happened to them, or that Ruth might have put their daughter in danger. 'I'll settle Bess for a sleep and you can wait here with her while I get you the things you need.' Leaving her baby with Leila feels like the most rational decision Ruth's made in months.

'But Farah, I must go to her quickly.'

'I won't let you, OK? Not like this anyway, not yet.' Ruth's anticipation gathers pace. 'We'll find somewhere for you to stay when I get back. There should be enough time before Giles gets home.' Bess's finger snags on a knot in Ruth's hair, and she pulls away. 'Just give me one more day. At least we can try to figure out where Farah's gone before you put yourself in any more danger. If you go back now, you'll both be trapped. This way you'll have a chance of getting her out.'

With pen in hand she looks for a piece of paper to write her number on.

'Here,' Leila says, holding out her arm. 'It is better here.'

Ruth writes her mobile number on the soft inside of Leila's forearm.

'Promise you'll be here when I get back,' Ruth says. 'And promise, on your life, that you'll look after my baby.'

'Of course. I am here with Bess. I will not leave.'

Low clouds draw in an early dusk. From the rear-view mirror of her car at the kerb, Ruth watches Liam on his phone in his mum's garden, the skin on his neck shiny and hot around the stubbly hair. He stomps from the gate to pace the pavement, the garden too constricting, and he stares down the alley from where Ruth and Leila made their earlier exit. Small dots of rain spatter Ruth's windscreen, the snow melting fast, but the ghost of her footprints will remain on the shaded path. Liam's phone drifts down from his ear to his thigh, and his head tilts to one side as he follows the trajectory of the prints. If he walks down the path, he'll see someone's been round the back of Frieda's, and after that he'll be able to trace those same steps in the opposite direction, directly to Ruth's front door.

Ruth jumps from her car and heads towards Liam, putting on her best smile. She pushes out her chest and places a hand on her hip. 'Hey, Liam, how are you? How's your mum?' His previous flirtation adds power to her performance, and he takes an encouraging step forward until they're a breathing distance apart. Ruth continues, 'I've been really worried about her. Is there anything I can do to help?'

Liam examines her face as if he's choosing what to buy, and she turns girly eyes up to his, straining with the pretence, but there's no depth to Liam's expression; it's almost

249

bovine, impossible to read. 'Anything come for my mum in the post?' he says.

'No, nothing yet.'

His sightline passes Ruth's shoulder to something more interesting, and she curls into the embarrassment of trying to play him at his own game. 'Nah,' he says. 'There's nothing I need from you then.' Men like Liam like to call the shots, and whatever interest he chose to turn on yesterday has vanished. The glimmer of a smile crosses his face, like he's enjoying letting her know she was easy to fool. 'But you can do something for Sandra.' He almost chuckles, the noise weirdly wet like it's stuck in his throat. 'I mean, what else does she need to do to shake you off?'

Ruth blanches, mouth open, shocked as well as shamed. Footsteps behind her. Ruth spins to see Sandra walking towards them, the bottom half of her face buried in the high-zipped collar of her padded jacket, and she's wearing boots that lace up to her knees, the same ones Ruth remembers from when the couple came to dinner once, when Ruth's wooden floor was still so new they were trying to keep it high-heel free. Liam had been the one to do up his wife's boots that evening before they left, as Sandra put out one foot then the other – not asking, only expecting – and Liam had knelt silently at her feet to tie the laces.

With only Sandra's eyes visible, Ruth can't tell if she's smiling or angry, can't unpick if Liam was simply trying to poison the friendship for his own sake or if Sandra's in on the deal too. Sandra looks different, and it takes Ruth a moment to understand it's the first time she's seen her friend without make-up. She looks younger somehow, and prettier. A rash of old acne scars runs up her cheekbones and her hair's wet and tied back – she must have come straight from the gym. Sandra's squint flicks between Ruth and Liam, and Liam does little to hide his shrug at Ruth's awkwardness. Ruth holds her hands together in front of her, arms straight, stepping away from Liam, who's landed her with all the blame for standing too close.

Finally Sandra lifts her head from her coat, mouth a straight, serious line. 'Everything OK?'

Ruth's shoulders tense. 'Yes, fine. I was just checking how Frieda's doing.'

'Where's Bess?'

'Oh, um . . . she's with Giles.' Ruth studies Sandra's expression, searching for any sign of softness.

'Really?' Sandra holds Ruth's stare, giving nothing away.

Ruth's head is so full of what she needs to do for Leila that she presses on. 'Yes, Giles took the day off,' she says brightly. 'He's taken Bess out.'

'Nice.' Even though Sandra's smaller than Ruth, her poise creates the illusion of height. There's a bruise on her jaw, the edges a little crusty. It's recent, but not that recent, and would have been easily covered by the foundation Sandra normally wears.

Ruth reaches out to Sandra's face. 'What happened?'

Sandra jerks her chin from Ruth's hand with a glance at Liam. 'Oh, nothing, just my Boxercise class.' She angles her jaw back into her collar to hide the bruise. 'More's the point, what's going on with you? You look a bit edgy. Do you need me to call the doctor?' Her words are clipped, and Ruth remembers that it was only yesterday Sandra likely witnessed the flirtation with Liam on her doorstep, and here, again, Ruth's betrayed her friend in plain sight.

'I'm absolutely fine,' Ruth says, guilt swelling. 'Absolutely nothing to worry about.' She tugs her coat across her chest, attempting if she could to hold her dignity inside, desperately wanting to tell Sandra that Liam's not her type, that friendship is more important than flirting with a man like him, but then that would be an insult to his wife.

'You sure you're OK, hun?' Sandra breaks into a smile and she strokes Ruth's shoulder. 'Haven't been seeing people who aren't there again?'

Ruth warms a little at Sandra's touch, but her cheeks redden too at the humiliation of being openly discussed in front of Liam. 'Oh no, nothing like that.' She laughs nervously, desperate to get away and get on with what she needs to do. 'In fact, I've never been better. You really don't need to keep an eye on me any more.'

'Oh, honey,' Sandra says, moving closer to Ruth with a wink. 'I'll always have my eye on you.' Her bubblegum-scented words are delivered with such playfulness, it's impossible to read them as a threat, so Ruth can't understand why she's uneasy. The way Sandra keeps blowing hot and cold in the space of only seconds has left her with nothing solid to hang on to. Sandra nods at the keys in Ruth's hand. 'Didn't know you were driving again.'

'Huh?' Ruth looks at her hand in the surprise of being

caught out. 'Yes, got the sign-off from Giles. It's great. Freedom at last.'

'He must be so relieved he can trust you again.' Sandra's words are still gentle, delivering her blows with such sweetness. 'Look at you, getting so much better.'

'I am.' Ruth's totally disorientated and her voice comes out high-pitched, attempting to convince herself as much as them that she's in control. 'All back to normal.'

The locksmith's van pulls up at the kerb. Sandra's attention follows the driver.

'San.' Liam's voice is a bark. 'C'mon, hurry up.'

Sandra presses her lips together, head high and regal. 'You what?'

Liam blinks hard. 'Sorry.'

Ruth thinks that for a couple who are so much in love, their relationship contains a hefty amount of griping. Perhaps they like it that way, perhaps the conflict keeps them hungry, with fall-outs followed by crazy make-up sex. She calls back to them, 'Look after the cat. Your mum didn't want her to go to the vet's.'

Sandra stops, spins to face Ruth. 'And what would you know about it?'

Ruth looks at the ground. 'Nothing really.' She kicks at some frozen moss on the pavement. 'She only mentioned it in passing one day.'

Sandra nods slowly at Ruth, and Ruth heads quickly to her car. Behind her she thinks she hears someone say, 'Mad as a box of frogs,' but when she checks over her shoulder, there's no one close, only the locksmith at the door and Liam, who's pacing in and out of the gate in a cross between a saunter and a stride, like he's cornered his prey and is itching for the kill. She hopes he'll be kind to the cat, though Ruth has bigger concerns for now. She starts the ignition, revisiting what needs to be done: drive to the shopping centre, buy a phone, take out some cash, set Leila up in a B & B. Simple. Sandra's marching back home as Ruth pulls out of the space and drives towards the end of the road, watching in her rear-view mirror as Sandra turns into her own front yard. Ruth waits at the junction, fingers drumming a restless rhythm on the steering wheel. Her neck prickles with the sensation of being watched, but she's just a woman driving a car – there's no way anyone can know what she's got herself involved in.

On the main road, the rain is falling harder now, the season having flipped within hours, its impermanence unsettling. Only the sooty bodies of snowmen remain, as unwanted as out-of-date currency. The sky darkens and Ruth grips the wheel, unpractised in the scrum of London traffic. Kids on bikes swerve in front of her and pedestrians launch themselves onto crossings. A Street light halos a figure in the car ahead as another vehicle zooms up behind, tailgating with headlights blinding her mirror.

Time is closing in on four, long enough to get what she needs and return home. She picks up confidence behind the wheel, steering through an endless high street of tanning parlours, charity outlets and cafes. Tender vegetables, crated on pavements outside convenience stores, absorb the fumes. All the butchers and greengrocers have disappeared, the web of local trade that would once have made a village erased by super-chains and small cheap shops. Fields and farms have been bricked over to create a seamless cityscape with no edge at the end of the tarmac, no coast with sea stretching towards the horizon, nowhere clean and light and wide open . . .

The minutes evaporate from her dashboard clock until finally she arrives at the shopping centre. She dives into a shop to pick out a pair of jeans and a couple of T-shirts for Leila. A jumper with a butterfly on the front, a pack of bikini briefs and a new bra, a warm parka and some basic trainers. Things a teenager might wear, clothes that will make Leila look her age. The total comes to three times what Ruth would normally spend on herself, but the expense makes an armour of the clothes, a statement of Ruth's care, and who would dare harm Leila if it's obvious she's loved?

Ruth's arms are buoyant and the carrier bag of clothes swings at her side as she strides across the concourse to the phone shop. Without a pushchair to hold on to or a baby to look after, there's so much space around her body, and a nervy excitement buzzes in her chest. Waves of people cross in front of her and a late shaft of sun drops through a skylight to illuminate the hair of a woman caught up in the flow. The sun-flare makes the woman pop out in the sea of heads, as if she's not of this world. Ruth strains for a closer look, her legs weightless in anticipation of a sprint: the woman is the double of Tam, or how Ruth imagines her sister would look now if she hadn't disappeared; if instead of drowning all those years ago, she'd been picked up by a fishing boat, amnesia setting her on course for a totally different life. Or perhaps she was washed up on another shore and decided to wipe the slate clean, reject her family and reinvent herself. Anything, Ruth would accept any of those scenarios over the finality of her sister actually being gone. The tsunami of people in the distance swallows the woman in its wake.

Ruth turns, continues to the phone centre where she paces the open-plan shop as customers fill out lengthy contracts with the few assistants available; young men and women with piercings and tattoos and hair that seems to have set in a strong wind. Her panic at having left Bess is growing – was it really right to entrust her baby to Leila? She calls home but the phone rings out. Of course Leila wouldn't answer, she'd have no idea it was Ruth and not someone else. Ruth fiddles with a display handset to take her mind from the worry. The phone drops, thumping to the floor on its coiled security cord. An assistant flicks a look in her direction as Ruth shoves the handset back in its dock. She perches on a padded cube in the centre of the shop, legs jiggling with impatience. More out of habit than any desire to reminisce, she opens up her phone and scrolls through her photos, the distraction barely denting her anxiety, but doing something is better than nothing at all. She pulls up pictures taken when Bess was little, images with flares and strange shadows, and a wateriness to some of the underexposures, as if her house was submerged. Her obsessional hunt for a figure in the lapping darkness – her brain's attempt to create form in the chaos – never turned up anything concrete.

Among the stream of photos are the couple of shots taken over Sandra's back fence, when Ruth had been paranoid enough to believe Sandra was hiding something from her.

The inside of the house itself is unclear, only the figure of Liam visible in his white T-shirt, but a deeper shadow in a corner always niggled Ruth. She stretches the image with her two fingers to zoom in. The mottled image blurs to indecipherable then snaps back to the closest focus it will allow. Even in sanity, Ruth's still questioning what's possible, what could have been in Sandra's house back then. She deletes the photos and shoves her phone to the bottom of her bag.

One of the shop assistants is chatting and laughing with a customer at the counter. Ruth goes over to them. 'How much longer until I'm served?' She stands close to the assistant. 'I'm in a real hurry. Please, I only need a pay-as-you-go phone.'

Paperwork is spread across the counter and the assistant leans into her hand that's placed on top of the pile. 'Someone will be with you as soon as they can.'

'But you don't understand—'

'You'll have to wait your turn.' The woman's nostrils widen as the customer in front of her smiles at his feet. 'Sorry, sir,' the assistant says, turning from Ruth and pointing to the contract. 'If you could just sign here . . .'

Ruth walks to the door as behind her the customer says, 'Who does she think she is?' Ruth swivels to challenge them. The couple at the counter smirk at each other. She clamps her mouth shut; they'll only take more time to spite her if she joins in their game.

She stands at the exit, arms tightly crossed. A cafe with a seating area occupies the centre of the concourse. Customers ferry past a fridge filled with sandwiches and fizzy drinks before ordering their coffees at the till. Such immaculate normality that Ruth questions how it's possible for Leila and all her problems to coexist, only a few miles from this bright, efficient world. She wants to shout at everyone to wake up. Or perhaps they already know what goes on behind closed doors, complicit through convenience, their guilt allayed by clean cars, painted nails, cheap vegetables and fantasies fulfilled. A young man in a suit sits opposite, feet tapping under the table as he flips the pages of a tabloid, taking more notice of his phone than the newspaper while he gulps his coffee. Would he pay to use a woman's body? Would Liam? The level of devotion he shows Sandra seems possible only with an element of falsity or objectification, and Ruth imagines him separating out the respect he maintains to have for his wife from going to watch a stripper. But would he go that step further? Her stomach tightens, remembering his statement about Sandra wanting Ruth to leave her alone.

Her phone rings. She digs out the handset from her bag: it's Giles.

She's here without permission, can't trust herself to speak to him without giving her anxiety away, and she mutes the call, replying with a text. *Sorry can't talk. Bess in meltdown. All fine tho. Speak later.*

Giles texts back immediately. *Call me now. I need to speak to you.*

The shop assistant taps her on the shoulder. 'How can I help?'

Ruth stares at the woman in panic, the phone hot in her hand, and the assistant tips back her head, eyes wide with alarm. 'Is everything OK?'

'Yes. Fine.'

'Right.' She flicks a pleading look over her shoulder before returning to Ruth. 'What kind of handset do you need then?'

The shop's tinny music rattles in Ruth's ears. 'Whatever's the cheapest pay-as-you-go. And the quickest to set up.'

Another text comes in from Giles. *On my way home. Where the hell are you?*

15

Ruth's heartbeat accelerates in line with her increasingly frantic driving, her urge to return to Bess a singular compulsion. Giles texts again – *You have so much explaining to do* – and Ruth fumbles to reply – *Home v soon* – terrified of digging herself any deeper into trouble. Will Giles make it home before she does, and if so, will Leila have stayed with Bess or panicked when she heard him coming and run away? She's promised to do both in the past and Ruth won't know exactly what she has to explain until she herself walks into the house. The girl's words replay in Ruth's ears: 'I am here with Bess. I will not leave.' She grips the wheel, fingers cramping with the pull of home as the vehicle flies over a speed bump, suspension wheezing as it hits the tarmac.

When Ruth reaches her road, she struggles to find a space, the street even more jammed than usual. As she passes her house, she glimpses Giles's bike leaning against the wall and her stomach flips. At least if Leila has run off, someone is home with Bess now. There's nowhere to pull over so Ruth

floors the accelerator, breaking sharply at the end of the cul-
de-sac, where a street light flares off the bonnet of a parked
police car. The officer inside the vehicle faces away from Ruth's
headlamps as she attempts not to hit his vehicle, her panic
swelling – he's here for her – before she sees the blackened
lump of a melted bin on the pavement. The officer must have
been called out to deal with more fire-starters; not everything
needs to be about Ruth, but worry is her addiction, an adrenal
response that puts her error at the centre of all problems.

Eventually she finds a space close to the main junction of
her road, parking without noticing she's turning the wheel or
shifting gears, her thoughts consumed by what's waiting at
home. She runs along the pavement. Ahead, Frieda's curtains
have been opened, lights switched off, and a wheelie bin put
outside the gate for the next collection. The lid won't close
over Frieda's twiggy bouquets and what looks like the rest of
her craft table supplies. A cannabis leaf blows across the road
and into the hedgerow, and the litter tray has been emptied
and left standing next to the bin – Liam's had a thorough
purge, only what does that mean he's done with the cat? Later.
Ruth will have to check on it later. At least she got Leila out
in time, though what problems has she brought the girl by
bringing her to her own house? Crumbs fill Ruth's fingernails
as she fumbles in her bag for keys and Bess's cry is a clear bell
through the window, the ever-unfurling cord pulling Ruth
home. Her muscles tense; she could simply run, now, leave all
this, but her fear is instantly trumped by guilt that she could
be so cowardly when Leila needs her, and when being away
from Bess would kill her anyway. A woman's voice, too soft

to make out what's being said, but it means Leila's inside; she's waited for Ruth after all. Giles's anger will be incandescent at this stranger left in charge of his daughter and Leila will be sobbing on the sofa as he paces in front of her with questions and recriminations, but at least this way Ruth won't need to convince Giles that Leila is real. Ruth's more relieved than she'd have guessed that at last the Leila dilemma will be taken out of her hands and given to someone with more tools to help. Giles is a good man, he'll come round to understanding why Ruth did what she did to help this vulnerable young woman.

The gate squeaks and bumps shut behind her. Giles has the front door open before she's even crossed the concrete yard. He greets her with flint in his eye. Ruth focuses on the floor as she passes into the lounge.

There on the sofa, now fully made up, bouncing Bess on her knee with all the vigour of an aunty at a wedding, is Sandra. Bess's face is scrunched in tears and she looks like she's going to be sick. Ruth wants to tell Sandra to stop, only her mouth won't work. Standing next to the sofa is the same policewoman who came before, legs planted in a downward V, arms crabbed at her sides in anticipation of what this crazy woman might be capable of. Behind Ruth, Giles comes into the room, blocking her exit to the kitchen.

I know this, Ruth thinks, *I know why they're here; this is a mutiny*. Giles wants to send her away, but it can't happen now, not without knowing Leila is safe.

'Thank you, Officer,' Giles says, rubbing his forehead. 'She's OK, obviously. I'm really sorry to have bothered you.'

The woman sidles past Ruth without making eye contact, the snub telling Ruth she's not the same as the rest of them, a patient consigned to her illness, not wholly human. 'I'll need to fill out a missing persons report,' the officer says. 'And the necessary agencies will have to be notified – social services will be in touch – but I'll give you some privacy for now.'

'Thanks, I appreciate it.' Giles shows the policewoman to the door. 'Again, I'm really sorry to have wasted your time.'

'Leaving a baby on her own in the house is not wasting police time, Mr Woodman. I'm just relieved everyone's safe for now.'

The officer leaves and Giles shuts the door behind her.

Ruth says, 'I can explain.'

'There is nothing' – a fleck of Giles's spit lands in Ruth's eye – 'you can say that will convince me you are well enough to look after our daughter for one more minute.'

No words will pass the stone in Ruth's throat.

'Jesus, Ruth!' Giles holds up his arms, bracketing the enormity of his outrage. 'This is the worst.' He looks to Sandra as he jams his fists into his hips. She's stopped jiggling Bess and is giving the baby a tight squeeze. Giles continues, 'Just as well someone used their intuition.'

Sandra's jittery in her seat, circling something that needs to be said. 'I'm sorry, honey.' That high girly voice with a whiff of Marilyn Monroe and none of the coldness she had for Ruth just a couple of hours earlier. She runs a hand over Bess's head to flatten the baby's sweaty hair. 'But I'm always looking out for you, you know that, so after I saw you earlier, my alarm bells went off. As soon as I got home, I called

Giles, just to check he was with Bess, and of course he wasn't.' A little laugh comes out as a sob. 'I got Liam to check on the house as he was only next door at his mum's.' She hugs Ruth's baby harder and Bess grimaces. 'He could hear her crying through the window . . .' Sandra puts a hand over her mouth to cover her tears. 'You'd left your little baby all alone in the house. Liam found her in her cot.'

Ruth switches her focus between Sandra and Giles before saying, 'Then how did he get in?'

Sandra catches Giles's eye and turns her face to the floor. Giles replies on Sandra's behalf. 'Sandra has keys, you know that. We got them cut for her months ago, just in case. Doctor Fraser said it was a good idea for someone else to have access in an emergency. Remember?'

Ruth says, 'And Liam just happened to have them on him, did he?'

'Yes,' Sandra replies. 'One of us has them at all times. It's what we discussed with Giles. I'm sorry, hun, but we all had Bessie's safety to think of, as well as yours of course. Anything could have happened today.' A mascara tear stripes Sandra's cheek as she says, more quietly, 'But Liam wouldn't have needed the keys anyway because you'd left the back door open.'

'What? No I didn't.' Bess reaches out to her mum and Ruth holds on tight to her hot little hand, her anger at Leila mounting, that she not only left Bess alone, she left her vulnerable too. 'Look, there's something I have to tell you, Giles.' Everyone's attention is now firmly pointed at Ruth. 'There was someone else—'

'Who?' Giles pushes his face close to Ruth's, like he's attempting to read her subtext. 'Did you think someone else was here? Was it one of your imaginary friends looking after our daughter?'

'No, of course not. I just—'

'Don't you understand?' Giles's voice booms in the small space. 'You are ill. These people you see don't exist. There was a girl in the wall, remember? You thought she was your sister. You nearly broke the house down to get her out.' He spins away from her, his movements fluid in rage. 'All these girls, Ruth, they're all invented, but the one you're actually supposed to be caring for is the least real to you of the lot.'

'That's not what I meant.' Ruth turns her thoughts to that day in the downstairs toilet when she'd been her most floridly psychotic and had tried to make a hole in the wall. She checks every recess of her brain where illness may linger. Nothing remains of that old fantasy. Leila is real, she's sure of this, though there'll be no convincing Giles or Sandra now. 'I was unwell then, I understand that. You're not giving me a chance to explain what happened today.'

Giles paces, shaking his head in the way a dog would to keep flies away. 'This is it, the end of the line. I'm so close to being finished with this, Ruth.' Sandra looks at the floor, a sheen breaking through her foundation, but Giles doesn't notice her discomfort, his anger too excitable, like it's been kept in for a long time and the rush of it is now an elation. His eyes glitter, the monologue turning into a rant. 'I don't think I can stand much more. You're always searching for something outside of all this, and none of what you're looking for makes any sense to me.'

'Ruth, honey,' Sandra says more quietly, eyes widening towards Giles, imploring him to bring the temperature down. 'You've just got it muddled in your head.' She reaches out and her touch jump-starts Ruth.

'Give me my daughter.' Ruth pulls Bess from Sandra's arms and hugs her baby. Tufty hair dances close to Ruth's nostril as Sandra blots her eyes with a tissue.

'Sit down, Ruth,' Giles says, gravel in his throat.

'I don't want to.' She sways a little with the now-familiar undertow dragging her feet; she's been cut adrift, marooned. Leila abandoned Bess and left Ruth with the blame. And after all Ruth has risked for her.

Giles takes Ruth's arm. 'I need you to do as you're told, Ruth.' He leads her to the sofa, her muscles oddly compliant in confusion. His hand gently and persistently pushes her down and her legs fold to the seat, arms still clasped round Bess. Giles pulls out a dining chair and he sits heavily, groaning with bone-deep weariness. 'Things are going back to how they were at the beginning and I can't let that happen.'

'I'm not ill,' Ruth says, anger whirling that Leila helped deliver this final blow. 'You can't send me away.'

Sandra stands to leave and Giles puts a hand out to her. 'Please, just stay for one more minute.'

'I'm not sure you need me here for this.' Sandra's cheeks are a high pink, like she's put on extra blusher. 'I have to get home to Ian, Liam's waiting for me.'

'Just for a little while,' Giles says, keeping his eyes on

Ruth. 'In case . . . well, you know.' Sandra hides her face behind her hair as she sits back down, and Giles continues. 'You need to get better, Ruth, and the only way for that to happen is for you to be with people who know how to help. Professional people. Because I'm all out of solutions.' He slaps his knees with his hands. 'I'm going to speak to Doctor Fraser. I'm sure they'll agree with me when they know how much worse things have got. They'll find a bed on a mother-and-baby unit somewhere – I doubt it will be the psych ward, but if it is, it is, that's what it's come to, I don't care any more. I can look after Bess. And whatever happens, it will be a darn sight better than what you're putting her through at the moment.'

'I'm not crazy,' Ruth says, her heart thumping against her ribs – this battered old muscle that will soon surely break. 'And I don't need to go to hospital.' She leans towards him, holds on to his fingers that remain slack in her grip. 'I've been doing so well recently and we've been good too, haven't we?' Giles pulls his hand away, blinking hard. Ruth continues, racing towards any excuse that might regain the tiniest bit of his trust. 'I'm sorry, OK? I wasn't supposed to go out, I realize that, but I didn't take Bess with me, just like I promised.'

'What? When did you promise?'

'That time I went out in the night, when it was late and Bess wouldn't sleep.'

'Jesus, Ruth, if that's your reasoning, then I'm even more worried about you. I mean, it's just unacceptable to leave Bess on her own.'

'I know, I know, I'm sorry. I made a really bad call, I can

see that now.' Her head is dizzy with tension. 'I just needed something for supper from the shops. You weren't due back until later and I'm banned from the petrol station, so I went to the Nisa on the high street.' Her words tumble out as she searches Giles's face for any sign of softening. 'I took the car to be quick. I left Bess asleep in her cot so I knew she'd be safe. I didn't want to wake her by putting her in the car seat because she's been teething and it had taken me so long to get her to sleep in the first place. I was only meant to be ten minutes, but there was a hold-up.'

He shakes his head, mumbling more to himself than anyone else in the room. 'You should have thought of that. It's totally unacceptable.'

'I made a mistake, that's all. It doesn't mean I'm ill. People leave their kids on their own sometimes. It's not right but it's not unheard of. They don't get the police called on them and they don't get sent to hospital. I promise I won't do it again, OK? Please, Giles.'

Giles sighs and leans forward. 'Apparently you've been camping out at Miss Cailleach's and sleeping in the spare bed. There was a nappy and an empty pouch of baby food in the bin.' His nostrils flare. 'Liam's mother's at death's door, for God's sake. He's not been able to get into her house and all this time you lied to him about having keys!'

'Frieda wrote a note telling me not to let Liam in. I didn't know what to do. It's not like I could question her about it, could I? I was only watering her plants and feeding her cat.' She straightens her back, looking between Giles and Sandra, whose eyes are locked on each other. Ruth continues, 'And

I . . . I changed Bess on the bed once. Must have forgotten to remake it.'

Giles turns back to Ruth. 'And what about the rest? These thoughts you've been having about losing control and harming Bess?'

'What? Who told you that?' Ruth checks Sandra, who's untangling a clump of hair with her fingers. That day at the cafe when Ruth had felt she was turning a tiny corner, finding the confidence to open up to a friend, and Sandra hadn't possessed the empathy to understand anything more layered than her own experience. Now she's turning that singularity back on Ruth. 'What did you tell him, Sandra? What've you said?'

Giles speaks first. 'Sandra's been looking out for you and Bess, that's all. She's filled in the gaps, put together a picture of what's been going on.'

Sandra carries on stroking the same piece of hair over and again, mouth curled down. 'I only repeated what you said to me, hun.'

Ruth stands. 'How could you? I trusted you.' She paces out her inadequacy, the shame of believing Sandra was an ally when all along she's been a double agent. 'You know I didn't mean it like that.'

Giles places both hands on Ruth's shoulders to keep her still and speaks softly as if trying not to spook a horse. 'Have you hurt Bess? Tell me, you need to be honest so I can get her checked out.'

'Of course not. Are you really going to believe someone like Sandra over me?'

'You know what?' Sandra stands and straightens her clothes. 'I don't care if you're not well, I've had enough of this now.' She flicks her mane of hair over her shoulder. 'I've tried and tried, even when I didn't want to, but I just can't do it any more.' Her words are breathy. 'You are such a snob, Ruth.'

'That's not what I meant.'

'Then what did you mean?'

'I . . .' She can't look Sandra in the face. 'I don't know, I'm sorry.'

'Anyway,' Sandra continues without even registering Ruth's words, 'I've seen you flirting with Liam, so don't give me this *wronged friend* stuff. He's told me how you keep coming on to him really strong. It's embarrassing.' She glances at Giles. 'Sorry, I didn't mean it to come out this way, but you should probably know. She's deluded about more than just seeing people who aren't there.'

Giles's mouth hangs open. 'I had no idea.' His eyes are on Ruth and he takes a moment before he follows Sandra to the door. She steps outside. Giles touches her arm. 'God, I'm so sorry.'

The door slams and Sandra marches from the gate.

The room is airless; Ruth's underwater, drowning. 'It's not like it sounds. Liam started it, I was just pretending.'

'I wish we'd never moved to this bloody place.' Giles's face brews with contempt. 'You've broken it, Ruth, you broke our marriage.'

'*I* broke it? We had a baby, we were supposed to be doing it together. Do you think what happened to me after I had Bess was my choice?'

'Well, it certainly wasn't mine.'

He takes Bess from Ruth's arms and a prickle of static jumps between the three of them. The little girl turns her head between her parents, the most confused Ruth's ever seen her, and Ruth's heart bursts with a love so fierce it's closer to pain than pleasure. In Bess's short life, she's witnessed behaviour Ruth's closest friends would have found intolerable, did find intolerable, and now Ruth's sweet baby is wise beyond her years, as the daughter of an addict or an abuser would be. Ruth has brought craziness into her family, whether real or imagined. She has put Bess in danger by leaving her with a relative stranger, and whatever it was that happened next, her baby ended up in the hands of Liam. Ruth does not work, she will never be fixed, she's not fit to be a mother.

'I'm going to give Bess some food,' Giles says. 'Then she needs her bed. I'm calling Doctor Fraser first thing in the morning.' He fiddles about one-handed in the kitchen making some baby food, clonking the bowls and cutlery on the worktop. 'I don't even think you're aware of the support you need or I wouldn't have to point it out. Think of Bess and how your behaviour is affecting her.'

Unworthiness tightens Ruth's gut. 'Giles, please.'

'The alternative is that I get you sectioned. I'll do it if I have to, but I'd rather you went willingly.' He stirs the cereal in tight circles. 'I wish you'd remember how much better you got last time you went to the unit, and how fast.' He shakes his head without making eye contact. 'This is going to happen, whether you like it or not, but I'd prefer you to be on board. Use the evening to pack a bag or something.'

At the back of the house, Barry's big security light snaps on. Hard white light streams through the window. Something's tripped the sensor; maybe Leila's been out there all the time, hiding in the chicken shed. Ruth presses her forehead to the cold glass, eyes darting over the allotments as she adjusts to the glare, unsure if she'd scream at Leila or rush to embrace her if she appeared now. A homemade animal trap at the centre of Barry's messy patch glints in the stark light. Then, from the corner of Ruth's vision, her fox streaks past the trap without setting it off and escapes into a hole under the railway fence.

Giles's phone is directly under Ruth on the windowsill. It glows with a text: *Shame you couldn't make it tonight*. Ruth can't help but be drawn to the words. *Everything OK at home?* The text is from Faye, and she follows it with a sad face emoji. Without a second thought, Ruth inputs Giles's password and clicks on the text to open the stream of messages between him and his boss. One yesterday from Giles – *Work won't be the same without you* – and last week – *You've been poached from me* – the thread between them lengthy, the messages always framed around work, but it's impossible not to intuit the longing. A tremor deep inside Ruth shoots to her hand and shakes the phone.

Giles is putting Bess in her chair to feed her as Ruth turns to face him, phone in hand. Another text illuminates the screen. Ruth reads it out loud, 'Come back if you can? Have your fave drink waiting.'

Giles bends from his waist to standing.

Ruth continues, 'Boring without U,' and she hisses the 'xx'.

Giles stammers. 'It's not what you think.'

'That's what they all say.'

'We're just really good friends. You know how it goes at work.'

'Do I?'

'Look, nothing's happened.'

Tears sting Ruth's eyes. 'That means you've thought about it.'

He falters. 'Of course not.' The hand holding Bess's bowl of food is stuck mid-air. 'I wouldn't . . . you know I—'

'You clearly have more nice things to say to her than you do to me.'

'I'd never do anything.'

'But you'd like to.'

He takes a deep breath. 'No, actually, I wouldn't. Whatever it looks like, I thought Faye leaving was a good thing.'

'Really, why's that? Because you can't control yourself, because she's so amazing compared to your useless wife?'

'Do we really have to do this now?' He slams the food on the table. 'After everything that's happened tonight?'

'Then tell me you don't want more!' Ruth moves closer, all of the rage and injury of this evening obliterating any caution. 'Come on, Giles, you owe it to me. Tell me the truth.'

He shakes his head at the floor and a huge sigh lifts his shoulders. 'It's just feelings, a silly infatuation, that's all. I desperately wanted it all to go away, and it will, as soon as she's gone.'

'So you're attracted to her, more than you are me.'

'No, of course not.' He looks Ruth directly in the eye. 'But could you blame me if I was? Faye's been a huge support these past months.' Even with Faye's name in his mouth, Ruth recognizes the desire in him, his readiness to protect her honour. 'Sometimes, I don't know, it's just such a struggle to want to come home, back to all this.'

A rock between them, of a size and density that will take more than the sum of this shabby marriage to climb over. Ruth grits her teeth, leaning into the problem: its power, her rage. 'So you lied.'

Giles rolls his eyes to the ceiling. 'Yes, if that's what you want to call it. It was a small lie. A white lie. I was dealing with it, though. What would have been the point in telling you, it would only have upset you.'

'But it affected me, our family.'

'Nothing was ever going to come of it.'

'Well, it already has. This *silly infatuation* has obviously been distracting you for weeks. You had the choice – no, the freedom – to swan off and get someone else to adore you, and all you had left for your sad mad wife was the dregs.' A car speeds down the road, engine screaming like it's stuck in the wrong gear. 'Then you dare to get all macho about me supposedly flirting with Liam!'

'Ruth, you're getting this totally out of proportion.'

'I don't think so.' She struggles to get words past her tears. 'You've been so . . . so separate, and you made out the problem was mine and mine alone.'

'I'm sorry, OK? I'm not perfect.'

'No, you're not.' Her spine lengthens an inch or two and her feet stand sure and solid on the ground. 'But you still expect me to trust you, when you've been struggling to control this thing that could take you away from us.'

'For Christ's sake.' He flops down on his chair, head in hands. 'It's not that bad, Ruth.'

'And yet I'm the one who always gets found out, who's told she's a liability. Why do you get to make mistakes and not me?'

'Don't stretch the logic on this, Ruth.'

'I'm not stretching anything, it's simply the truth.' Barry's security light shuts off and the night filters back inside. 'You know what?' She points a finger at him, lips pulled back to frame her teeth. 'You don't get to tell me what to do any more.'

16

That night, in the last minutes before the sun rises again, Ruth's mobile rings. She jolts from a feathery sleep and into the panic of darkness. The ringing continues, her phone close, and she takes a moment to remember it's in her bag at her bedside, airplane mode disabled. She shoves her hand inside the bag, receipts, wallet and keys tumbling before her fingers connect with the cool slim rectangle of the handset. The display flashes up the familiar *No Caller ID*. Ruth hesitates, heart hammering, remembering the time she imagined Tam's voice on the other end of the phone, but she has to listen now; it might be Leila. She swipes to answer, pressing her ear to the receiver. A high rattle, like someone's holding a hairdryer up to the mouthpiece, behind which might be a voice, almost inaudible: 'I'm drowning.' Then a rapid scrunch as the call cuts off.

'Ruth?' Giles pulls himself up on an elbow. 'What's going on? What are you doing?'

She spins to face him. 'My phone.'

'What?'

'It was ringing.' She's shaking.

'I didn't hear it.'

Her jaw tightens. 'What a surprise.'

He takes the jab, his guilt over Faye still a hangover between them. 'Who was it?' he asks more quietly.

Ruth searches for any angle to explain an unknown voice possibly saying two words. His face across the darkness is more exasperated than worried, eyes burning into her. She takes a deep breath – 'There was no number' – and chucks the handset on the bed.

'I wouldn't worry about it then. Probably just a pocket call.'

Ruth digs in, because she can, because his betrayal has given her back some power, and Giles is the only other place apart from herself where she can grind her anxiety. 'Is there really nothing that gets to you? Is your life really that simple?'

'Look, what do you want me to say? I've got as little idea who it was as you have, so why don't you for once just accept the call was nothing important and stop trying to read anything into it?'

'But what if it was important? What if someone's trying to get in touch?'

'Then they'd have left a message. And anyway, who could it possibly be? Who would call you in the middle of the night without leaving a number?'

She runs her tongue round dry lips – 'You're right' – and puts her phone to sleep on the bedside table. 'Sorry.'

Giles moves his elbow and collapses on the mattress without the support. He turns from her, snoring within seconds.

Ruth flops back onto her pillows, wide-eyed at the ceiling, the flicker of the street light over the plaster cracks now so familiar it's a torture, and for the millionth time her mind probes the day's events and what could possibly have happened to Leila. The girl's image is unfaded; urgent and defiant even in absence. Ruth swings between anger and fear as she's done all night, unable to decide whether Leila simply panicked and ran out on Bess or felt she had no other option but to hand herself over to the petrol station. And then what about the phone call? Was Ruth imagining her sister again or is Leila in even deeper trouble than before? Ruth is still no closer to knowing where or how to find Leila. She envisages the confrontation at the shop if she went in and demanded they give her Leila, the way they'd imply she was mad, manhandle her outside in front of watching customers or call the police to accompany Ruth on her walk of shame home. Last evening, she finally managed to talk Giles down from calling the doctor about another stay at the unit, but the truce they've agreed is shaky and any misstep now will re-engage that process. More than anything, Ruth needs to be here, alert and on guard for Leila.

She shoves the covers aside and sits on the edge of the bed with her head in her hands. Behind her, Giles mutters in his sleep. He's probably dreaming about Faye and their lust that's been incubated by secrecy, although perhaps it's easier for him now everything's out in the open and he no longer needs to hide the fact that his love for Ruth is – and always has been – conditional. The duvet rises and falls with his gentle breath. Once, a lifetime ago, Ruth would have reached out to him, stroked his back, taken the comfort she needed, blind faith in the desire she could inspire in him. Now she rubs her face, fingers sandpapering her cheeks as she struggles to connect to her jealousy; she knows it's there, wrapped so tightly in anger, defeat and this strangling loneliness that only sadness makes it through.

Ruth stands, creeps into Bess's room where her baby is fast asleep. At the window, she pushes the curtain to one side to rest her forehead on the cold glass. Outside, the night sky is fringed with dawn, the ground below still in darkness. Metres in the distance, though, on the sidings, a small glow. Ruth's heart quickens – someone's lit a fire. An aura surrounds it, and something passes through the glow, impossible to tell what from this distance. Perhaps Leila's hiding out in the scrub like a wild animal, waiting for Ruth to come and rescue her. Ruth runs downstairs for a closer look and tries to open the back door. It's swollen shut again and she can't budge it – God knows how Leila got it open earlier. Through the floorboards, Ruth hears Giles turning over in the bed, and she holds her breath for a few seconds until he settles, then puts her face to the window to squint into the night. The fire is hidden from this angle by the trees, but she recalls the picture on Frieda's wall of the kestrel, backdropped by the roofs and chimneys of the terraces, the perspective only possible if the photo was taken on the other side of the fence. In the far right-hand corner of that picture was the suspended roof of the petrol station. The only place Ruth's never been on this street is the back of the shop. Somewhere there, hidden from view, is the entrance onto the sidings.

Ruth grabs her coat and boots from the lounge and puts them on over her nightclothes, not wanting to wake Giles by opening drawers in the bedroom. She inches the front door closed until the latch clicks softly into place and runs round the back of the house, pushing the spare set of keys she found in the kitchen into her pocket. Behind the railway fence, dark trees swing in the wind, their trunks and branches moving in unison as if they're formation dancing, or being pulled by a tide.

'Leila.' Her voice is a loud whisper. 'Where are you?'

She jogs down the back path, feet thumping on the paving stones as she checks to her right for the fire she saw from her bedroom. The dawn is beginning to loosen the blackness and a form crosses Ruth's vision; substance in the woods, a shape moving through the lapping trees. She crashes across a neighbour's allotment and grabs the fence struts, squinting into the dark to make sense of the shadow among shadows. It's fast, the edge of it in the distance apparent by a linear speed at odds with the smooth sway of the trees. Shorter too, and more compact than the trunks and branches. A head and shoulders perhaps. Of a woman? 'Leila!' The shape dissolves into the undergrowth. Ruth races back to the path in the direction of the petrol station, legs powering her across the forecourt, past the closed-up shop and round the back of the building where a haul of litter has been dumped in weeds by the wind: disposable coffee cups, sweet wrappers, plastic bags – the filth everywhere and endless. One of the shop windows is covered in hardboard, the one Leila must have broken, and at the fence a larger piece of board has been propped against the railings. Ruth lifts it to one side to find the entrance, a small break in the bars that have been cut through and heaped to one side. Her whole body is shaking, with fear or cold she's not sure, and she squeezes through onto a narrow path that cuts into thorny scrub, refusing to engage with her busy brain, sustaining only the motion of her hands and legs to do the thing that needs to be done. A drift of smoke in her throat. She calls a little louder now. 'Leila, it's me, Ruth.'

A few metres of heavy undergrowth hugs the fence before Ruth steps into the woods. Cold air holds the promise of day and last night's moon fades into the brightening sky like spilt milk. Soft leaves stroke Ruth's face and the ghost of something passes through her, like walking into a story that's been tidied away, the edges of it tugging at her, telling her she needs to pay attention: she's submerged, a forest of kelp, a figure ahead she can't reach. 'Tam.' Ruth's off-balance on the waterlogged ground. 'Why didn't you . . .' She trips, jolting back to the present. Carrier bags stuck in branches catch the wind like fat, rustling sails.

In the distance, movement again, a shock of colour running away at speed. Ruth chases through the trees. To her right, the railings are high and smooth to deter climbers, and through the metal struts Ruth spies trampolines and compost heaps, the dirty obelisk of her chicken shed in the distance. Beyond this is the roof and walls of home. Ruth's husband and daughter will still be asleep, as unreachable to her in this moment as they would be if they were on another planet. She's crossed over to the other side, antimatter to her reality. Her family pulls at her, the impulse to run home reined in only by the need to find Leila, this girl who's secured a place inside Ruth as firmly as if she were made of her own flesh and blood. Ruth is torn between her two girls, the instinct to protect her own rooting her in this netherworld, though it's dangerous being on this waste ground with no one knowing she's here. In her rush to leave without disturbing Giles, Ruth left her phone in the bedroom, and she imagines if she fell now and banged her head, she'd lie unconscious and undiscovered, never returning to Bess who'd grow up thinking her mother had abandoned her. Immaculate Bess, who has been undone daily, minutely, irreversibly by her mother; perfection misplaced, though at least Ruth was present, at least she tried. All those times she'd fantasized about disappearing, and now that the choice might no longer be hers, she realizes with lightning clarity that all she really wanted was to leave her useless self behind and begin again. *Bess, my sweet, sweet girl.* Ruth wipes the tears from her eyes.

Hanging from a shrub near her house is the twiggy remainder of the dreamcatcher Frieda gave as a present, which Ruth threw away. Its feathers are limp with damp and the circle is incomplete, perhaps chewed by an animal. A glint of something on the matted ground underneath, where Ruth once discarded the corkscrews, the broken mirror and knives, items she'd imagined her thoughts alone could mobilize to violence. She crouches, hands skimming the grass before coming into contact with one of the smaller knives, its handle rusted, blade clogged with dirt. Holding it again now, Ruth still senses its potential, how every sensor she'd possessed had been switched to high alert, confusing her love for her daughter with fear and convincing Ruth that even the tamest situation could turn bad if she were to make the wrong choice – when really all she was trying to do was protect Bess from anything and everything, even the inconceivable possibility of Ruth herself. Ruth knows this now as surely as she once doubted herself; she was never a threat to Bess. Ruth was simply on her knees in front of the lioness she'd become. She turns the knife over in her hand. Mud makes dust in her palm.

Behind Ruth, a snapping. She spins to face whatever's come for her, but there's no one there, only the trees reeling in an aftershock of wind. In the distance, a small clearing and a tail of smoke. Ruth tucks her mouth under the collar of her coat and moves quietly towards the glade. She steps into the clearing, the space vaguely familiar, like a memory of a memory, then her eyes take on the perspective of Frieda's photos.

A fire pit at the centre. Wind skims embers from the ashy heap and the strap of a bag reaches out, as if it had tried to fling itself away from the flames. A charred envelope – the kind that would have held a set of developed photos – blows past her shins. She crouches, sifts through the embers with the blade of the knife, pushing over a large hot stone. Underneath is a piece of fabric that's been protected from the fire. She lifts the material on the point of the knife. It's silk. She dusts off the ash and holds it up to the lightening sky. Still visible under the dirt are the spots of Farah's scarf. Ruth stands slowly, the circle of trees soughing, the sound so pure it amplifies her confusion as to why Leila would have burnt her sister's scarf. She looks left and right. A small, battered metal trunk has been dumped at the edge of the ash, the initials

F. C. on the lid. Ruth recognizes it from somewhere, her head so full it's hard for the memory to take shape. Whatever was inside the box has been emptied, the contents now ash. Just beyond the clearing, an area of uneven ground. Ruth clambers across to find a patch of freshly dug earth, the smell of the damp soil here ripe, as if the centuries of stories that have played out in this place are finally coming to the surface, revealing their secrets. A prickle of instinct tells Ruth to be afraid, but there's no time to pause and unpick what any of this means. It's Leila she has to find and, with a gathering urgency, she needs to get home to her baby.

As quiet as a fox, Ruth backs away from the clearing and stumbles over a fallen sapling. The wind rallies and the trees roar with its energy, the woodland as desolate as when she first entered. 'For God's sake, Leila, where are you?' She rights herself, turning towards the exit as a flicker of something swoops down near the fence and disappears. Her homing instinct at once sharpens to a point and she breaks into a run, lumbering at first then gathering speed with an animal energy she didn't know she possessed. She needs to grab Leila before she gets away, tell her she's safe, take her home to Giles – enough secrecy, it's time he knew. None of what's gone between him and Ruth seems to hold any importance any more, all that matters is home and family and making it work. Houses flash past on Ruth's left, and through the trees she counts their numbers, the perspective from this side of the fence unfamiliar and throwing her judgement. A few bedroom curtains are backlit as Ruth's neighbours begin to wake, and the last house before the exit is Sandra and Liam's. A light is on in their lounge downstairs.

As Ruth comes level with their house, the gruff of Liam's voice, even at this distance, reaches the sidings. It's followed by a fragile female reply. Ruth's panting, she can taste her blood, and she pauses for the briefest second to catch her breath. The high wall obscures most of Sandra and Liam's window, but from this angle on the sidings Ruth can see more than she'd be able to from the path: the top of the window pane, plus the ceiling and its light fitting. Shapes move across the ceiling inside, shadow-boxers twisting and rebounding along with Liam's growing volume. Ruth pulls up fast, then onto tiptoes, but she can't see any more detail. A couple of thumps and a high cry – Sandra is stuck in the house with that man. Ruth sprints to the exit where the pale dawn reveals the entrances to several animal dens. The bushy tail of a fox disappears inside one of the holes.

Voices in the distance, a car door slamming, engine firing up. Ruth leaps through the exit and onto the tarmac, sliding the hardboard back into place, then she scurries along the back path to where the terraces begin. Liam's shout again, clearer now she's closer. Ruth thinks about running round to the front of the house and banging on their garden gate, demanding Liam give her Sandra, only her legs have turned to lead. Liam will cut her dead if she turns up at his door. Ruth knows he's possessive, never worried before if that might translate into violence, but there's always a first time.

The wall is high and topped with a solid trellis a couple of inches above Ruth's head, the whole window obscured from this angle on the path. Ruth tries to pull herself up a couple of times. There's no footing and she slips back down, scuffing her knees through her trousers. She kicks the crappy wall that looks like it was put up in a hurry. Mortar sprinkles to the ground. Ruth kicks again and something gives. She crouches, brushing the crumbling area with her hand. A small section of brickwork, about knee height, wobbles. She grips one of the bricks; it's loose, one edge still set in the wall. She looks to her other hand, at the knife she'd forgotten she was holding so tightly it's almost fused inside her grip. She digs it into the mortar, scraping away until she can fit her fingers round the edges of the brick, and she works at the back of it until a piece has loosened. She tugs. Cement dusts her hand as a small chunk of masonry breaks away.

She drops the knife to the ground and puts her foot in the space she's made in the brickwork, gripping the ledge where the wall ends and trellis begins. Without a sound, she levers herself up. Her forehead breaches the top and she blinks hard. Directly in front of her, Liam's stood in the centre of his lounge with his fists at his sides. On the ground with a protective arm over her head, face angled towards the window in alarm, is Leila.

17

Giles is slumped on the sofa, as if he's collapsed there and been set in plaster. Bess is in his arms, crabby as she tries to free herself, both dad and baby with their coats on and cheeks glowing with the heat. At Giles's feet is a holdall and a couple of supermarket carriers, clothes shoved next to a few bits of food from the cupboards; a hasty and angry pack-up, and it's still so very early.

'No, Giles.' Ruth slams the front door behind her, breath-less from the sprint home. 'Please.' Déjà vu crowds in on her, coming in with yet another emergency, and to a version of Giles's anger, but there's no way to indulge it, she'll simply have to convince him this time. 'I can't do this now.'

Giles's head sinks further into his neck. 'Well, it's happening whether you like it or not.' His expression is hard, determined, with no trace of sympathy or last night's guilt, their fragile truce clearly over.

She looks from the bags up to Giles's face a couple of

times, her husband's eyes stung red with tears, and she says, 'Giles, you have to listen. I need your help.'

Giles doesn't rise up or shout as Ruth crosses to him, the fight all punched out of him. 'You've got a bloody nerve.' Bess cries and he holds her close. 'I thought we were finally getting somewhere last night, being honest at last, and then you go and disappear on me in the middle of the night. Like everything we went through yesterday meant nothing.'

She crouches at his knees, waves his words away. 'You've got to come to Liam's. Now. He's got someone inside the house. You have to make him open the door. He won't be able to refuse if it's you.'

'Huh.' Giles laughs breathily. 'Of course whatever this *problem* is would be about *them*. You know, Ruth, perhaps it's time you accepted the friendship is over. In fact, as far as I can see, Sandra's been trying to distance herself for ages, but you keep reining her back in with your never-ending issues.'

'This has got nothing to do with her. She wasn't even there.' Ruth grips Giles's knees. 'But that might mean Liam's done something to her too!' She dips her head so Giles has nowhere else to look but at her. 'I'm sorry, OK? I should have told you before but I knew you wouldn't believe me. This time I'm telling the truth.' She pulls his hand. 'I can't do it on my own any more, Giles. You have to help.'

He snaps his hand away from her, his face sullen and drawn.

'There's a girl,' Ruth says. 'A real girl. I was looking after her. I thought she ran away but Liam took her. He's been burning her stuff on the sidings too, trying to make her disappear. I knew she wouldn't have left Bess on her own.'

Giles groans, his patience straining at the seams. 'No, Ruth, not this again.'

'Stop dismissing everything I say. I'm not ill.'

'Really?' He swings his knees from Ruth's hands and she falls back.

'Yes, really.'

He looks at Ruth with his head to one side, then takes a breath. 'When I woke up this morning and you were gone, I called your phone and it rang where you'd left it, in the bedroom. After what you put me and Bess through yesterday, you promised things would change.' Giles shifts uncomfortably to the other buttock as Bess holds tight round her dad's neck, eyeing Ruth with a wide stare. 'Then I had this terrible sinking realization that this stuff with you is never going to end, and you're never going to accept you need help. The nightmare is just going to keep going on and on until you ruin the lot of us.'

'Look, none of that matters. Please, Giles, I've never been more sane or serious.'

'I'm just so tired, Ruth. I almost don't care, not about you anyway. Or us. But I won't give up on Bess. She deserves better than this constant chaos.'

'Giles, there's a reason—'

'There's always a fucking reason.' Giles twitches – he's never sworn this deliberately in front of Bess, and the bile is jubilant on his face. He gets to his feet, a little unsteady, and Ruth slides out of his way then stands back a pace. 'Who is it this time?' Giles says. 'Who's this new girl who needs rescuing, or is it the same one it's always been, your sister who was in your photos then came out of the wall? Oh, and let's not forget when she climbed out of the ground!'

'You don't understand.' The fan in the downstairs toilet rattles, like ball bearings in a tumble dryer. 'But you'll see for yourself if you come with me to Liam's. If we don't get there soon, he might hurt Leila or take her away, then I'll never be able to find her again.'

'Oh, this one has a name, does she? And why would Liam hurt her? Why has he got this *Leila* at his house in the first place?'

'Because he's trafficking women.'

'Jesus, Ruth.' He turns to the wall laughing, as if he'll find consensus there. 'It's never simple with you.'

'Call the police then, I don't care.' She hands him the landline. 'They'll take you seriously. But we have to do something. Please, I'm begging you, before it's too late.'

Bess is squirming in her dad's arms, and still Giles refuses to let go, jigging up and down to keep her quiet. 'You've gone too far now, Ruth, way too far. It's enough. I have had enough.' Giles's words are ringed with exhaustion. 'Nothing's going on with Liam, and even if it was, it's got nothing to do with us, so leave it alone, stop bloody poking it.' He lifts the holdall that's next to the sofa and moves it to the front door.

'No,' Ruth says, standing in his way. 'You have to help. You can't leave.'

'I can and I will.'

290

Bess reaches for her mum and Ruth puts her hands out for her little girl as Giles sweeps the baby to one side. 'Get away from her.'

'What? You're taking Bess?' Ruth's voice rises. 'No. You can't. I won't let you.' She tries to grab her baby as Giles holds Bess to his chest, circling her with both arms, muscles taut. Ruth would have to pull hard to get her daughter from him, perhaps even hurt Bess in the process. Precious little arms and legs, her soft, soft skin. 'She's mine.' Ruth's words are clogged with tears, arms shaking with the effort of keeping them at her sides. 'I made her.'

'Well, guess what? So did I. And there's not a lawyer or doctor who would disagree with my decision to give my daughter a better life. It's done, Ruth.' He puts a hand on Ruth's arm to move her out of his way, his grip firm, but underneath he's shaking with an uncertainty Ruth's not felt in him before. 'You made me feel so guilty about Faye, when it was just a kiss. It doesn't give you permission to carry on dragging everyone else into your madness. And I won't be held hostage because I did one bad thing.'

Ruth jolts her arm from his. 'So something *did* happen between you and Faye. It *has* gone further.'

'Well, what did you expect? I'm not an endless pit of sympathy.'

'Christ, I haven't got time for this.' She runs her hands through her hair then drops them to her thighs with a slap. 'Leila's in danger.'

'I don't know why you're refusing the help, Ruth, but you need to rein this in. The doctor will be in touch, I've left a message with the perinatal unit to let them know you're on your own now. Maybe tough love is the only way you'll take me seriously.'

'You bastard.'

'Whatever.' He picks up one of the carriers and a doll of Bess's falls to the ground.

Ruth picks up the toy. 'I don't care what you do, but I won't let you take Bess.' She holds the doll to her chest, smelling the dusty sweetness of her baby on the fabric. 'All that pussyfooting around I had to do in case I scared you away with some problem or emotion that was unattractive, but you'd checked out months ago anyway.' Giles tries to take the soft toy, and Ruth yanks it back, shouting, 'No, you can't have it. I won't let you take it.'

He stares at her with an open mouth. 'I don't know who you are any more, where the illness ends and you begin.'

'I've been caring for a baby. Nothing about my life will ever be the same.'

'Well, mine neither.'

The radiators throw out heat, warming the yeasty air. Ruth presses her fingers to her skull, wanting to weep at this argument, this same mountain of issues they've had in one form or another since the day Bess was born – who does what, who gets what and why none of it is fair – only now her anger tunnels through. 'It's all about you, isn't it, the weight my illness put on you, the fun you wanted to have but couldn't. Only now there's something more important than any of that, and you're going to leave? Leila's in danger. We're the only ones who can help.'

Giles pinches the brow of his nose as tears fall to the floor. 'I can't take this any more.' He picks up the last of the carrier bags and moves it to the door. 'I didn't sign up for this.'

'No, you just signed up for the fucking fairy tale.'

He opens the front door and moves the bags outside. 'I'm done.'

'You don't get to take my baby.' Ruth's voice is shrill. 'You can't take her.' She tries to grab Bess, tugging her little arm as Giles staggers backwards. Bess begins to cry hard.

'Really?' Giles faces Ruth across the threshold. 'You're going to make this scene in front of Bess?' His expression, on the other side of their door, calcifies, shutting Ruth out for good. Ruth's fingers try to connect with her little girl, but Bess is sobbing into her dad's shoulder and won't look at her mum. Giles's voice is almost a whisper. 'I'm going, Ruth, and I'm taking Bess. You cannot and will not stop me.' He places a hand on Bess's back and the baby softens onto her dad's chest before turning her sweaty little face to Ruth, eyes wide with fear. 'Look what you've done to my daughter. Stay where you are, don't you dare come after us.'

Ruth's breathing too fast and she chokes, throat burning like she's swallowed seawater. All this time she's been afraid, unreasonably so everyone kept telling her, that Bess would be taken away, and now the one person who's supposed to have Ruth's back is doing just that. Her vision blurs with rage. She bows her head so Bess can't see and with a shudder she hangs on to the kitchen counter to steady herself, dislodging a package that's been stacked there behind other mail. It falls to her feet where she can't avoid but look. The name above the address is Miss Cailleach – that name – not Mr Smith as usual. Giles must have accepted the package from a courier in the last couple of days without telling her. The flap is partly torn at the top, perhaps damaged in transit, or Giles started to open it by mistake.

Even here, even now, the presence of this delivery prods Ruth, refuses to be ignored as Frieda's words play out in her ears: *something's coming for me, keep it safe.* She squints at the parcel on the floor, wants to rip it apart, tear it with her teeth, and she kicks it with all her might. It spins and crashes into one of the kitchen cupboards. A white envelope from 'Express Photos' pokes out, the same branded envelope that was under Frieda's bed, and that blew past Ruth less than an hour ago on the sidings.

While Giles struggles back and forth with the bags to the pavement, takes out car keys, peers left and right from the gate attempting to locate the car that Ruth parked right down the other end of the street, Ruth crouches, picks up the package, and like magnets her fingers take out the envelope of photos and break the seal. A strip of negatives in a con-certina sheaf. She tosses them aside and removes the pictures, shots that Frieda must have sent away to get developed. Ruth quickly shuffles through the amateur photos, sketchy with focus, some birds only black dots in a pale sky. She slows as she comes to a picture of the glade from where Frieda once took her favourite shot of the kestrel, where Ruth stood so recently. The image is of the fire pit at the centre of the clear-ing, a debris of bottles and a T-shirt with RAY'S HAND WASH AND VALET in the dirt. Then night-time shots, a view through the fence slats onto the forecourt of the petrol station – Ruth's elderly neighbour must have been crouched in the undergrowth, staking out the scene with her long lens. The fast-film stock has made the photos grainy in the low light, but the action's unmistakable. An image of a Transit van on the forecourt under the street light, then another shot of the exposed manhole – Frieda told Ruth she'd seen happenings at night before. Next, the back of a woman climbing out of the ground. Just as Ruth had seen that other night. One photo is zoomed in on the driver who's replacing the manhole, the detail clear even at this distance, to a standard that Ruth's phone could never maintain, and even if his face wasn't in close-up, Ruth would have guessed by the glowing white T-shirt that it was Liam.

'Shit.' Ruth wipes away the tears to clear her vision; Frieda's been trying to protect the girl she rescued while attempting to not get her son arrested in the process, sorting things out her own way, just as she was grasping at anything to stay well on her own terms. No wonder Liam was desperate to get into his mum's house; Frieda must have been bartering with him over these photos that were coming. All along, the old woman's had the proof.

The final photo is of another figure on the forecourt. A woman in trainers and tracksuit with her hair tied back as if she's about to go for a run. Still groomed, though, still undeniably Sandra. Ruth slams the pictures down on the worktop as they're shaking so hard in her hand. Sandra's got her knee in the back of the woman who's just come out of the manhole, pinning her to the ground, and the truth of it snaps into

Ruth's focus; Sandra's fluffy edges, which Ruth had interpreted as her friend's kindness and vulnerability, were nothing more than a distraction from her poisonous core. Ruth squints at the image of the girl on the tarmac. Tied round her neck is a polka-dot scarf, the same one Liam tried to burn on the sidings. That bruise on Sandra's cheek – she's never needed protecting, it's everyone else who needs to be afraid of Sandra.

Ruth puts a hand to the wall to brace herself against the wave, spreading her feet wide, refusing to let it upend her.

The sound of the gate slamming and Giles's footsteps as he comes back to the door, eyes glinting with tears, and for the briefest moment Ruth thinks he's going to apologize before he says, 'Where the hell is the car?'

Ruth pushes the photos towards him. He flinches as if he's expecting her to hit him, this man who she's loved and made a child with. 'Look,' she says, thrusting the shot of the van on the forecourt close to Giles's face.

'Enough, Ruth.' He brushes the pictures away. 'Leave me alone.'

Ruth holds the photo of the open manhole directly in front of his eyes, then shifts to the next shot of the woman climbing out of the hole. Giles stumbles for a second, then rights himself. He pulls his chin up as Ruth presses the last two pictures, unmistakably of Liam and Sandra, into Giles's free hand. He moves inside the kitchen and leans under the light, rebalancing Bess on his hip. Ruth reaches for her baby. Giles frowns at Ruth, his face hot and confused, and he offers the smallest resistance before loosening his grip on

Bess and refocusing on the images in his hand. Ruth slides her baby into her arms, wraps her close, breathes her in as if Bess is oxygen, as if Ruth is finally coming up for air.

One by one, Giles goes through the pictures, then hurriedly repeats the shuffle. He turns to Ruth, his tongue moving inside his mouth without making words, a penny dropping behind his eyes.

18

Ruth can't abide Country and Western music, and today the mawkish twang of the singer's broken heart grates even more than usual. She doesn't need to be told to be sad, but the song was a choice and needs a little respect; it was someone's theme tune to life's big moments.

The small curtains winch round the coffin as the group in the chapel bow their heads. Feet shuffle. A person in the next row to Ruth checks his watch. It's a scant turnout, to be expected, though, for someone who was cut off from almost everyone, whose outlook became hemmed in by circumstance.

The music ends abruptly, as if someone simply decided to press stop. The mourners hesitate; no one wants to be the first to leave, though it's obvious by the way heads are turning to the door that everyone's itching to get back into the fresh air. Ruth puts the order of service in her bag, taking a last look at the photo on the cover: a joyful, even playful shot that's impossible to square with the frail person she knew at the end. She wipes her eyes on a tissue and shoves it in her pocket. She nearly didn't bring a handkerchief, wasn't even sure if she'd need one today, and inwardly she berates herself for her selfishness because the truth is that she's ended up crying for a lost part of her own life rather than the person who's gone.

Bess is reaching for her mum. 'I don't mind taking her outside for a bit,' Frieda says, the bracelets on her arms stacking and jangling as she bobs the little girl up and down to keep her quiet. The woman holds on tight to Bess, the longing for her grandson visible in every knuckle and finger. 'If you need some more time to yourself.'

Ruth sniffs up the last of her tears. 'Sure, thanks.'

But Bess is cranky, grabbing at her mum's sleeve, and Ruth nods a folded smile at Frieda who relents, sliding the little girl into Ruth's arms. 'There you go, wean,' Frieda says. 'Go and see your mummy.'

The toddler settles instantly into a tight hug round her mum's neck as Ruth absorbs her little girl, tingles with her softness, the effortlessness of this love that gathers pace every day, never ceasing to amaze her with its ability to find more space in her heart. She kisses Bess's head, gently repositions the little girl on her hip and puts her free arm round Leila's shoulders, the young woman crying the hardest of anyone in the room.

She looks to Ruth with red eyes. 'I'm so sorry, I keep trying to stop.'

Ruth tightens her hug. 'You don't need to be sorry about anything.'

'It just reminds me.' She blows her nose loudly. 'I can't help it.'

'I know, I understand. It's still so recent.'

She pulls the girl close, the sob in Leila's chest moving through Ruth, and she again questions why she allowed Leila to come today, but the young woman was so insistent that Ruth thought it might help her to be part of someone else's grief. 'I want to be there for you too,' Leila had said, although Ruth's young friend is already coping with more than anyone ever should.

The gathering files out of the chapel into the sunshine. It's a crisp winter day, the chill a tonic, and people turn their faces up to the sky, reminding themselves that it's good to be alive. Ruth stands Bess on the ground to do up her coat. The little girl started walking at fourteen months, and now she's nearly a year and a half old; her legs fidget with the impatience of needing to run. Ruth won't let her go, though. She doesn't want to lose her daughter to this crowd.

Ruth's stepmum is the last to leave the hall. She's basted in perma-tan even though it must be cold in Spain now. A couple of women Ruth has never seen before comfort Beverly, and they stand among a small gathering of similarly aged and expensively dressed people who've formed their own unit. These must be Ruth's dad's friends from the community in Spain; it's not as though he's been survived by or bothered to keep in touch with many friends in England. Ruth takes Bess by the hand and walks over to Beverly.

'Ruth, darling.' Beverly air-kisses Ruth's cheeks without a millimetre of skin touching Ruth's face. 'And sweet Bess.' The woman takes Ruth in for a moment before her chin crumples. 'Oh, look at you, you're the spit of your dad.' She dissolves into tears. 'What am I going to do without him?' Ruth reaches out, brushes her stepmother's arm as Beverly swabs her eyes, takes a breath, pulls herself upright. 'Don't mind me.' She waves her tissue, giving Ruth a weak smile. 'Me and your dad hadn't known each other long, but when you get to my age and you meet someone you get on with, well . . . you have to grab hold of them while you can.' She sniffs and dabs a nostril. 'It's going to take some getting used to being on my own again.'

'I can imagine.'

Beverly blows her nose in tiny little puffs. 'I know you never made it out to us while Bess was little, but you must come and visit. Promise me. Your dad would have loved that.'

Ruth smiles back. 'I'm sure he would.' The two women survey each other, not unkindly, simply confirming that these are formalities never to be followed through. 'And thanks, I'll bear it in mind.'

A bird sings in a tree close by and Ruth finds herself searching for it in the bare branches, wondering how long she and Beverly will have to go through the motions, how much of her time quantifies the correct amount of respect. 'I'm sorry I can't come to the pub for very long,' Ruth says, trying not to sound too bright. 'But I have to get back for Giles.' Beverly frowns sympathetically as Ruth continues. 'Everything needs to be timed down to the nth degree these days. Giles sends apologies he couldn't make it too, but he's in the middle of a big project and just can't afford any more time off work, what with . . . well, you know.'

'It's OK, darling,' Beverly says, tying her camel coat tighter round her waist. 'I knew it would be hard for you both today.'

Giles isn't due to have Bess until the weekend, but he's offered to watch their little girl tonight as a favour while Ruth goes to the gallery, so he's coming straight from work to the house rather than back to his own flat. Ruth's exhibition opens next week, comprised of the shots she took when Bess was about six months old, and she still has lots to organize: last-minute invitations to send out, a meeting with a sponsor that couldn't be rescheduled, Prosecco and glasses to order. Ruth wants the fizz to be decent quality as her old work friends are coming, although they're so excited for Ruth it probably wouldn't matter if she served them cheap cider. Even Minnie told Ruth at lunch the other day, 'You're the envy of the office. Everyone dreams of doing what you're doing, but no one's actually brave enough to give up the day job.' To Ruth, though, the career change was less of a conscious choice and more a psychological purging, her illness forcing her to shed old skin and grow into a new self, soft and raw, where she's learning to be comfortable with her imperfection.

Yesterday, when Ruth had stood at the centre of the exhibition space with the images surrounding her, it was like peering through a window onto that difficult time. Finally she could witness the breadth of beauty she'd so ravenously sought to counter her old depression, and she sensed she was at last exorcising most of what her illness had imposed on her – most, but not all: two photos still at the framer's and yet to be hung are from further back, with camera flares and shadows creating an ethereal liquid quality. In the exhibition catalogue, these pictures are titled, *Sister*.

Beverly says, 'I've brought that box of old things I was telling you about, the one I found when I had a clear-out. I'm sure your dad would have wanted you to have it. It's in Janet's car. Do you want to get it now or later?'

'Where's she parked?'

Beverly points in the direction of the fleet of hire cars next to some bushes. 'Just over the back there.'

Ruth says, 'My car's almost the next along. I can put it straight in my boot.'

'Great. Let me find Janet for you.' Beverly cranes her neck, searching the tight bundle of people as if they are a crowd rather than a smattering. 'Ah, there she is' – and she goes to extricate Janet from cousin Dick's golf blather.

Ruth crosses to Frieda and Leila, who are sitting on a bench. Leila's stopped crying and Frieda's clutching the girl's hand, her other arm round Leila's back. Between Ruth, Frieda and Leila's foster mum, Penny, they've created a rota that means Leila's never alone, never unsupported, never needs to question if she's safe; a small lifeboat in the ocean of Leila's grief. Ruth understands the pain of losing a sister – the missing limb, forever a twinless twin – but the manner in which Farah was taken means that Leila will always risk sinking deeper.

As Ruth approaches her friends, her heart expands with

a sudden warmth, like wading out of freezing water into the hot sun. What a funny little family she's made, but it's the best she could have wished for, plus she got to choose them for herself. She slides Bess onto Leila's lap without asking or warning, and Ruth's two girls cuddle into each other, the shockwave of love that always passes between them the same as it was the first time they touched palms on Frieda's back porch. Leila can't help but smile.

'I'll be as quick as I can,' Ruth says, giving her baby a kiss on top of her curly hair and running a quick hand over Leila's head. Janet waves to Ruth over by the cars and Ruth marches across to her.

Inside Janet's car is an old cardboard box that Ruth puts straight inside her own boot only a couple of vehicles down. 'I'll leave you to it,' Janet says as she walks away. Ruth should wait until later but can't resist peeking at what her dad had hung on to all these years. She opens the flaps to find a top layer of books. Yellow dog-eared editions of *The Secret History* and *High Fidelity*, the sight of them bringing a flutter of familiarity to her chest. She checks over her shoulder to see if her friends are OK. Bess is jabbering to Leila, who's now laughing. Ruth puts the books to one side and digs through another layer of magazines, finding a plastic Eiffel Tower that Tam used to keep on her bedroom shelf – Ruth's sister had bought it on a school trip to Paris. There's an old Rimmel lipstick too, and Ruth scrolls up the half-used stick, examining the tip up close. Minuscule stripes have hardened into the red wax, ancient imprints from Tam's lips. Ruth blinks away tears, puts the lid back on the lipstick, lays it gently in the box. A couple of posters have been folded and are ripped at the edges where they were taken off the wall, the Blu-Tack hard greasy lumps at the corners. As Ruth unfolds the band pictures – Sonic Youth, Sleater-Kinney – she tumbles down a rabbit hole of memory: holding hands with Tam, swaying to the music, throats sore as they shouted along to the CDs, putting on their favourite tracks over and again, because they wanted to and because they could. She laughs through a sob. She'd forgotten all the happy stuff, the power she'd felt then, of being untouchable, magnified, and the memories gather inside her. She slots them back into place, making herself a little more whole.

At the bottom of the box is a bright-red notebook, carefully wrapped in layers of tissue paper, perhaps never taken out again since it had been stowed away. The sight of it now zooms Ruth back to another moment she hasn't thought about for years: stumbling into Tam's room months after her sister had disappeared, Ruth's mum sitting on the bed surrounded by Tam's things, boxes in various stages of being packed covering the floor, and this very book open on her knees. Her mum had looked directly at Ruth, tears in her eyes, and said, 'I don't want you in here. You've done enough damage already.'

Ruth unwraps the book and turns the pages of Tam's journal, the smell of old paper wafting up. Her fingers tremble across the tiny indents made by a biro Tam once pressed on these very pages. One passage is about boys and school and not being allowed to go to a party because she had to revise, the language overwrought with clumsy longing, but it's heartfelt and open too, the emotion on the page pure Tam, and Ruth's sister's voice rushes inside her head, like Tam's carrying on a conversation they were just having over breakfast. Ruth shivers, holds her breath, can't help flicking past the entries, until there it is – the last thing Tam ever wrote:

> *Mum and Dad want me to go and see the doctor*
> *again, but I don't want to keep dumbing myself*
> *down just so I can get through my bloody*
> *exams. Every time they have friends over, they make*
> *me come down and tell them all about my science*
> *award, like I'm some kind of performing monkey. It's*
> *so embarrassing, I hate it and I hate them. Some-*
> *times I feel like running away or just disappearing.*
> *Perhaps I'll give them a fright. Then they'll take me*
> *seriously.*

Ruth slams the book shut. It falls from her hand. She holds the edge of the car boot and leans over as fat dark circles of her tears stain the journal. Tam the golden girl was coming unstuck and Ruth's parents couldn't stop it, were actively ignoring her pleas to falter or fail. Maybe what happened to Tam in the sea that day was the deliberate and desperate act of a young woman who felt she would never be heard – it's possible Tam was that ill or unhappy – but Ruth's stronger suspicion is that her sister simply miscalculated the size of a provocative dare; Tam being Tam, she probably thought she was stronger than the sea. And after

Tam died, it became easier for Ruth's parents to live inside the lie that they had nothing to do with Tam's pain, so they ended up creating their own alternative story where their part in her unravelling was absent, and they got caught up in the fantasy and ran with it; it was certainly easier to bear than the truth. Plus, they found an easy scapegoat in Ruth. Ruth not telling her parents that Tam was in the sea was a devastating mistake, a childish error that she will regret to the end of her days, but her intention was never malicious. She tenses her hands, thumps her head on the open boot, screams behind her teeth.

A hand on her shoulder. 'Ruth?' It's Frieda. 'Are you OK?'

'No.' She wipes her eyes. 'But I will be as soon as I get away from here.' She slams the boot and takes Bess from Leila, who's standing next to Frieda. 'Come on,' Ruth says, moving round to the side of the car.

'Are we going to the wake now?' Leila asks, opening the door opposite Ruth.

'Nope.' Ruth slides Bess into her car seat and secures her daughter's straps, hands working fast as she clicks the buckles into place, her sense of relief mounting. 'My dad's had the last of me he's ever going to get.' All Ruth has ever had to mourn is that her mum and dad were not the kind of parents to command her grief.

Frieda and Leila look at each other then back at Ruth.

'It's OK, I'm fine.' Ruth gets into the Prius and places her bag in the seat well behind. 'Anyway, this way I've got time to drop you at college, Leila. If you still want to go in, that is?'

'If you're sure, that would be great.' Leila sits in the back

307

next to Bess and yawns loudly. 'The library's quieter in the evenings and I need to catch up.'

Bess returns the yawn, her eyes growing heavy; it's been a long day and she's missed her sleep. Leila strokes the toddler's hair and, like magic, the little girl's eyes close.

'No one will mind if you get your essay in a bit late,' Frieda says, leaning through the front passenger door to put her bag on the floor. 'Especially if you explain where you've been today.'

'I don't want the other students to think I'm a snowflake.'

'What?' Ruth's voice is shrill and Bess startles awake for a second before dropping instantly back into sleep. Ruth says, more quietly, 'You take all the time you need, no one has the right to judge you. Where did you even hear that? Has someone said it to you?'

'No, it was on TV. Penny likes *Question Time*. We watch it together.'

'Huh.' Ruth nods, puts her seat belt on. 'Preferable to *EastEnders* for an insight into British culture, perhaps?'

'We watch that as well.'

Ruth and Frieda laugh, and Ruth says, 'Well, between the two programmes, you've got everything you need to know.' She leans over her seat to straighten Bess's coat that's rucked up under her seat buckle. Bess doesn't stir. 'What time do you need to leave, Frieda?'

'I've got a couple of hours until my bus.' Frieda hangs on to the sides of the door as she begins to lower herself into the passenger seat, her colourful sleeves billowing, grey hair longer and wilder than ever – a totally unedited version of the woman Ruth first met – the sight of which had prompted startled glances from some of the more conservative mourners. 'I have to feed the cat and give her her medicine before I go out, so there'll be plenty of time for me to do that now.'

'You're going out?' Leila says. 'But it will be late. And it's cold.'

'It's OK, hen.' Frieda's breath wheezes in her chest. Ruth reaches out to help her sit, but Frieda bats her away. 'I'm only meeting a friend at the pub. I'll make sure she gives me a lift home.'

The woman gives her weight to the seat and her eyes connect momentarily with Ruth's. Ruth looks at her lap; there'll be no talking Frieda out of her plans and it would cut Ruth deep inside to help in any way. Frieda's getting a bus to the station as she does every month, then a train to a B & B close enough for visiting hours tomorrow – the nearest prison with space at a mother-and-baby unit was outside London. 'The rest of Sandra's lot have washed their hands of her,' Frieda said when Ruth first found out she was visiting. 'So I'm the only family Ian's got.' 'But Sandra?' Ruth asked. 'How can you bear to be near her?' Frieda shook her head gently. 'She's sucking up to me now, like everything that happened between me and her was all in my imagination, but only because she thinks I might help her case, give her some kind of character reference, as if that could stop her losing her son.' The old anger fizzed-up in Ruth at this talk of her ex-friend. Frieda continued, 'It's a miracle she's persuaded them to let her keep Ian with her this long, but then you know Sandra, she's got them dancing her dance. I'm on to her, though, have been all along. As soon as Ian's eighteen months and the foster carers take over, she'll no' see me for dust.'

Ruth's sure Frieda visits Liam too, although she's never told Ruth directly. 'I love him,' was all Frieda said after he was first arrested. 'I can't help it. Somewhere along the line I must have done something to make him turn out like this.' Frieda's earlier paranoia about involving the police had been tied into protecting her son, but she hadn't fully grasped the seriousness of what he was involved in then, and neither did she know about Farah. None of them did. Things would have been very different if she had. Ruth senses now that it's deep guilt rather than bloody-mindedness that keeps Frieda secretive about her son. Ruth can't judge her friend, though, because if it came to Bess, Ruth would be blind to her daughter's faults too, would do everything in her power to keep Bess safe and close. And keep her free.

But Ruth can judge Liam and Sandra all she likes, Sandra the most of all.

Liam's defence is that Farah's death was a terrible accident, a struggle that got out of hand and he panicked; he's taking all the blame, still bowing to Princess Sandra who disguises herself behind vehement denial, gaslighting the lot of them to the point where even the prosecution are questioning if it's her in the photos. 'Why didn't you tell me you knew Liam was Ray, was Rainbow?' Ruth asked Leila after the girl was first rescued, and Leila shrugged as she replied, 'I thought he was your friend. Frieda said Ray's wife could make you believe anything she said.' When the case finally goes to court, Ruth will be at the front of the public gallery for Leila's testimony, waiting for the drop in Sandra's face when her story comes crashing down. Leila told Ruth that when she'd been trapped at Liam's, Sandra was the one egging him on, threatening to do to Leila what they'd done to Farah if Leila didn't go back to work. 'She called me faulty product,' Leila said. 'Plenty more where me and Farah come from.' Ruth doesn't doubt it, knows first-hand the dark, manipulative heart under Sandra's airy exterior. After the arrests, the police downloaded the log from Sandra's phone and found a stream of calls to Ruth's number. All Sandra had to do was turn off her caller ID and pretend to be a voice from beyond the grave, so that Ruth doubted everything she heard and saw. *It's Tam*. How dare Sandra use Tam's death to chip away at Ruth's sanity?

And all the while, Sandra was reining Ruth in by playing on her loneliness, keeping an eye on her because she knew too much, even after Sandra had washed her hands of the friendship weeks earlier. That same Sandra was able to carve off her love for Ian, weighing his needs against those of others, attributing more value to her own child than to someone else's. To have been born across a border, to speak another language, for skin to contain a different amount of pigment, made Farah, Leila and the rest of the girls deserve less, feel less, bleed less, their only crime that they'd escaped and naively put their faith in compassion. The maternal impulse is supposedly a great equalizer, though Ruth knows too well how the reality of caring for a child pitted her against the role she'd imagined for herself. Motherhood became a madness for both her and Sandra, Sandra choosing money to protect her family, slavery her alchemy, transmuted into cars and clothes, that shiny new pram, down payments on a big house. Ruth, on the other hand, chose fear. Neither was right, but even though Ruth's mothering fell short of what she'd hoped for, she takes comfort in the fact that her actions were always selfless.

A text lights up Ruth's phone. It's from Giles. *I'm at the house* – he still has keys – *Want me to do food? You should eat before you go out.* Dear Giles, always trying to counter his betrayal and mistrust, and now Ruth finds she's living this strange reversal, him waiting nervously, doubting himself and wondering if she'll ever come back to the marriage, the one she once wanted with him – she lost out too – before the months of illness and trauma bent the family so far out of shape it's no longer clear if they still fit together.

Another text: *And when did the petrol station come down?* Ruth normally drops Bess to his flat, so Giles hasn't been to the house for a couple of weeks, and this will be the first time he's seen the shop levelled, the awning and forecourt dismantled in preparation for the development being rolled out across the sidings. Young professionals are flocking to the area with promises of a tram line, and architects' plans for acres of glass balconies have ensured the gentrification Ruth predicted is finally taking place. The council's banner on the forecourt shouts REGENERATION. Monica next door calls it *social cleansing*. 'None of my kids will be able to afford those flats,' she said to Ruth over coffee one day. Ruth's had leaflets from estate agents offering a tempting price for her place too, but she won't let another home on the street be fitted with dark-grey windows and have its brickwork obliterated by a slick of new white render.

She pushes the power button to start the ignition, spinning the car towards the exit. The narrow lane leading to the main road is lined with tall pine trees and sunlight strobes through the branches onto Bess's eyelids. Leila's forehead is pushed against the window, Frieda's eyes close against the glare. Ruth thinks about her choices this past year and a half: her illness wasn't her choice, her mothering ceased to be her choice, helping Leila was more of a compulsion. But her life – whether she lived or ended it – that was always in her control.

Another vehicle is coming from the other direction. Ruth pulls up on the verge to let it pass. The Prius's engine cuts out as it idles on solid ground and silence rolls through the car; Ruth has no power over tomorrow, but this moment could be hers. She picks up her phone, sends a text to Giles: *Supper would be great.*

The road clears. Ruth taps the accelerator, the engine springs to life and she steers back onto the tarmac. Winter sun through the windscreen warms the car's interior with golden light. Ruth glances round, taking in each of her friends and her beautiful daughter in turn, and with a smile she says, 'Time to go home.'

ACKNOWLEDGEMENTS

Huge thanks to my wonderful agent, Sue Armstrong, for much hand-holding and the best advice, and to Emma Finn for great feedback on that early draft. To my brilliant and wise editor, Sam Humphreys, unbound thanks for helping me dig this story out of the words, and also to Maria Rejt, Josie Humber, and all at Mantle for their enormous patience and advice while I took my time to get the book right.

Thanks to my fellow writers and friends, Kathy Andrew, Jacqui Burns, Laura Darling, Rosalind De-Ath, David Green and Kate Wesson for reading and support, and to Susannah Waters and Catherine Smith for guidance and inspiration. Jo Bloom and Alex Hourston, thank you for endlessly picking me and the story up, as well as for noodles, wine and chats – more of that, please!

To everyone else I've badgered with emails, phone calls and questions, thank you for being so generous with your time and advice, I couldn't have got there without you: Clive Autton, Graham Bartlett, Rosie Cole, Jamie Cruisey, Andy Cummins, Dr Sam Fraser, Dr Richard Fraser, DC Jayne Hayes, Carly Houston, Eirene Houston, Rich Lancashire, DC Brad Loyzinski, Ellen Nolan, Elaine Ortiz, Charli Regan, Jeanette Rowsell, Caroline Smith, Joanne Squire, Steven Wise and Ian Woodgate. I hope to have done you credit; all errors are my own.

And to Rob, Bea and Billy, for being the family I wished for.